A BEAUTIFUL FALL

LAURIE WINTER

ISBN-13 e-book: 978-1-7357438-2-0

ISBN-13 paperback 978-1-7357438-3-7

DEDICATION

I give you my hand!
I give you my love, more precious than money,
I give you myself, before preaching or law;
Will you give me yourself?
Will you come travel with me?
Shall we stick by each other as long as we live?

Song of an Open Road
by Walt Whitman

CHAPTER 1

Does life get any better than this?

For a boy who'd come up from South Boston, Colin Moynahan's life had turned out pretty damn good. For eight weeks, he'd hung out on the beaches around Santa Barbara, catching waves and relaxing. But there was no beach or surfing on his upcoming schedule, and no relaxation for at least two months. Work would take up most of his time. Once his contract as a private duty nurse was completed, though, he might decide to book a room at a high-end resort and stay awhile longer. He loved winter sports, and Polaris, Utah boasted some of the best ski and snowboard runs in the world.

Colin drove his rented Jeep Wrangler over a winding freeway, through a mountain pass. He rounded a lengthy bend and caught his first glimpse of his destination. The resort town was even more beautiful than the photos he'd seen online. Up ahead, a long street lined with two-and three-story buildings cut through the center of town. The area bustled with activity. Must be the famous downtown

Polaris he'd read about, filled with a mix of high-end restaurants, expensive boutiques, artisan shops, and hip bars.

Since he skipped lunch, he'd head to the downtown area and grab some food and a cup of joe before checking into his hotel room. After parking on a side street, he strode along the busy walkway until the smell of fresh-baked bread greeted his nose. His reflection shone on a window decorated with painted flowers. Inside the café, a display case filled with baked goods stretched the width of the space. Customers mingled around small tables. The sign above the door read: *Downhill Delectables*. Clever name.

As he opened the door, a bell rang. He was instantly enveloped in a cloud of the most heavenly aroma of yeast, sugar, and flour. Colin approached the counter and stopped behind the woman who was first in line. While he waited, his gaze wandered over the curves of her pink dress before lowering to her tan calves and ankles.

Since her back faced him, he let his imagination construct a beautiful profile. Her voice was soft, and Colin strained to hear her conversation with the bakery worker.

If she was as beautiful as he imagined and sat at a table once she ordered, he'd ask to join her. He was good at small talk, a skill that made him successful in his chosen profession as a caregiver. Going with the assumption she was a local, he'd inquire about the area. Get the lay of the land, so to speak. A perfect excuse to strike up a conversation.

The woman peered into an open box set on the counter. "The cake looks and smells delicious. I also ordered two dozen raspberry tortes. Oh...I'll take a large chamomile tea to go as well, please."

"You got it, Nina. Be right back with the rest of your order and your tea." The tall, skinny bakery employee disappeared behind a swinging door.

The mystery woman slowly turned and gazed past Colin, toward the windows facing the street.

At the sight of her face, amazement hit him like an unblocked blow to the chest. His imagination had not done this woman justice. She wasn't simply beautiful, she was gorgeous. Her eyes were framed with long thick black lashes. Surprisingly, the color of her tawny eyes matched the color of her hair, which looked like raw honey dripping off a saturated comb.

Her mouth was wide, creating a nice balance with her high cheekbones and defined jawline. She wasn't tall, maybe five foot four, but her legs were long, and made even longer by her high heels.

He racked his brain for something witty to say, but his mind had been reduced to mush. If he did talk, he'd say something stupid. *No rush. You'll be in town for several months.* Although, for the first part, his focus would stay on work. But after his contract was done, he could make time for romance along with skiing.

The bakery worker returned, holding another large box and a covered paper cup. "Okay, Nina. I think I have everything on your order. Sorry for the confusion."

Nina returned her attention to the man behind the counter. "No problem, Nick. We got it all figured out." She handed the bakery worker her credit card. "The last thing I want to do is show up at a bridal shower with thirty women and no raspberry tortes."

Colin's pulse accelerated at her husky laughter. Her well-polished dialect held a tinge of northeastern coast hauteur —incredibly sexy.

Once she'd finished paying, she studied the two large boxes sitting on the counter, then the tall cup. "Hey, Nick, I'll need to make two trips. Can I leave the cake box here for a few minutes?"

Colin stepped forward before Nick could answer. "Let me help you carry these out to your car." He gave her a smile he knew from experience made women's hearts melt.

She jumped at the sound of his voice. With a turn of her head, she met his gaze, and her shoulders slackened. She coolly glanced over him, from his dark hair to his scuffed boots. "Thank you for the offer, but it's not necessary." Nina lifted one box and grabbed the tea with her other hand. "I don't want to inconvenience you."

Colin swept up the second box. He had one shot to impress this woman. "Taking a short walk while carrying a cake is no inconvenience. No reason you should make two trips in those shoes when I'm right here, willing and eager to help." Just like a Boy Scout, which he was anything but.

Her doe eyes widen. "While I'm perfectly capable of walking for miles in these shoes, I am in a time crunch, so I'll accept your offer." Nina began walking toward the door. "I parked several blocks away. Hope you don't mind."

"Not a bit." While holding the door open for her, he smiled. Second time might be magic.

She simply breezed past him, and then turned her head to make sure he was coming with her cake.

Two other women approached, and Colin held the door while they entered the bakery. Once they'd passed through, he jogged to catch up to Nina, careful not to drop her cake. "Are you from around here?" Start off with an easy question.

She glanced from the box in his hands to his face. "I've lived in Polaris for ten years, so I guess that makes me a local."

Her slight smile left him struggling for breath. "I just

arrived today...for work. I have a two-month contract, but want to stick around for a little while longer and do some skiing. Do you ski?"

"I do." She shifted the box in one hand while keeping a firm hold on her cup with the other. "I tend to avoid the runs during the holiday tourist season, though. Going at twilight is the best, on a weekday when it's not busy, right when they turn on the lights and the sky grows dark. You glide down like you're the only one left in the world."

"Got me sold." He reached over and grabbed the torte box from her hands, gently placing it on top of his. The lid for the cake box held sturdy under the added weight. "What are the best restaurants around Polaris? I'm deciding where I want to get dinner tonight. They all look top-notch."

She slowed her pace. "What are you in the mood for?"

You. He grinned at the thought. "Nowhere with snobby waiters where I have to wait forever for three tiny pieces of food on a weird-shaped plate."

"Polaris has a few of those." She laughed and stepped to the side, making room for an elderly couple to pass. "If you want good food at a decent price, I'd recommend The Chute. It's three blocks farther down Main Street. You won't leave hungry." She turned to the left and continued along a side street. "I'm parked right up there."

The road had a sharp rise in elevation, and Colin worked to keep from huffing. Exercise in this high an altitude was something he had to get used to. His gaze dropped once again to her legs and the slope of her tan calves. Those heels did incredible things to her legs. "My name is Colin, by the way. Colin Moynahan."

"Irish boy, huh?" She gave him a sideways glance and arched an eyebrow. "I caught a slight Boston accent in your speech. Subtle, but it's there. You drop an R every once in a while."

He grinned. "I've worked hard to keep my Rs up where they should be." Her dialect was crisp, but with a slight Boston inflection. Small world. Wonder where she originally called home? With her polish, he'd bet a Benjamin and some change she grew up far from the rough section he'd lived in.

"I'm Nina." She reached into a pocket on her purse and pulled out a key fob. "Thanks again for your help." She set her tea on the car's roof, then unlocked and opened the back door before taking the top box in Colin's hands and carefully setting it on the back seat.

"Nina's a lovely name." *If you're going to ask her out, now's the time.* "How about you join me for dinner tonight? I'd love to hear about all the spots not in the tourist brochures."

Bent over, with her top half still in the car, she froze. While Colin waited with a lazy smile, Nina gradually stood and straightened her back. Despite the tight set of her mouth, his confidence held firm.

"I'm sorry if I gave you the wrong impression." She strode around her car to the other side and set the cake on the driver's side rear seat. "But I don't go out with men I've just met."

"Then don't think of it as a date." He stuffed his hands into the front pockets of his jeans. *Be cool, man. You got this.* "I'm new in town. You'd simply teach me about the area. Think of it as a charitable act."

With the grace of a dancer, she rounded the front of the car and returned to the sidewalk. Her cheeks burned a bright pink and her golden eyes glowed, giving her the look of a delicate but angry doll.

She set a hand on her hip. "Mr. Moynahan, between the women who live in Polaris and all the tourists in town, you'll have no problem finding someone to share your meal with tonight. Good day."

Before he could open his mouth, she hopped into the driver's seat of her car, started the engine, and pulled away from the curb.

"Nina," he shouted, trying to catch her attention.

She glanced over her shoulder with a dismissive look before accelerating down the road.

He cringed as he watched her teacup teeter back and forth on the roof of her car. The thing held on for longer than he expected before finally tipping over as she rounded the corner. Liquid dripped down the side of her cream-colored car.

As she disappeared from view, Colin missed the sight of her. He was attracted, but what red-blooded male wouldn't be? And she possessed a cool haughtiness, which only increased his curiosity.

Strolling back to the bakery for lunch, he grinned. He didn't blame her for being cautious with a strange man. Actually, he admired her guardedness. Made her a greater challenge, and he was game.

During the next few months, he'd find a way to run into Nina again. Warm her up to the idea of spending time together.

He gazed at the yellow leaves of the aspen lining the street. Pumpkins and huge baskets of mums decorated the sidewalks outside shop windows. Colin tipped his head towards the sun and inhaled, filling his lungs with clean mountain air.

Taking the job in Polaris had been wicked smart. Especially if he managed to spend some time with the graceful and lovely Nina. This season, he'd be surrounded by natural wonder and fascinating people, which for him certainly meant a beautiful fall.

CHAPTER 2

hile Nina Pettit fussed over a flower centerpiece, arranging and rearranging the pink-and-white blooms, she couldn't get the handsome Colin Moynahan out of her mind. When she'd first seen him in the bakery, after recovering from her momentary startle, her jaw had about dropped to the floor.

Colin wasn't simply a Bostonian; he was dark Boston Irish, like a full, frosty bottle of Guinness Black Lager. His hair was the color of coal, overgrown with a hint of wave. And his eyes... She'd never seen a pair so blue.

He was tall and muscular, with wide shoulders and big hands—a body built for manual labor. If she had to guess, and she'd given it a lot of thought, she'd say he was one of the many construction workers who temporarily called Polaris home while building some new resort or restaurant, and then would leave once the job was completed.

The Boston accent in his speech was subtle, as if he'd worked hard to polish it out, but it was there. Judging from the scar slashed through his left eyebrow and the rough look about him, she doubted he'd rubbed shoulders with the same high-society snobs she'd been raised with. Which came as relief. Right now, she didn't want to reconnect with anyone from her old life in Boston.

"Nina, child, you keep messing with those poor flowers and they won't have a petal left between them." With the help of her cane, Beatrice Maxwell shuffled over to where Nina stood and rested a hand on her shoulder. "Come sit down and rest awhile with me before our guests arrive. You can tell me what's on your mind."

Sighing, Nina slipped a baby-pink rose into a bare spot between two springs of freesia. The flowers smelled divine, filling the room with a heady fragrance that was feminine and romantic. Perfect for a bridal shower.

With one last glance, she decided the arrangement looked full and well balanced. She'd bring this last center-piece outside to join the others already decorating the round tables filling Beatrice's backyard.

She sat on the sofa while Beatrice eased herself into her well-loved armchair. Nina couldn't love her neighbor any more than if Bea were her real grandmother. Honestly, she loved Bea more than her own ice-veined grandmother.

"How's your hip feeling today?" Nina recognized the too-familiar look of pain furrowing the woman's face.

"Hurts like someone's stickin' pins into a voodoo doll of my likeness." She rubbed the offending hip. Her black-and-silver hair was pulled back into its usual bun, showcasing her face and its luminous complexion. "Two more days to my surgery and before you know it, I'll be dancing the jive at Celia and Captain Luke's wedding."

"Are you sure you don't want me to come stay with you while you recover?" Nina would, if needed. She'd do anything to make sure Bea was well cared for.

"You got plenty to do already." Bea reached for a tissue

from the box on the side table and blew her nose. "I have a private duty nurse coming tomorrow. My doc arranged for one from a fancy nursing service out of Chicago, but you're very welcome to make a trip across the street and visit. I'll need someone to fill me in on everything I'll miss."

"You can count on me." Nina smiled despite her worry.

"Enough about my hip. You've got a troubled look about you." Beatrice pointed at Nina while her other hand gripped the top of her cane. "Tell me what's weighing on your heart."

Nina considered telling Bea about Colin. Even at eighty years old, Bea wasn't past swooning over a good-looking man. The weight pressing on Nina's chest was the result of something darker than the sexy Bostonian. "Erich was released from jail yesterday. I try not to dwell on the fact he's free again, but I can't block him from my brain."

"Oh, child." Bea rested her cane against the side of her chair and leaned forward. "No wonder you look so troubled."

"I hate feeling sick with dread, like everywhere I look, I expect to see him. What if he finds me?" Nina swiped away a tear from the corner of her eye. "While he's been locked in prison, I've felt safe and in control. Now, everything inside me is a jumbled mess."

"He doesn't know where you live or your new last name. Rest assured you're safe here, surrounded by people who love and care for you, like Captain Luke and Celia Batista right down the street, and all the parents of your music students." Bea pointed the end of her cane at Nina. "And don't forget about me. I may be old and have a bum hip, but I still got some fight left in me. Plus, this cane can be a very dangerous weapon if need be."

The welcome feeling of laughter bubbled up inside

Nina. "I'll remember that. Does your new private nurse realize what a troublemaker they're getting?"

"No idea." The sound of Bea's deep laughter filled the room. "Don't spill my secret. At least not until after I'm back on my feet."

The doorbell rang. Nina stood and motioned for Beatrice to remain seated. "You stay there until it's time to go outside." She smiled at Bea as she opened the front door. "And here is our guest of honor. Celia Batista, you are positively glowing."

Celia stepped inside and wrapped Nina in a strong hug. "I feel like I'm glowing."

Behind Celia stood Gabrielle Joyce, more often known as Gabs. For the party, she replaced her normal blue police uniform with a very feminine dress, which showed off her tall, lean frame. "We really lucked out with the weather."

"We sure did." Beatrice stood and walked to Celia, leaning heavily on her cane. "Our Nina's got everything looking so pretty out in my backyard. Wait till you see all the flowers and twinkle lights."

Nina cupped Bea's elbow. "Since you're already up, let's walk outside and find you a comfortable chair. You can direct the party from there."

With her cane in one hand and Nina supporting the opposite arm, Bea hobbled through the house and out the back door, onto the porch.

Hopefully, Beatrice's hip replacement would improve her quality of life. Nina didn't mind helping care for her. In fact, she enjoyed their time together, but she knew the elderly woman was in pain. Plus, Bea was a woman who loved her independence.

Nina pushed all thoughts of Erich from her mind. Today was a happy day. A day to celebrate love and family. Not a

day to relive the kidnapping nightmare she'd survived—
especially after working hard to ensure her ex would never
find her.

˜ˌ˜

Not wanting to eat at a table alone, Colin situated
himself on a stool at the end of the bar. The Chute was busy,
and he purposely picked a spot with a good view of the
action. If he couldn't enjoy his dinner with a beautiful
companion, he'd keep busy people watching. Try to figure
out which couples would head home together and which
would go their separate ways after the bill was paid.

"What can I get you?" A hipster bartender with thick-
rimmed glasses, shaggy brown hair, and a neatly trimmed
beard stood on the other side of the dark-stained bar. He
rested his palms on the wood top. "Our house drink is
bourbon cider. We add a touch of honey for the right
amount of sweetness. Perfect for fall."

Honey. The image of Nina's long, flowing hair came to
mind. Shame he was here alone. "Sounds good. Can I get a
dinner menu?"

"You bet." He reached under the bar and pulled out a
tripod menu. "My name's Dex. Drink's coming right up."

As the bartender stepped away to grab a clean glass from
the shelf behind him, Colin let his gaze wander the crowd.
Thankfully, no one knew him here. There'd been a time
when he wouldn't have been able to be out by himself. If the
fans looking for autographs weren't bad enough, there were
the idiot guys looking to prove their manhood by picking a
fight with Colin Moynahan, the Irish Fist—Boston's hard-
hitting boxing champion.

Years ago, he'd left the boxing ring behind him, and his

star slowly faded. He'd gotten what he wanted out of his boxing career, as well as a few things he'd tried to avoid but were inevitable. Colin flexed the fingers on his left hand, the hand that had taken the most abuse in the ring. A pins-and-needles sensation traveled from his fingertips into his wrist and up his left arm. His hand was stiff, and he rubbed his knuckles, helping to ease the ache.

Dex set a full tumbler on the bar top with a clinking of ice cubes. "You ready to order?"

Glancing down at the closed menu, Colin shrugged. "I'll take whatever you recommend. First night in town." He slid the menu over to the bartender.

"River trout with butter sauce and wild rice pilaf it is." Dex scribbled on his order pad. "Welcome to Polaris. How long are you here for?"

"At least two months for work. Think I'll stay longer and get some skiing in before my next job starts." Which wasn't until January, when he'd leave to care for an elderly gentleman on the tropical island of Maui. After some time riding powder, he'd be ready to switch back to sand and surf.

"You came to the right place if you want some excellent skiing. Heard about some sick black diamond runs up behind the North Star Resort, if you want a steep, fast ride. But all the slopes here are cool, or at least that's what I've been told." He tucked his pen behind his ear.

Colin smiled. "I haven't skied in a while. I'll take a few slow runs before riding a black diamond."

"No shame in that, man." Dex nodded and tapped the bar top with his fist. "Be back with your food."

"Hey, can I ask you a question quick?" Colin's growing curiosity about Nina, the woman from the bakery, might be satisfied by a local. Take away the tourists, and Polaris was a small town. "You know a woman who lives here named Nina? She's medium height and slender, with long blonde hair. Very pretty."

"Sorry, man. I've only been in Polaris for a month. Took a break from college in Spokane to make a few bucks before heading back to finish. Tuition keeps going up and so does my student loan debt." Dex adjusted the knot in his dark purple tie.

"College was expensive when I went over a decade ago. Smart to take a break and earn some money to pay upfront. I worked hard to put myself through school." His gaze dropped to his lumpy knuckles, and he felt the ghostlike sensations of each blow his body had absorbed during those years.

With a nod, Dex left to put in his order.

Colin sipped the amber liquid. Nice and crisp, with a hint of sweetness to balance out the tang of bourbon.

"Why are you asking about Nina?"

A feminine voice sounded from his right, and he turned to see a dark-haired woman in a tight black dress take a seat on the stool next to him. Another beautiful woman. Luck was a friend today—or maybe Polaris had a highly disproportionate share of attractive women.

Colin gave her a lazy smile. "Nina who?"

Her mouth hardened, and her body stiffened. "Do I need to speak more clearly? Why did you ask about Nina?"

This time, her tone was less friendly. He decided not to push his luck, good or not. "I met her at the bakery this afternoon and helped carry a cake out to her car. She declined my dinner invitation for tonight, but I'd like to give it another shot."

The woman's gaze raked over him. "Police Lieutenant

Gabrielle Joyce." She reached over to shake his hand. "Nina's a friend of mine." Her grip was firm.

Point taken. He held up his hands, palms facing her. "I'm not a stalker or weirdo, if that's what you're thinking. My question about Nina is totally innocent."

"Make sure it stays that way. Enjoy your drink." After one last glance, the statuesque police lieutenant slid off the stool and strode away.

Okay, got it. No more asking about Nina. At least not tonight.

He was a patient man, so he'd wait for another chance meeting. Though, he wasn't one for leaving too much to chance.

CHAPTER 3

Today was too beautiful to stay indoors. Nina put on her hiking boots, grabbed a bottle of water and a small canister of pepper spray, and headed out the door. The air temperature had dropped since yesterday, and she wore a faded Juilliard pullover to ward off the chill. Low clouds moved quickly across the sky, sporadically blocking the warmth of the sun.

She didn't see a car in Beatrice's driveway, which meant the private duty nurse hadn't arrived yet. If the nurse showed by the time she finished her hike, she'd go over and introduce herself. Just because the nursing service was highly rated didn't mean Nina fully trusted her friend's care to a stranger.

After a mile of walking through neighborhoods, she came to the entrance of her favorite trail. The hike was moderately challenging, and the peaceful scenery always left her with the sensation she'd stepped into heaven. At the end waited a rambling waterfall. She usually stopped for a rest on one of the large boulders at the bottom and listened to the rhythmic pattern of the falling water—a reward for her endurance. If she closed her eyes, she heard a wonderful symphony of notes in various tones.

As she turned toward the trail, a car horn sounded. Jumping, she covered her heart with her hand. "Geez, Gabs, you scared the living daylights out of me."

Gabs leaned her head out the open driver's side window of her squad car. "Sorry, didn't mean to startle you. Just wanted to get your attention before you disappeared into the trees."

Nina walked back to the street and grinned. "I'm not under arrest, am I?"

Climbing out of the car, Gabs was all smiles. "That would be the day." She laughed. "You don't even drive over the speed limit."

"Because they are speed limits, not suggestions."

"I'll introduce you to several people around town who'd dispute that." Gabs rested her hip against her car and shifted the weight of her duty belt. "In all seriousness, I didn't want to bring this up yesterday at Celia's shower, but I know Erich was released and wanted to make sure you're doing all right."

"I'm as good as I can be, given the circumstances." Nina tucked her hands into the front pocket of her pullover. "I knew he'd get out someday, and that's why I moved from Boston and changed my last name. Finding me won't be easy."

"You still have your protection order, right?" She reached over and put a hand on Nina's shoulder.

Despite the warmth of her sweatshirt, she shivered. "Yes, but I had a restraining order on him before, and the piece of paper didn't stop him from taking me...and killing Seth."

Picturing the face of the man she'd dated years ago, she choked back a sob. Seth's only crime had been showing romantic interest in her, and he'd paid with his life.

"I got your back, Nina. You need anything, or that sick bastard reaches out, call me...okay?"

The chill inside Nina's body faded, replaced by the reassuring warmth of friendship. She nodded. "I will. Promise."

"I'll let you get back to your hike." Gabs started to get back into the driver's seat but paused. "Hey, I almost forgot. I overheard some guy asking about you at The Chute last night."

Her heart pounded against her ribs, and her vision blurred. Had Erich found her already? Panic swirled. "Who was it? What did he want?"

"Don't freak." Gabs reached out to hold Nina's trembling hand. "I overheard him mention your name, and being the hard-ass that I am, I went over to see what he was all about." She grunted. "The guy told me he'd helped you with a cake from the bakery yesterday. Dark hair, blue eyes, really good-looking, with a hint of bad boy."

The image of Colin's sexy face flashed in her mind's eye, causing her anxiety to fade. "Oh yeah, he stood in line behind me when I picked up the desserts for the shower. He did help me." But what if the scenario had been a setup? Had Erich sent him? Why was she being so paranoid? Normally, she was a very rational person. *Erich's release is driving me crazy.*

"When I questioned him, he seemed genuinely perplexed. Honestly, I think he wants to see you again to ask you out."

"Really?" She felt her cheeks warm. "He did ask me to join him for dinner."

"Then why was he at The Chute alone?" Gabs winked. "The guy's a tall, dark glass of whiskey."

One she might enjoy looking at, but would definitely decline to drink. "Not exactly my taste. Thanks for being a good cop and a great friend." Nina gripped the car door as Gabs got seated. Once Gabs was inside, Nina leaned in the open window. "You and Troy doing okay?"

She sighed. "I guess. He's still on me to quit the force, which I won't. He knew what he was getting when he started dating me. I'm not sorry I refuse to change in order to make him more secure about his manhood."

Nina reached in and rubbed her shoulder. "You are perfect, so don't change." She turned her gaze to the neglected trail. "Catch you later."

"Enjoy your walk."

As Gabs drove away, Nina shook off all her unsettling feelings. Instead, she focused on the serenity she'd achieved since moving to Polaris ten years ago. She filled her lungs with the fresh mountain air. Around her, birds fluttered about and sang. She walked by hundreds of white-trunked aspen trees, some topped with golden leaves.

Her life now was simple—nature, friendship, gratitude. She'd rediscovered her love of music, not by playing herself, but through teaching. Seeing the faces of her students light up when they played set her heart free.

She'd left her trauma behind in Boston. And that was where it would stay.

Ninety minutes later, she turned the corner onto her block, feeling pounds lighter. Could be the cleansing sweat she'd worked up and a release of tension with her exertion.

Up ahead, she noticed a forest-green SUV parked in Beatrice's driveway. Looked like the nurse had finally arrived. Bea's doctor had applied for a special grant from Health Shield Nursing Service, and she'd been selected to receive the highest quality in-home care at no cost. After a life of struggling with diabetes, a courageous fight for civil rights during the sixties and seventies, losing her husband to cancer, and still finding the time and energy to volunteer in the community, no one deserved the gift more than Bea.

Picking up her pace, Nina walked up to the front door. She knocked twice, then waited. The sound of quick footsteps alerted her that Bea was not the one who would open the door, which earned the new nurse a point of favor in her mind. The less walking Bea did, the better. At least until after she healed from her hip replacement.

The front door swung open, and Nina planted a smile on her face and raised her gaze. At the sight of Colin Moynahan, she blinked. Wait. What was he doing inside Bea's house?

"Well...hello again." He lifted his eyebrows. "You must be the pretty neighbor Mrs. Maxwell was just telling me about."

His grin sent electric pulses across her skin. "What are you doing here?" She stepped past him and into the living room. "Bea, where is your private nurse?"

Bea chuckled and pointed to Colin. "Sweetie, you're looking at him."

~ ᵧ ~

What a wicked bit of good fortune. Colin's gaze swept over the woman he hadn't stopped thinking about since yesterday at the bakery. Today, she looked more relaxed, in jeans, a baggy hoodie, and dirt-stained hiking boots.

She stopped on the entry mat, untied her boots, and slipped them off one at a time. "This man is not a nurse." Her narrowed eyes glared at him.

Colin ignored her snippy tone, as well as the finger pointed in the direction of the door. Instead of being offended, he was amused. Colin took out his wallet and retrieved a business card, and then handed it to her. "I have a master's degree in nursing with a specialty in gerontology from the University of Massachusetts Boston. Along with some training in physical therapy. For the past eight years, I've worked for a company called Health Shield as a private duty nurse."

Nina stood with her arms crossed over her chest, jaw hanging slack. She glanced down at the card, and then back at him. "I don't believe it."

"Mr. Moynahan, please meet my neighbor, Nina Pettit." Bea turned her attention to Nina. "Sweetie, his company came highly recommended by Dr. Brown. Health Shield is one of the top private healthcare providers in the country. I learned that on Google." She tapped her cane on the carpet. "You know what else I read on my computer, Nina? Colin here cared for an English lord after the old geezer fell off his horse and broke both his legs."

Nina leveled her gaze at him. "May I speak to you outside?"

He found her more attractive by the second. The hot temper dancing in her eyes set his blood on fire. "Please excuse us, Mrs. Maxwell. As soon as I'm done convincing your neighbor I'm not a shady criminal posing as a nurse who's here to seduce you and steal all your money, we can finish going over your medication schedule."

"Being seduced sounds like more fun than getting a hip

replaced." Beatrice winked. "Now go with my Nina and put her mind at ease. I'll close my eyes and rest a bit."

Nina slipped her boots back on, and he followed her out the front door. The late-afternoon sun was mostly hidden behind the rise of the mountains, casting long shadows across the ground.

"If you don't believe me, I have a list of references." He stopped underneath a tall maple and leaned against the trunk. Chilly air blew from the north, sending dry orange and red leaves tumbling down the street.

"You're a man...not at all what I expected." She tucked her hands inside the long sleeves of her hoodie.

The stitching on the faded yellow fleece read Juilliard, and he wondered if she'd gone to school there. Was she a dancer? She definitely had the body of one. He could do a quick internet search and find out, but learning about a person the old-fashioned way was more fun.

"That's kind of sexist." He grinned as her big honey-colored eyes met his, giving him another blow to the chest. This woman hit harder with one look than any opponent in the ring. "But I'll let it slide since I know you're only worried about your friend."

"Yes, I am worried about her, and you're not a local, so no one around here knows you." Her gaze lowered to his chest. "Plus, I've never seen a nurse who looks like you."

His already healthy ego swelled. "I am one in a million."

She arched a light-brown eyebrow. "I wouldn't go that far."

"Don't judge a book by its cover. I'm very good at my job." His playful grin faded. "And I don't say that to brag, only to prove my qualifications."

Nina tilted her head toward Mrs. Maxwell's house. "How long have you been a nurse?"

"Have dinner with me tonight, and I'll go over my résumé." Colin pushed off the tree trunk and stepped toward her. Worth another shot.

"I'm not going out with you." She moved from the lawn onto the driveway. "I heard you were asking about me at The Chute last night. Why?"

He released a deep-throated chuckle. "You're drop-dead gorgeous, if you haven't noticed. You're also fascinating, and I wanted to see you again."

"No one sent you out here to search for me, did they?" She picked at the pills on her sweatshirt.

At the sight of her face lined with concern, he stopped laughing. His flirtation was meant to be good-natured, but she appeared on edge. He'd stepped over the line. Better pull back. "I have no other motive for being here other than to care for Mrs. Maxwell after her surgery."

"I believe you." Nina's shoulders slackened, and she walked toward the front porch steps. "We're both from Boston. I no longer have connections there, and I'd like to keep it that way." She stopped on the porch and rested her forearms on the white wooden rail, then leaned forward.

Colin stood beside her, keeping a foot of distance between them. His curiosity turned into protective concern. He'd dedicated his life to caring for people. It was the reason he'd learned to fight and the reason he'd trained to be a nurse. Growing up, he'd gotten little nurturing from his parents. His grandmother had been the only one who'd made sure he had enough to eat, clean clothes to wear to school, and completed his homework to the best of his ability.

Nana Rose, as weak and poor as she'd been, had provided him a lifeline. She'd made him want to be a better person, which was why he took high-paying jobs with rich clients who wanted a private nurse who looked more like a bodyguard. Those clients helped fund the grant program for patients like Mrs. Beatrice Maxwell, who, judging from the grant proposal written by her doctor, deserved to be treated like royalty.

His career was a small payment in honor of his deceased grandmother, who'd been the light of his life.

"We may have grown up in the same part of the country, but I doubt we ran with the same crowd." He rested a hip on the porch rail and allowed his gaze to wander over her. When her lips tilted in a small smile, he relaxed. "I'm a Southie. Spent every day of the first fifteen years of my life within a ten-mile radius of home. Once I got my driver's license, I started moving around more. Me and some friends would take off to New York for the weekend and find trouble, which isn't hard to do when you're sixteen and lookin' for it."

Nina angled her body to face him. "I'm from Wellesley."

When he opened his mouth with pretend astonishment, she laughed.

"Is it that obvious?"

"That you were raised with money? Not just by looking at you." He stared into her eyes and detected hurt and wariness in their depths. "You got a polished, high-class vibe. When I was in college, I dated a girl who lived out in Wellesley. Old money." Colin smiled at the memory. "Her daddy wasn't happy when I showed up for family dinner, but I think that was the point."

She chuckled. "I had friends in high school who would have really liked you." Tipping her chin, she met his gaze. "I love Bea, and I want her to have a swift and easy recovery. If you can help make that happen, then I'll stop the inter-rogation."

"She's lucky to have you watching over her."

A beam of sunlight backlit her head, giving her hair an angelic glow. Fine strands blew around her face, and his hand burned with the need to sweep them away, if only to touch her soft skin.

Growing up, Nina was the type of girl he would have admired from a distance, knowing she was way too good for the likes of him, a kid from South Boston with no money. A kid who boxed on the streets and in the ring to earn his college education. And after all the struggle and pain, he'd made something of himself. He wasn't rich, but comfortable. He traveled the world for work, only taking jobs that appealed to him. But standing next to Nina, he still felt unworthy.

Could be why at thirty-six, he'd never fallen in love. He assumed he was missing the essential part of a person's soul that opened before connecting with another. Or maybe he avoided deep relationships because he'd enjoyed most of his adult life without a permanent address and no desire to settle down. Probably a solid combo of both.

Nina pushed off the porch rail and moved to the front door. "I'm the one who's lucky to have Beatrice in my life. She's my family."

Standing close to her, he crossed his arms so as not to be tempted to reach out and touch her. "I'll care for Beatrice like my own grandmother. You have my word." Grabbing the knob to open the door, he paused. "You know, I don't officially start until tomorrow, when I take Mrs. Maxwell to check into the hospital at six a.m." He cleared his throat. "If you want to avoid cooking dinner tonight...I hear the Backcountry Bar has great burgers and fries. I'm heading over there after I'm done here."

She lifted both her eyebrows. "You don't give up, do you?"

With a crooked grin, Colin held the door open for her and enjoyed the view as she walked by. "Ms. Pettit, the word *quit* is not in my vocabulary."

CHAPTER 4

What am I doing? Nina had been asking herself that question ever since she'd left home for the short walk to the Backcountry. Now she stood at the entrance of the bar, doubting her normally acute judgment.

She peered inside through one of the long, narrow windows flanking the front door, not sure if she hoped to see Colin or not. He had her all mixed up, and she wasn't sure how she felt about the addition to her already off-balance psyche. Since half walls blocked the tables towards the rear of the building, she couldn't see the entire space. The bar was busy, and Nina saw several men with dark hair, but no one with Colin's tall, athletic build. None who made her heart race and her palms sweat.

She loved the way his smile lit up his entire face and made his eyes twinkle with some secret mischief. He was a man of contradictions. Tough looking and strong, as well as a private duty nurse who treated Bea with the same dignity, kindness, and respect she imagined he showed all his patients.

She could trick herself into believing she'd only come to

discover if he was good enough for Bea. But honestly, she was standing outside in the cold because she was attracted to a nice guy who killed it in the looks department—double trouble.

Why hadn't she listened to her head and warmed up a plate of leftover lasagna for dinner like she'd originally planned? Wanting one last look before she decided whether to go in or run for home, she leaned toward the window. *This is a bad idea. Time to go.* Feeling a tap on her shoulder, she jumped a foot clear into the air.

"Didn't mean to scare you." Colin's deep laughter sounded from behind.

She pressed her hand over her heart to keep it from bursting out of her chest and slowly turned. His wide smile made her knees shake. "Good grief. I'm not normally so jumpy." While catching her breath, she checked him out— black boots, slightly faded black jeans, a long-sleeve blue shirt that brought out the color of his eyes, and just enough red-tinted scruff on his face to send heat pooling into her belly. Air rushed out of her lungs.

"Are you coming inside?" He grabbed the brass antler handle and swung open the door. "Break my heart if I had to eat alone."

"I have a feeling you wouldn't be alone for long." Shooting him a sideways glance, she strode into the bar. A cloud of cheery noise greeted her. She didn't frequent the Backcountry often, but she knew several of the waitstaff and bartenders, meaning she'd feel comfortable here with Colin. If he tried anything inappropriate, he'd be quickly tossed out on his ass.

He scanned the room, and then his gaze fell back on her. "I don't see anyone else here I'd rather share a burger and beer with than you." Pointing toward an empty table set against the wall, he led her through the crowd. "Easier to talk at a table than sitting at the bar."

She removed her coat and slid onto the booth seat, all while trying to ignore the quickening of her pulse.

He sat on the other side of the table and grabbed a menu. "What do you recommend?"

"They make a really good veggie burger. But if you want something with meat, I won't be much help." A small rise of panic fluttered inside her chest from sitting alone with him at a table. Trusting people, especially men, did not come easily, no matter how nice and good-looking they were.

"My last patient was vegan. He's a retired movie star who lives in a beach house in Southern Cali. His private chef tossed together quinoa, grilled vegetables, and some Middle Eastern seasoning for one of the best meals I've ever eaten." He ran his finger down the menu and tapped on a color photograph of a thick, juicy burger topped with lettuce and a tomato slice. "But right now, I'm really craving some red meat. I won't order it, though, if it will bother you."

She shook her head. "Order what you like. Thank you for asking." A thoughtful gesture. She couldn't tell if he only meant to impress or was genuinely respectful of her feelings. Guess she'd need more time to figure him out.

Their waitress swung by to take their drink order, and then returned with a pitcher of Sam Adams and two frosty mugs. Colin poured amber liquid into one mug and slid it across the table to Nina.

She took several sips. The cold liquid slid down her throat and sent a relaxing sensation through her body. "Sounds like you travel a lot for your work. Do you still call Boston home?"

"My buddy, the owner of Health Shield, lives in Chicago. I crash at his place every now and then when I have nowhere else to be." He shrugged. "I still own my grand-mother's rowhouse in South Boston, which I rent out. I stay busy enough with patients that I travel most of the year. It's why I love my career."

"Sounds like you have a strong case of wanderlust." She lifted her mug and took a long swallow. Her upper lip tingled, and she licked off a spot of beer froth before taking another drink. "I traveled a lot when I was younger. Some-times for education and sometimes for performances. But these days, I like staying close to home." Traveling had always given her anxiety. Since moving to Polaris, she'd taken one trip to Seattle. After two days of gut-twisting nerves, she'd moved up her flight and headed home.

"I noticed you in a Juilliard sweatshirt earlier today. Were you a student there?" He smiled as the waitress approached with a notepad to take their food order. Once she left, he folded his hands on the table and turned his full attention to Nina. His bright eyes contrasted against his dark lashes, brows, and hair, making them look like two moons set in an inky-black sky.

She avoided talking about the time in her life when music was everything. With Colin, though, she'd offer a small peek. "I played the cello...and studied music educa-tion at Juilliard." Inhaling deeply, she attempted to block out any memory of Erich, but it was no use. He was always hidden in the recesses of her mind. His demands she play only for him still echoed in her head. The memory made her sick.

She'd dated Erich after her graduation from Julliard. He'd seen her final solo performance at the school and sent her flowers the next morning. He was older and sophisti-cated, and Nina was totally taken in by his charms.

Six months of dating went by before she recognized the

pattern of his abusive control. Especially regarding her music. By then, he'd become her sponsor and the center of her musical world. When she broke off their relationship, she soon discovered his confident demeanor disguised a brutal obsession.

The day Erich was convicted of assault, kidnapping, and involuntary manslaughter, she locked her cello case away for good. Her love of playing had been permanently corrupted.

Nina closed her eyes and pushed away the toxic feelings. She reopened them to the gorgeous sight of Colin.

The corners of his mouth lifted with a small grin. "I can picture you as a cellist."

"I teach music at the Polaris elementary and high school, but haven't played myself in years."

"What made you stop?" He rested his forearms on the table and leaned in.

"I lost the desire." She exhaled. "Now I find joy in teaching children and seeing their smiles when they learn to play a new song or perform in front of their families. Whether my students have natural musical ability or not makes no difference. Music opens doors to many parts of life that are too often overlooked. Music is about closing your eyes and feeling the rhythm of your heartbeat and your breath. You listen to the melodies of nature instead of tuning them out because you're too busy and distracted."

"You paint a pretty picture." He lifted his mug and winked. "Almost makes me want to learn how to play an instrument. You interested in teaching me?"

"Sure. How about the piccolo?" She reclined further in the booth in an attempt to fight off her attraction to him— one neither welcome nor wanted.

"Piccolo." Grinning, he rolled up the sleeves of his shirt. "Doesn't sound very manly."

"It's not." She glanced at his exposed muscular forearms. A circular tattoo resembling a compass marked the underside of his right forearm. Very fitting for a man who didn't stay in the same town for more than a few months. Someone who seemed allergic to putting down roots.

Taking a glimpse at his hands resting on the table, she noticed they were larger than the average man's, and his knuckles looked misshapen. Despite their rough appearance, they must be gentle enough for him to be an effective nurse, especially to the elderly.

A stocky man with a long braid down his back walked toward their table, carrying two large plates. "Who got the veggie burger with extra onions?" He glanced from Colin to Nina.

She raised her hand. "That would be me."

He set the plate on the table and chuckled. "Hope you brought some breath mints, miss."

As he handed Colin his burger, Nina felt her face heat. Surely her cheeks glowed cherry red. Once the man was gone, she let out a long breath. "The last thing I want is for anyone to think we're on a date."

"So being the town's music teacher makes you ineligible?" He cocked a black eyebrow.

"No." She unwrapped her silverware from the napkin. "I can date. I just don't." Nina didn't date casually. Although, on the other hand, she'd closed herself off to a serious relationship in the years since Erich.

Tonight was definitely not a date, because Colin was the walking, talking, breathing embodiment of a casual hookup —which made him an interesting dinner partner, but nothing more.

~ ᵥ ~

Colin shook his head. "You don't date. What a waste of a perfect woman who is not only attractive, she also gives piccolo lessons."

Nina's cheeks darkened with a pretty blush, and she dropped her gaze to her onion-loaded veggie burger. Did the woman have any idea how smoking hot she was? No. She acted like she wanted to be invisible. As she sat across the table, her posture slightly hunched, he wondered who'd hurt her. Someone obviously had. The damage was subtle, but it was there, hidden just below the surface.

He was fascinated by her, and the more time he spent in her company, the more he wanted to know. Why had she left Boston? What had happened to cause her to stop playing the cello? If she was a gifted musician, why hide in a small town like Polaris and teach music lessons to kids?

He wanted to know everything about Nina Pettit. Unfortunately, his time here was limited. His next patient lived in Maui. After his contract there was over, he'd take another job in another city and forget about Nina, with her honey-colored hair and wide doe-eyes. Just like all the other interesting people who'd entered and exited his life at various points.

She lifted her burger and smirked over the top of the bun. "Enough about my choices of extra onions and what they mean to my nonexistent dating life. Why did you decide to become a traveling private duty nurse?"

He finished chewing a french fry before answering. "My Grandma Rose was a saint of a woman. Had to be to raise the likes of me." Colin smiled at the memory of Nana Rose waving a rolling pin in the air, yelling at him to sit down at the kitchen table and finish his homework. "She only stood five feet tall on a good day and wore either a floral print dress or a housecoat, depending on whether she was going out or staying in. When she hollered, which was mostly either at me or the guy who lived next door, the woman had a voice like James Earl Jones. Mostly thanks to a half-a-pack-a-day habit of Marlboro Lights and a redheaded Irish temper."

"Sounds like one heck of a woman." Nina dabbed a napkin at the corner of her mouth.

"That she was. My folks didn't like having me around, so I spent most days at Nana Rose's house. She pushed me hard to do well in school and go to college."

A burst of noise sounded from the back of the bar. Several couples were engaged in a seemingly competitive game of darts. He watched as Nina's gaze flickered to the group and noticed a hint of longing in her eyes.

"Anyway." He waited until her attention was fixed back on him. "If not for her, I would have never finished high school, let alone college. I decided to become an RN with a specialty in geriatrics. Her health was failing, and I wanted to care for her the way she cared for me for so many years."

"That's very sweet." She swirled a fry through the mountain of ketchup on her plate.

"It was the least I could do." After downing the remaining drops in his mug, he grabbed the pitcher and topped off Nina's beer and then his own. "Since I had to work to make money for school, I took longer than usual to get my degree. Once I graduated, Nana's lungs were failing. Remember the half-a-pack-a-day habit I told you about?"

Nina nodded, her mouth bowed downward in a frown. "How long did you have with her?"

"Not long enough...less than a year, but we made those days count." His spirits lifted with good memories. "She loved to dance. I played every jazz record in her collection at least once. When she was feeling good, I moved the sofa against the wall and we had a little dance party in her living room."

"She sounds a lot like Beatrice."

With a hitch in his heart, he tapped his chest. "After Nana was gone, I had no reason to hang around Boston. I got a job as a private duty nurse in Manhattan and worked for rich folks with apartments ten times the size of my home back in South Boston. I made connections, got good referrals. My buddy James started Health Shield and established the Angel Grant for deserving elderly patients who needed private care but the cost was above their means." He took a drink of beer. "I love moving around and seeing all the different parts of the world and meeting new people. Nice, beautiful people who can teach me to play the piccolo."

She blushed again and looked down at her almost empty plate.

He took a bite of his burger and realized he'd been doing most of the talking. Why did he constantly babble on and on, telling one story after another? Nana Rose had been the same way—always a story to tell, like she had them stored in a filing system inside her brain. She'd talk for hours to anyone who'd listen, or anyone who'd strike up an innocent conversation, then unwittingly become a captive audience.

"How long have you known Mrs. Maxwell?" he asked, hoping to nudge out some more information about Nina.

"I've lived across the street from her for ten years. Bea was the first person who came over and greeted me after I moved in." She twisted a napkin with deft fingers.

Colin imagined those same fingers gracefully moving across the neck of a cello, her other hand sliding a bow across the strings, creating a haunting melody. He'd seen a cello performance several years ago and remembered the passion with which the female cellist had played. Now, he practically felt her fingers plucking across his chest, playing him like an instrument. His body flashed with heat, and he forced himself to look away until he pulled himself back under control. "Your house is the funky purple one, right? Was it already that color when you moved in?"

Her face brightened with a smile. "I can't take credit for the color. My house belonged to an artist. It sat on the market for some time before I came along. I fell in love with the purple exterior and white gingerbread molding the moment I saw it. The flower gardens are my contribution. Each year I add a little more. Next spring, I want to build an arbor with a bench in the backyard rose garden."

"I'd love a tour...someday. I'm clueless when it comes to flowers. Can't tell the difference between a daisy and a sunflower."

"You can't possibly be that bad." Nina pulled out her phone from her purse and checked the time. "I should get home. I need to find our waitress and get my bill." She craned her head to search the room.

"This is my treat." Reaching across the table, he set his hand over her purse.

Shaking her head, she slid her wallet out from under his palm. "We shared a table and ate dinner together, but you're not paying for my share." She raised her hand and waved at their waitress.

"Don't panic. I'm not calling this a date." Although, he'd like to. He also didn't want their time together to end. Fortunately, he'd be seeing Nina a lot during his time working in Polaris. "Being new in town, I appreciate the company. Paying for your veggie burger and a pitcher of beer is an easy way to say thanks."

"I always pay for myself. I don't like feeling obligated to anyone." Her attention turned to the waitress now standing at their table. "Please split the bill. I'll pay mine as soon as it's ready."

He opened his mouth to protest, but decided his best bet was keeping it shut. His male pride wasn't that easily damaged. If Nina wanted to keep the lines sharp and clear between them, he'd respect her wishes.

It wasn't like he was looking to start anything serious. He simply liked hanging out and getting to know new people.

Admittedly, her attitude was better than the opposite reaction—where a casual friendship was misinterpreted as something more significant. There'd been a few times he'd broken a woman's heart right before leaving town. Bad scene all the way around, and one he did his best to avoid.

Nina set cash on top of the paper copy of the bill and slid out of the booth seat. "You were good company. I loved hearing the stories about Nana Rose. You'll have to tell me more sometime." She buttoned up her jacket.

Tonight, she'd worn dark blue skinny jeans, brown boots, and a turquoise shirt. Her hair was straight, as if she'd flattened out all its natural waves. Looped around her neck was a copper chain necklace, and scattered on its links were crystal beads that sparkled in the light.

He liked the way she looked tonight as much as he liked how she looked at the bakery, dressed in the pink dress and heels. And as much as earlier today, when she wore an old pullover sweatshirt and faded jeans.

"Maybe we can do this again." He grinned, looking up at her. "I have an endless supply of stories."

"Sure. I guess I'll see you tomorrow at the hospital." After a brief hesitation, she walked away, weaving through the crowd toward the door.

Once she'd left the bar, Colin grabbed the pitcher and refilled his empty mug. He needed something to put out the fire inside him. One that had started in his gut and was slowly burning a path to his heart. Might take time to earn her trust, but he'd learn at least some of her story—why she was both skittish and fiercely independent. As someone who loved a mystery, he vowed to leave town knowing as much as he could about Nina.

CHAPTER 5

*O*nce Nina got the word Bea's hip replacement had gone well, she breathed normally again. A nurse arrived and escorted Nina out of the waiting area to the hospital room Bea would occupy for the next two days. Hopefully, she'd be discharged to finish healing in the comfort of her own home under Colin's care.

With Bea still in the recovery room, Nina settled into a semi-comfortable chair and went through her emails. She hated replying on her phone, with its tiny keyboard. Half her time was spent deleting the wrong letters she mistakenly pressed before retyping her message. She had several emails from parents of her music students that needed a reply. Her students' concert was less than two months away, which meant she'd spend a lot of time from now until then planning and organizing dozens of small details.

She'd been eight or nine years old when she'd taken part in her first cello concert. As she walked onto the stage on trembling legs, she filled with a mixture of fear and excitement. Once seated and ready, she gazed into the crowd, wanting a glimpse of her parents to steady her nerves. The audience, spread out on auditorium chairs, waited for her to begin. Absent were the familiar faces of her mother and father. After a minute of panic, her music teacher, Mrs. King, walked onstage.

"You can do this, dear. I believe in you," Mrs. King whispered in her ear.

With the small encouragement, Nina began playing. Not perfectly, but she played with all her heart and soul. After finishing her last song, she looked once more into the audience. Again, not seeing anyone from her family, she ran off stage—her tears creating a trail.

She was grateful all her music students had parents who loved and supported them, even if the children would never become professional musicians. These parents volunteered to help with decorations and put together post-concert receptions full of homemade foods. The opposite of her own parents, who'd been too busy to attend her early performances.

Growing sleepy, she put her cell back inside her purse and checked the time. Bea should be brought in any moment now, and Colin would arrive shortly to meet with Bea's doctor to discuss her plan of care. If Nina moved quickly, she could sneak away for a cup of coffee to wake up her brain.

She had a music lesson back at her house at four. After a long day of sitting around the hospital, she wasn't sure her brain could function at a high enough level to teach a flute lesson to a very talented thirteen-year-old girl without a shot of caffeine.

Before leaving, she took a moment to check out her reflection in the small mirror inside the bathroom. Good grief, she looked as pale as a marble statue. After a quick pinch on each cheek and a few light slaps to get the blood flowing, her skin flushed into a more natural-looking pink. She combed her fingers through her hair and wished she'd brought a hair tie. And Colin had called her drop-dead gorgeous. *Ha.* Either he needed his eyes checked, or he was a talented and experienced flirt.

Still, she had to admit she didn't look half bad for thirty-something. In another year, she'd round second base and do the slow creep toward forty. No worries, though. Age was simply a number. Bea had taught her that.

Exiting the room, she made her way to the bank of elevators and took the first available one down to the main floor. She cut through the lobby, heading in the direction of the café. Without warning, the sound of a familiar voice calling her name brought her to a lurching halt.

Meg? No. She hadn't seen her sister in over ten years. Her family, even though estranged, knew she'd moved to Polaris, Utah in order to start her new life. The threads holding them together were weak, but she hadn't been able to sever them totally. Perhaps someday, she'd wish to repair their relationship. She just wasn't ready for that day yet.

"Nina." The voice sounded again. "Are you going to stand there all day?"

The woman's laugh was unmistakable—pretentious with an undercurrent of cruelty. Nina turned to see a familiar face. Meg had put on some weight since the last time they'd been together, and the added fullness was a vast improvement to the gaunt girl she remembered. Her hair was the same white blonde, but styled in a sleek bob. Better suited to a woman in her mid-thirties than the curly mass of hair she'd had as a teen.

"Meg? What are you doing here?" She gulped out the question. Seeing her sister at the Polaris Hospital lobby, in a setting totally out of context, left her feeling like she'd been hit with a stun grenade.

Rushing forward, Meg reached Nina with arms spread wide. "Is that anyway to greet your sister?"

Nina sidestepped Meg's embrace and put several feet of distance between them. "You're acknowledging me as your sister now?"

"Oh, Nina," Meg whined. "Don't be like that. We haven't seen each other in forever. Let's start over."

She stifled a laugh at the absurdity of Meg's question. Put the past behind them? That's why she left Boston and was now living in Polaris. Away from all the people who'd alienated her, including Meg and the rest of her family. "You want to make amends? Is that why you're here?"

"Amends?" Meg's voice rose. "Why would I need to make amends? I never did anything wrong."

Inside the small lobby, she noticed heads turning in their direction. Although she hadn't hidden her past since moving to town, she still didn't want strangers overhearing. "Let's step outside and talk in private." Nina lifted her arm and motioned toward the large glass sliding doors.

"Fine." Meg pulled the front edges of her cardigan together and folded her arms across her body. "And I thought you'd actually be happy to see me." With a lift of her chin, Meg marched towards the doors, waited for them to swoosh open, and stepped outside.

Nina followed closely behind, debating how to verbally approach her sister. Their relationship had never been good. Growing up as the youngest, Nina had felt left behind by her brother and sister. She'd lived with her family, but they never were a true family. It wasn't until she gained fame for her cello playing that her parents, grandparents, and siblings paid attention to her.

Meg stopped next to a cement planter filled with lemon-yellow Heliopsis blooms. "I'm vacationing in Polaris with a friend and thought we could reconnect." She reached into her purse and pulled out a pair of large-lensed sunglasses, then slid them on to cover her blue-gray eyes. "I got your address from Mother, who, of course, disapproves of my trip to see you, but then again, what doesn't she disapprove of? When I stopped by your house earlier, I rang the doorbell a few times, but no one answered. A nice lady walking her dog told me you were at the hospital. She said she didn't even know you had a sister." Meg snorted. "Figures."

Had she given her address to her mother or only the name of the town? She honestly couldn't recall. The time right after she'd moved away had been filled with emotional turmoil, so perhaps she had provided it in the hopes her parents would wish to see her again. No surprise, that never happened. "You once told me I was dead to you," Nina replied. "Remember?"

"That was so long ago." She shrugged. "I'm here now, right? I want to see how you're doing. What's it like living out West? Are you married?"

Meg's saccharine smile accentuated the tightness of the skin covering her forehead and cheeks. She'd obviously had some surgical enhancements. But under the surface of Meg's beautiful face was an unhealthy pallor. Despite her makeup, she appeared sallow and worn.

"My life here is great. I teach music lessons, volunteer at the library, and I have a large flower garden. And I'm happily single." A little information about herself couldn't hurt.

"Are you playing again?" Meg sat on a nearby bench and crossed one long leg over the other.

Sighing in resignation, she sat beside her. "No. Haven't

touched my cello since—" Her mouth refused to form the words *kidnap* or *Erich*.

Meg shook her head. "What a shame to waste such a gift. You worked so hard to get to a high level and then just walked away like it meant nothing."

"You think leaving my music career was easy?" She pivoted and angled her body to face Meg's. Years ago, when she'd been a little girl, Meg's words had gone unchallenged. No longer.

"You think what happened was easy on anyone in the family?" Meg pushed her sunglass up to the bridge of her nose.

"No. Kidnapping and murder have that effect." During the two weeks Erich had held her captive, she not only worried about her own safety, she grieved for Seth. When law enforcement finally rescued her, Nina was sent home to recover, but home proved not to be a safe haven for healing. Instead, her parents blamed her for igniting Erich's obsession. The media buzzed outside her house like gnats at a summer picnic. Both her brother and sister had resented the imposition and gossip.

Nina worked closely with the authorities to ensure Erich's conviction, which was another black mark against her. As her parents had expressed many times, if she just stopped talking about what happened, everything would go back to normal.

Normal. She'd never had a normal life. Neither before or after Erich. But once she came to the realization her life was her own, to build how she saw fit, a new path emerged. One that led her straight to Polaris.

"Mother and Father took down every photograph of you in the house but one," Meg said. "The portrait of you with your cello on stage at Carnegie Hall. So I suppose you're still a small source of pride, despite it all."

"Is this why you're here under the pretense of reconnecting? To poke a stick into old wounds?" Her temper flared. "You must know Erich was released from jail four days ago, and I'd be unnerved."

"You always thought everything was about you." Meg shot to her feet, whipped off her sunglasses, and pointed a finger at Nina. "Because of what happened between you and Erich, our family became a fountain of society gossip. And not just in Boston, but the entire East Coast." She blew out a breath. "Did you know I got married five years ago and have a beautiful daughter named Charlotte? Do you even care? I thought we could try to mend our relationship. Obviously, I was wrong."

Trying to ignore the tremors inside her body, Nina stood and faced her sister. "I'm glad you found happiness, but Meg, you're a stranger to me. As far as I'm concerned, we have no relationship to mend."

~ᵧ~

Even from fifty feet away, Colin could see Nina shaking. She stood off to the side of the main hospital doors, next to a vignette of a park bench and flowers, talking with another woman.

Normally, he didn't get involved in someone else's tense conversations, but in the short time he'd known Nina, he'd grown protective of her.

"Hey." He approached and came to a stop at Nina's side. His arrival should put an end to their discussion. "I thought I'd find you inside. How's our patient?" As he spoke, he noticed the other woman's eyes widen and her eyebrows arch up a smooth forehead. Her face looked a lot like Nina's. No doubt these two were related.

Nina tipped her chin and glanced up at him. Her lips were pressed together like they were holding back a flood. "Bea was still in recovery when I came down to grab a coffee from the café." She sighed. "Colin, this is my older sister, Megan. Meg, this is Colin."

"Older but prettier." With a wide smile, Meg reached over to shake his hand. "Pleasure. Nina just told me she was single."

Nina opened her mouth, but Colin rested his hand on her arm. A silent gesture that he wanted to take this one. "We're at the hospital caring for a neighbor who's just had surgery. Why are you here?"

Meg's momentarily offended expression shifted into a humored grin. "Looking for my sister, of course. We haven't seen one another in years, and I was hoping we could spend some time together while I'm in town on vacation."

"Are your husband and daughter here too?" Nina asked, moving a step closer to Colin.

"Oh, no." She chuckled. "Keith is working. He's a corporate lawyer and very busy. And sweet little Charlotte is at home with her nanny. There's really nothing to do for a toddler around here."

"That's too bad," Nina said. "I'd like to meet them."

Meg reached into her purse and pulled out a card, then handed it to Nina. "I'm staying at the North Star Resort. If you decide you want to talk, you can reach me there." She pointed to the card. "Room five hundred thirty."

After turning to leave, Meg took about ten steps before coming to a halt. She spun back to face Nina and Colin. "I hope you can be a big enough person to bury our past disagreements."

Once Meg was out of sight, Nina sat onto the park bench and hung her head. Tears dropped onto her legs, darkening the denim where they landed.

After a short internal debate, Colin wrapped his arm around her shoulders. He watched for any sign his touch caused her discomfort. Instead, she leaned into him.

"She caught me so off guard." Nina sniffled. "I was going for a coffee, and my sister was waiting for me in the lobby. We haven't seen or spoken to each other in a very long time."

"I take it you two aren't close."

Her shoulders shook with a brief snort of wry humor. "Meg and I were never close, even growing up. I envied her because she was older, prettier, and always had a boyfriend. She was jealous of my musical talents and the attention they brought me."

"Grass is always greener."

Nina lifted her head and looked at him with her large, honey-colored eyes, and his mouth went dry. Did she have any idea how innocently beautiful she was? She reminded him of a magical fairy in a children's illustration. The kind he'd seen on the pages of Nana's extensive storybook collection.

"Being a caregiver has made me a very good listener. I also respect confidentiality, so if you feel the need to talk..." He nudged her leg with his knee.

After about a minute of silence, she blinked a few times to clear her eyes, then shuddered out a breath. "I had a stalker...an ex-boyfriend. After he was sent to jail, I left Boston." Nina wrapped her arms around her body and rocked slightly. "All my family cared about was the scandal and gossip I'd caused."

A stalker... No wonder she acted guarded around others.

He hated men who placed their own desires ahead of respecting a woman. And then during and after her ordeal, she lacked support from family. "Loved ones can inflict the most painful scars."

Nina lowered her head and rested it on his shoulder. "I left everything behind and changed my last name to start a new life." She wiped her eyes with the sleeve of her sweater.

"Which was extremely brave." Being near Nina produced a heady dizziness. Touching her made his heart pound like he'd finished a race. He struggled to catch his breath. "You're a fighter and a survivor. That's something you should be proud of."

A small smile tugged at the corners of her mouth. "Products of trauma mixed with a dysfunctional family."

"Sounds like you and I have something more in common than coming from Boston."

"I like that we come from the same city," she said. "I find it strangely comforting."

"Wellesley is a totally different planet than South Boston, but I'll give you credit for being in the same solar system." He purposely exaggerated his Boston accent. "You'll earn extra points if you can recite *I drove my cah to the Gahden to watch the Celtics and eat some chowadah* without enunciating a single R."

She covered her mouth with her hand, stifling laughter. "I haven't heard someone talk like that in forever."

"Come on now." He bumped her with his elbow. "Or I'll start quizzing you about Red Sox history. I know it all."

"Okay." Nina took a deep breath and then recited his Boston tongue twister like a born-and-bred Southie. "Oh... what I wouldn't give for a real East Coast grinder—a good chicken Parm dripping with cheese and sauce."

He pretended to lick his fingers, almost tasting one of his favorite meals. "Stop. You're making me hungry."

A sweet giggle came from her lips, and he fought the urge to kiss the source of the sound.

"Thank you." She gazed off toward the rise of mountains in the distance. "I was upset, and you made me laugh. Your humor is a gift."

"My specialty." When Nina turned back to lock eyes with him, his breath hitched inside his chest. If he wasn't careful, he'd fall hard. Standing, Colin forced an easy grin. "A good sense of humor and a strong left hook were the reasons I survived high school."

She stood as well and faced him. "Let me guess... If you couldn't joke your way out of a confrontation, you were forced to fight?"

He shrugged. Now was not the time to relive his rise from street fighter to legitimate boxer. He had a feeling Nina was not the type of woman who'd be overly impressed by his fame, which had come from beating the crap out of another human. "I found nothing stops a tense situation like a funny story. And I had plenty of them."

"I'm sure you still do." She hitched her purse up her shoulder. "We should go back inside the hospital. I'm sure Bea has been brought to her room by now. I don't want her to be there too long by herself."

"I'll walk with you up to her room." He checked the time on his watch and flexed his fingers to work out the ache inside the joints.

Nina rested her hand over his, her touch as gentle and warm as a candle flame. "I'm glad you're here for Beatrice. I'll rest easier knowing you're staying with her." Her cheeks blushed a rosy pink, and she pulled her hand away.

He instantly missed the connection. "Caring for people's

medical needs is my job, and I take pride in my skills and education." When he noticed her open her mouth to speak, he held up a finger. "But caring for a person's heart and dignity is just as important. I've found healing takes place more rapidly when the patient is happy, comfortable, respected, and surrounded by loved ones. So I hope you'll visit your neighbor often over the next weeks." Colin winked.

Nina's gaze dropped to her feet. "I'll be over there every chance I get." She walked next to him towards the hospital doors. "You can count on that."

CHAPTER 6

The next morning, Colin entered Mrs. Maxwell's hospital room holding a vase filled with fresh flowers. The lady at the florist shop said the bouquet was made up of lilies, roses, and gerbera daisies. He'd have to take her word on that. "Morning, beautiful. How're you feeling?"

"Wonderful now that you're here." She shifted in her bed to sit upright. "No matter how old you are, a woman always likes being called beautiful first thing in the morning."

Setting down the vase on the counter, he smiled. "You able to get much sleep last night?"

She shook her head. "Only off and on. I had a hard time finding a comfortable position. My hip aches and so does the incision, but I guess that's to be expected."

Colin pulled up a chair to the side of the bed and sat. "Let's see about getting you released today. The doc will want you to take a few steps with assistance first, but considering you're otherwise strong and in good health, I expect you'll be sleeping in your own bed tonight. The longer you stay in the hospital, the greater your risk of infection."

"I'll do my best to get on my feet." She smoothed the white blanket over her legs. "I do appreciate you working with me until I recover. Since my husband passed, I rely on my friends to help me out. I know my sweet Nina would have dropped everything to stay and care for me, but she's got other people who need her too. Like those talented children she teaches music to. I just love in the summertime when she gives music lessons. I sit by my open window and listen to the wonderful sounds drifting from her house."

"Nina told me she used to play the cello."

"Oh, yes." Her dark brown eyes misted over. "I've seen videos on the computer of her concerts. She has a special gift, a way of bringing music to life. When you listen to her play, you feel it here." Mrs. Maxwell placed her hand over her heart. "I wish I had the opportunity to hear her perform live."

Colin reclined in the chair. He could almost picture Nina's small frame seated on a large stage, holding her instrument, her eyes closed, as she single-mindedly worked the bow across strings. The image stirred his own passion, and he forced his attention back to his patient. "Have they brought your breakfast yet, Mrs. Maxwell?"

She clicked her tongue. "You better get used to calling me Beatrice or Bea, young man."

"Yes, ma'am." He grinned.

"And no. I haven't eaten yet." Bea tucked a lock of silver hair back inside her purple silk overnight bonnet.

"Then I'll go ask what's the holdup." He stood and stretched his legs. "Can't leave you hungry my first full day on the job."

"Thank you, dear. Even if you're bringing me hospital food."

"Hang in there." Colin opened the door. "Once you get home, I'll make you a western omelet that will make you forget your own name."

As Bea closed her eyes, she let out a deep laugh. "Honey, at my age, that's not saying much."

~ˎ~

As Nina stood in front of her closet, trying to decide what to wear to music class, her mind drifted to Colin and his attractive charm. He seemed too good to be true. No one was perfect. Instead of perfect, though, he was only good-looking, kind, and had a great sense of humor. And, judging by the size of his biceps and chest, very physically fit.

She wondered about the scar slicing through his black eyebrow and the story behind the bump on the bridge of his nose. Colin Moynahan was a fighter. Even if he hadn't told her about his rough years in South Boston, he had the look of a man who didn't back down from a challenge. He carried himself with confidence and a hint of swagger, like he wasn't afraid of the damage others could do to him because he could do worse.

Nina wished her outlook on life was as brave.

She picked out a nice pair of jeans and a sweater, since the morning's weather report had predicted highs only reaching the mid-fifties. Once dressed, she checked the time and realized she didn't have to leave for a good hour yet. The toddler music class she led at the library on Wednesdays was her favorite part of the week. She reveled in seeing the babies' delight as they shook and pounded the various plastic and wooden instruments she provided, as well as the sparkle in the parents' eyes while they watched their precious children.

Though once class was complete and the formerly vibrant room empty, she was left fighting her sorrow over not having a child of her own to love. She often wondered what her child would look like if she was ever blessed with one. Would the baby have her coloring—blonde hair and tawny eyes? An image flashed in her mind of a chubby baby boy with a head of dark hair and big blue eyes.

Where did that come from? She shook her head, attempting to clear any thoughts of procreating with Colin.

If she did have a baby before her reproductive clock ran out, she'd want the whole package—love and marriage to go along with the baby carriage. And Colin Moynahan was as likely to settle down and get married as she was to play the cello again.

Her cello—once her most prized possession—resided on a shelf in the basement. If she tried to play, would music flow from her like it did years ago, or was the magic gone forever? Just the thought of holding the instrument and bow left her weighed down with anxiety.

With her thoughts of music trailing off, she wandered into the kitchen and poured a second cup of coffee. Hers didn't taste as good as Celia Batista's, whose Café Cubano was a sweet taste of heaven inside an espresso cup.

As she sipped, she looked over at her sister's card lying on the kitchen counter. Picking up the card, she twirled it with her fingers. The name on the card read Megan Montgomery Sawyer. Yesterday, she'd called her husband Keith. So, her sister had married Keith Sawyer. She vaguely remembered him hanging around the house with Meg and her group of high school friends. Keith's parents were new money, having made millions in the video-game arcade machine business.

Back then, Nina had gotten the impression Meg had simply tolerated him because he had money even though he lacked the pedigree of the right family name. Since she married the guy, she must have changed her tune. Maybe Meg finally realized there was more to a person than who their great-grandparents were and how many generations back their relatives had socialized together in the same high society circles.

Deciding rehashing her history with Meg at this point in time would not be positive for her mental health, she tucked the business card into the front pocket of her purse. Maybe someday she'd reach out and connect with her sister, but not now—not so soon after Erich's release had jumbled up her emotions.

After she downed the last drop of coffee, she grabbed her box of instruments for class, her purse, and her car keys, and headed out the back door. She loaded the box into her car and opened the garage door. Out of the corner of her eye, she saw a man standing at the base of her driveway. When he turned to face her, Nina felt her stomach heave. *Erich?* Before she could take a strained breath, the man angled his body and strode down the sidewalk, away from her house.

She stood frozen, blinking, as cool air swirled around her body. A chill traveled up her spine and settled at the back of her neck. With all the stress brought on by seeing Meg, she must be imagining things.

That man had been too short and thin to be Erich. And he'd worn a black stocking hat and hooded sweatshirt— items the pretentious Erich would never own in his finely tailored wardrobe.

Despite the nausea rolling in her belly and snaking up her throat, she sprinted down the driveway. Her gaze darted down the sidewalk, in the direction the man had taken. She saw no one. A black car approached, driving slowly toward her. Nina glanced through the lightly tinted windows. An elderly woman sat in the driver's seat and waved as she passed.

"You okay?" A deep voice sounded from behind.

She jumped, clutching her chest. Turning, she saw Luke Veldkamp, her neighbor and the Polaris police captain, striding towards her. "Yes." Her tongue stuck to the roof of her mouth, and she swallowed a few times before she could speak again. "I thought I saw someone."

Luke shifted his stance to gaze over her shoulder and down the street. "No one's there."

She hugged herself, trying to stop shivers from taking over her body.

Luke studied her. "You look like you're going to be sick. Come on, let me walk you back home." He cupped her elbow and guided her along the sidewalk and up her driveway.

Once she was back inside her garage, she leaned against her car and exhaled. "Erich, the man who kidnapped me back in Boston was just released on bail. I'm feeling on edge knowing he's no longer behind bars."

Luke crossed his arms and scowled. "If he's on parole, he can't cross state lines without permission, and I doubt his parole officer will sign off on a trip to see his victim."

She didn't like the term victim when referring to her, but she understood in the legal sense, she was a victim of his crime. Inside her heart, Nina only thought of herself as a survivor. "The man I saw only glanced my way for a few seconds, and the distance made it hard to make out his features. When I saw him, I felt a punch in the gut." Panic constricted her chest. "It wasn't him, right? It couldn't be him."

"You're never wrong to trust your gut instincts." Luke stood at arm's length, and his strong, reassuring hand rested on her shoulder. "I'll contact his parole officer and confirm he's still reporting as required. I'll follow up with you once I have reassurance he's still in Boston."

"And if he isn't?" Sick dread stabbed her like tiny shards of glass.

"Then we act. Polaris is a small town with a police force dedicated to keeping you safe. Okay?" He gently squeezed her arm.

"Thanks, Luke. I feel better knowing you're keeping an eye on me." She lifted herself on tiptoes and kissed his cheek. "Say hi to your fiancée for me. Tell her she still owes me for ditching girl's night last week."

"Roger that." He winked. "I'm not sorry I kept Celia otherwise occupied that night."

She swatted his arm. "Go on now, you lovestruck man. I don't need to know the details."

Luke strode away, and Nina's brain immediately switched back to worry.

Do not let fear and paranoia back into your life. Erich doesn't know where you live.

Once upon a time, his obsession with her had turned deadly. Surely, his time spent in jail had cleared his mind. After ten years, he probably didn't think about her anymore. *Yes, he doesn't even remember your name.*

Deep inside her heart, she knew that wasn't true.

CHAPTER 7

olin supported Beatrice as she sank into her favorite chair. He gently raised her legs and rested them on the ottoman, then placed a small pillow under her knees. "You did great. I'm very impressed by how many steps you took today being only three days out of surgery." He was equally impressed at her combined independence and willingness to place herself into his care. Normally, a female private duty nurse would have been placed with Bea, but due the fact she was a larger woman, he was better suited to offer physical assistance and support when needed.

"*Whew.* I just went around the living room twice, but my body thinks I ran a marathon." Bea rested her head on the back of her chair and closed her eyes. "Not that I've ever run a marathon." She snorted with laughter. "My only experience with running was when I was a young girl, trying to beat my big brother home from school. Oh...he and I would race down the sidewalk to see who'd touch the front door first. Loser had to help Momma with dishes that night."

"And how many nights did you help with dishes?" He

leaned Bea's walker against the wall and lowered himself onto the sofa.

"More than Solomon, my brother. He had skinny legs and such a long stride. The boy moved like he floated above the ground."

A relaxed smile gave her face a dreamy appearance. Colin turned to look at the black-and-white photograph displayed on the side table, and saw the same expression on the teenage version of Bea. She wore a knee-length dress, belted in the middle. Her glossy hair was parted on the side. An array of large curls adorned the ends. She stood next to a lanky teenage boy. Their body language—hands clasped together and shoulders leaning in—hinted that the boy had grown up to become her husband.

Bea noticed his attention focused on the old photograph set in a silver frame. "Didn't we make the most beautiful couple? Love does that, you know. Makes you sparkle and glow. Right before that photograph was taken, Clyde said he loved me for the first time. I still remember how my heart soared hearing him confess that he felt the same crazy love I did."

"How old were you when you married?"

"I wanted to wait until I finished college, but Clyde was in such a hurry. He finally convinced my parents, particularly my father, to give their blessing. When we married at our church in Milwaukee, I was a fresh-faced twenty-year-old...so excited to start my life as a wife and someday a mother."

Colin tidied a stack of magazines on the coffee table. "You were lucky to find the love of your life at such a young age. Mine's still hiding out there somewhere."

She grinned. "Young man, you have to be searching for her in order to find her."

"True." Up to this point in his life, he'd never felt a strong, natural urge to find his soul mate. Single suited him. He wasn't even sure what love felt like. Seeing other couples in love was different from experiencing it himself. He'd never met a woman he couldn't live without. When the time came to end a romantic relationship, he usually parted on good terms. What did that say about his ability to fall in love? Defective heart, perhaps?

"Then again, maybe you'll find your treasure when you're not looking." Bea took a rainbow-colored crochet blanket off the table next to her chair and draped it over her lap. "Clyde and I were married for almost fifty years. We were blessed with mostly good times together, but there were a few troubled times when I feared our marriage wouldn't survive. First was after six years of trying for a baby, I got the news from my doctor that I'd likely never get pregnant." She exhaled a long breath. "The news broke Clyde's heart. I was a teacher by then, so I had dozens of kids to love. He took a long time to come to terms with the fact he wouldn't be a father."

"I can only imagine." Colin hadn't given much thought to fatherhood. His old man had been a miserable excuse for a dad. Could be the trait was genetic. Or a behavior passed on from generation to generation of Moynahan men who never should have reproduced.

"Another source of disagreement between us was my activism in the civil rights movement. Those were dangerous times. Oh, very dangerous times for an outspoken woman of color." The brown skin on her cheeks flushed rose. "You see, in the nineteen-sixties, when I taught in the city of Milwaukee, both the school system and housing were segregated. I taught at an all-Black school, and those students could not attend a school for white children.

Clyde and I couldn't buy a house in a white neighborhood. When we spoke out against segregation as individuals, no one listened. But when we banded together, Blacks and whites marching in the streets, they had no choice but to pay attention."

"And I assume some of that attention was negative." Colin leaned forward, resting his forearms on the tops of his thighs.

"Sure as the rain falls in spring. Over my years of teaching and community activism, I saw some big improvements. People putting things right. Things that should have been right all along. Of course, there's still more work to be done." Gazing at the sepia-toned wedding picture propped on the fireplace mantel, she smiled. "When Clyde and I retired, I wanted to stay in Milwaukee, but he'd fallen in love with Polaris during a summer vacation here. He used to love hiking in the mountains, especially this time of year, when the leaves change color and the air turns cool and crisp. Looking back, I'm glad we moved here. Polaris gave me some wonderful memories. It's a good town, with good people."

Colin stood and retrieved his calendar book out of his messenger bag. "The people I've met so far in Polaris have been very friendly." He glanced out the window at the purple house across the street and thought of Nina. If she was the only other person he got to know during his time in town, he'd be content. She radiated beauty and kindness, and he felt a natural high whenever with her.

While he opened the calendar to the folded corner that marked today's page, he reminded himself of the reason he was in Polaris—for work. Which meant he had to focus on his patient, not the attractive woman he couldn't get off his mind. "Looks like we have an hour before the van arrives to take us to your physical therapy appointment. I'll need to check your blood sugar before we go, and you should have something to eat."

"Let me close my eyes and take a short nap before you start in on more nursing." She chuckled. "I need rest before I go see that drill sergeant of a physical therapist."

"Marcus isn't that bad."

"I'm sure he's a perfectly nice young man when he's not torturing me with those darn exercises."

With a laugh, Colin closed his calendar. "Okay, okay. You have a thirty-minute reprieve. Take a well-deserved nap. I'll be in the kitchen catching up on my emails."

Bea waved her hand. "Before you sit down in front of your computer, would you do me a quick favor? Nina left the centerpiece jars from the bridal shower here, and I want to get them back to her. They're packed up in a box sitting on the bench in the mudroom. Would you take them over? I don't think she's left yet for the day."

He caught an unmistakable glint of amusement in her eyes and clearly understood her intention. He'd play along, but only to sneak a look inside Nina's house. He was curious. "Sure. As long as you don't think she'll mind me dropping by."

"Why would any woman mind a handsome man like you knocking on her door?" With a smile on her face, she closed her eyes. "Now shoo, before my thirty minutes are up."

He flipped off the light in the living room. "Snore away, sleeping beauty. I'll wake you with a kiss when your time is up."

With her eyes still closed, she clucked her tongue. "You best save those kisses. Never know when you might want to plant a few on a pair of young, pretty lips."

His mind pictured Nina's perfect mouth, and her slim body, and her incredibly long legs. Great. Now, he needed a cold shower before walking over with the box of breakable glass jars.

Unfortunately, he didn't have time for a shower, so he settled for a cold drink of water before grabbing the box and heading across the street.

~,~

A loud rapping on her front door sent Nina's heart leaping. Her breath became quick and shallow. With her back against the wall, she stepped quietly towards the door. Then she craned her neck to peer out the small window overlooking the front porch. At the sight of Colin, her muscles relaxed. She exhaled a long breath.

He held a large cardboard box. Bea must have sent him over with the centerpiece jars. She planned on delivering a casserole to Bea's tonight and grabbing them then, but Colin was nice to bring them over, even if Bea had likely put him up to the task.

She twisted open the dead bolt, then slid the chain out of the latch. "Hey," she said after opening the front door. "Come on in."

Colin stepped into the entryway. "I come bearing gifts. Where would you like me to set them?"

"I'll take it." She accepted the box, which was heavier than it looked, then walked back to set it on the kitchen table. "Since these jars are already mine, they're really not gifts."

After slipping off his shoes, he joined her in the kitchen. "Promise I'll do better next time. Nice place you got here." He glanced around the room.

"Thanks. I like it." While he studied her house, she studied him. Colin Moynahan had taken a starring role in her recent fantasies. A fact she'd keep to herself. Especially now, with him standing inside her kitchen, looking way too fine. "You want something to drink?"

"No, thanks. I'm good." His head swiveled back toward her, and he smiled. "You sure like color, don't you?"

Yes, she did. Right after she bought the house, she'd gone on a painting spree. The woman working at the local paint store had gotten a kick out of seeing Nina come in almost every day, each time ordering a different color paint. She'd picked a burnt umber for her kitchen, which contrasted nicely with the white cabinets and cinnamon-flecked granite countertops.

"All this color is my little rebellion." She motioned with her hand for him to follow her into the living room. "The house I grew up in was stark and bland. My mother was into the modern look, even though our house was over a hundred years old. I felt like I lived in a museum and hated it. When I bought this place, I wanted to make my home comfortable and fun."

"You accomplished your goal." He pointed to an oil painting hanging over her fireplace, which featured a cluster of pink peonies set against a lime-green background. "Are flowers another one of your rebellions?"

Laughing, Nina nodded. "That painting is a Nina Pettit original. I went to one of those classes where you drink wine while learning how to paint. After three glasses of merlot, I was surprised at how well it turned out."

He stepped toward the fireplace and studied the painting. "I think you've discovered a hidden talent."

"Drunken Monet." She studied her handiwork and did feel a sense of pride. If she could no longer play the cello, painting might be a new creative outlet. Then again, her artwork might look like a toddler's if she tried to hold a brush sober. "I think I'll stick to teaching music."

His gaze locked onto her, and she melted into his summer-blue eyes.

Colin wandered over to her small yellow sofa and took a seat. "I'd like a painting of the view from on top of one of the mountains around here. I bet it's spectacular."

"The view is amazing, but where would you hang one? No house means no walls." The fact that she'd let a man she didn't know very well inside her home should send her anxiety through the roof. Instead, his presence draped a blanket of calm over her.

He reclined against the back of the sofa and rested an ankle on his knee. "I might settle down and buy a house…someday."

Someday, a good reminder he was here temporarily, meaning her attraction was temporary too. Really a shame. He looked so bad-boy delicious, with messy black hair, baby-blue eyes, and a dusty-red-stubble-covered jaw. "Someday, meaning when you're the same age as your patients?"

He tipped his head back and laughed. "I doubt I'll wait that long. I've always assumed a time would come when I'd find a spot on the globe that I wouldn't want to leave. But for now, there's still a lot out there left to discover."

Nina lowered herself onto an upholstered chair and situated herself to face him. "Where's your favorite spot so far?"

"Hmmm." He scratched his chin. "Probably Providenciales in the Turks and Caicos. About two years ago, I cared for a wealthy couple who'd both had a few nips and tucks. They escaped to the privacy of their tropical vacation home to recover. The job was fairly easy, so I had time to scuba dive and explore. It's a beautiful island, with bright turquoise water and powder-white sand. The people who live there are beautiful too."

"Got me sold. Too bad I don't travel—"

"*Ahhhhh,*" Colin squeaked and hopped off the sofa. "Did you see that?" He pointed towards the vertical piano pushed against the far wall. "You have a rat inside your house."

She turned to see her sweet pet ferret poking her nose from behind the piano. "That's Ariel. She's not a rat, she's a ferret." Nina knelt on the aqua-and-orange area rug. "Come here, girl, and meet our guest." She looked up at Colin, whose face had turned an ashy color, like papier-mâché paste.

Little Ariel scampered over to Nina and jumped up onto her lap. Scooping up the furry bundle, Nina held her pet in the crook of her arm.

Keeping his feet firmly planted, Colin studied the animal. "She looks like a rat."

"Don't listen to him, Ariel," she whispered.

Ariel stuck out her head and sniffed in Colin's direction. She made a clicking noise before wiggling out of Nina's hold.

Nina set the white-and-gray bundle of fur onto the floor and stood. Ariel scampered back to her hiding spot behind the piano. "A few years ago, I went to the pet store with a friend who needed some supplies for her cat. I walked past Ariel, sitting in a display cage all alone. She looked sad, so I brought her home."

"I'm still convinced she's a rat. I think the pet store might have tricked you."

"Stop." She swatted at his arm. "Rats are short and round. Ariel is long and thin, with cute little ears and a furry tail."

He grinned. "I'll take your word on it. Why the name Ariel?"

"In *The Little Mermaid* movie, Ariel's a mermaid who collects things. Ferrets are the same way. Whenever I can't find something around the house, I check Ariel's nest behind the sofa, and most times, it's stashed there."

"No kidding." Colin moved towards the front door. "I like animals and always wanted a pet growing up. Maybe I'll put a pet on the list of things I'll get once I settle into a permanent address."

"Along with one of my paintings." She watched him tie his shoelaces, saddened he was leaving. Talking with him was comfortable, and he made her laugh.

"Can't forget the art." He turned the handle of the front door, then hesitated. "Will you be over to visit Bea later today?"

A fluttering sensation filled her chest. "After my lessons. See you again soon." *Not soon enough.*

After one more dashing smile, he exited outside.

Nina rested her back against the closed door and sighed. What harm was a little innocent flirting? None, as long as she remembered to leave her heart out of it. A knock sounded on the door behind her. Instead of panic, anticipation rose. Had Colin returned already? Maybe today was a lucky day.

She reopened the door to see Colin's face—a version that didn't look as flirty as the one he wore only a minute ago. "What's wrong?" Her thoughts jumped to Bea. "Is Bea all right?"

"Yes, I didn't make it back to her house yet." He extended his hand. On the palm rested a cream-colored envelope. "I ran into your sister just now. As I was walking across the street, she drove up and parked alongside the curb in front of your house." Turning his head, he gazed toward the now-empty street. "She must have recognized me from the hospital because she called me over and asked me to give you this letter."

Strange. Why would Meg have come here and not bothered to get out of her car to deliver this personally? She took the letter from Colin. The paper was thick and felt like expensive stationary. Gazing up, she returned her attention to Colin. "Did she say anything else?"

He shrugged. "I asked her to give the letter to you herself. Maybe she wanted to avoid another confrontation. I finally agreed to bring it to you, and she drove away."

Nina huffed. Figured. Probably for the best. She didn't have the emotional bandwidth right now to deal with family drama. With a flip of her wrist, she turned it over to look for writing on the front. Her blood froze at the sight of a backward bass clef shaped like the letter E. The floor underneath her feet tilted, and her balance wavered.

"Hey." Colin took hold of her arm. "You okay?"

She couldn't breathe. Couldn't talk. Pressing a hand against her stomach, she fought the impulse to vomit. With numb fingers, she let the envelope slip out of her grasp and let it drift to the floor.

CHAPTER 8

Nina swayed on her feet.

"Sit down." Colin guided her to the stairs and helped her into a seated position. "Stay right there. I'll get you a glass of water."

Nina mumbled something he couldn't understand, and she lowered her head to her lap.

He raced into the kitchen and rummaged through her cabinets until he found a glass and then filled it with tap water. When he came back into the entryway, he found Nina still sitting on the stairs, breathing hard and fast. "Take a drink." He waited until she was upright before handing her the glass of water. *I should have never given Nina that letter.*

While she drank, he retrieved the discarded envelope lying on the floor. He held it between his fingers and studied the object, seemingly benign in his eyes. Besides the swirling letter E on the front, the envelope was blank.

Nina held out the empty glass. "Thanks."

He set the glass on a narrow console table by the staircase, which held a few decorative items and a framed photograph of Nina and Bea sitting on a bench in a flower garden.

"Talk to me. What's got you upset?" He sat beside her and wrapped an arm around her slight shoulders.

"This." She pointed to the envelope in his hand. "A letter from the devil."

Gazing down at the paper, he got a kick in the gut. "I'll toss it in the trash."

Nina shook her head. "Read it to me. Please." She peered at him with wide, glossy eyes, which resembled two polished gold coins.

He tugged open the envelope and pulled out a folded notecard, the same color and weight as the envelope. After opening it, he scanned over the handwritten words, then balled up the letter in his fist.

"It's all right." She rested a hand on his arm. "Go ahead."

Colin uncrumpled the paper and cleared his throat

Dear Nina,

I hope this note will not cause you stress. My only intention is to make recompenses. Please finally accept my apology. What happened between us was years ago. I've changed and become a better man.

You are so precious, and I realize now I didn't value you and your talent like I should have. Again, I'm sorry.

Always,

Erich

Colin's stomach soured from speaking the words of the man he assumed was Nina's stalker. He wanted to set fire to both the letter and envelope, and hoped she'd give him permission to do just that. Concerned, he turned to her. The unmistakable flush of anger colored her face. Her lips were pressed together, creating a hard, straight line. Two small creases furrowed her brow.

Without warning, she jumped to her feet. "That son of a

bitch. How dare he?" Her hands were clenched at her side. Her face burned with murderous intent.

"Breathe, Nina." He stood. "Breathe."

"My sister brought this garbage to my house." She whirled on him and grabbed the envelope out of his hand. "If he thinks he can upset my life, then I have news for him. He will never get near me again. Never touch me again." A tremor passed through her body, and she drew in a sharp breath.

"Come outside and get some fresh air. You need to cool down." He opened the front door and held it for her.

She moved through the doorway and stepped onto the porch. Her hands grasped the wood railing, fingernails digging in. "Why won't he leave me alone? How can he possibly think I'd want to do anything other than kill him?"

"Do you feel comfortable sharing?"

Nina blew out a breath and lowered her head. Her gaze stayed fixed on the ground below. "I met Erich Everett out east, and he became a big supporter of my music. We dated and traveled together for my performances. He became controlling, and I broke it off."

"Let me guess... He didn't take rejection well."

"He was of the opinion that I owed him for everything he'd invested in my career. I disagreed. When he began stalking me, I reported him to the police, but they couldn't catch him doing anything threatening." She shivered. "The nightmare went on for almost a year, and then I began seeing another man. Erich became extremely jealous. He warned me not to date Seth, but I would not allow my life to be dictated by anyone, let alone an ex-boyfriend. I should have listened."

Colin's temper heated his blood until he no longer felt

the chilly autumn wind. "You had...have...every right to date anyone you want."

She made a sound in her throat like a strangled groan. "Erich killed the man I was seeing and then went after me. When the dust settled, he earned fifteen years behind bars for manslaughter, kidnapping, false imprisonment, and several other charges. He paid for really good lawyers, who not only got him a lenient sentence but out early on parole."

If only Colin had known Nina back then, he would have enjoyed one last fight, giving Erich a bloody send-off to jail. From the creepy tone of Erich's note, Colin still might get a chance. "He's out of jail now, and you're worried he's found you."

"I always knew he'd come after me when he got out." She pushed off the railing and stood straight. "Luke Veldkamp, a police captain here in Polaris, reached out to the Boston PD and Erich's parole officer. Erich has to report twice a week, so they'll know if he left town."

"Why would your sister have brought along a note from him?" Back at the hospital, he'd witnessed the bad blood between Nina and Meg. Still, he struggled to believe Meg would intentionally put Nina in harm's way after she'd been through so much trauma already. They were still family, after all. The idea made him sick.

She pinched the bridge of her nose. "I honestly don't know. Now, I understand why she didn't want to give it to me directly but pushed the job onto you."

Which, deep down, he was grateful for. Being here for her now dulled his anger at Nina's sister. "You have a friend who's a cop, right? The woman who practically read me my rights at The Chute my first night in town." He smiled at the memory.

Her gaze swept the street from east to west and then

settled on him. "Yes, Gabs. She'll want to know about the letter and so will Luke." She stepped toward the door and halted.

A brisk wind lifted a few orange leaves off the grass and carried them into the neighbors' yards. The branches of the maple tree planted in front of Nina's house waved with the strong movement of air, leaves bristling.

Sighing, she wiped a tear from the corner of her eye. "I hate that he still has the power to make me feel weak and vulnerable."

"Take back control." He brushed a finger over her hand. His skin sparked on contact. "You are strong."

Across the street, the handicap accessible van pulled into Bea's driveway. How could it already be time for physical therapy? He took out his cell from his back pocket and checked the time. He didn't want to leave Nina, not while she was upset, but Bea's care was his first responsibility. And he still had to check Bea's insulin level and get her something to eat before they left.

"Bea has a PT appointment starting soon. I need to go." He reached over and rubbed her arm. "Promise you'll call someone to come over."

"I'll go inside, lock the door, and call Gabs." Nina trembled and stepped toward him. "Thank you, Colin."

He wrapped his arms around her. She molded to him perfectly, like brandy poured into a glass. She filled his heart with warmth. Despite the damage from abuse, Nina was one of the strongest and most open women he'd ever met. "No need to thank me. I brought you that damn letter." Her laughter vibrated against his chest.

"Go on now." She kissed his cheek before backing away. "Bea's probably wondering what's taking you so long."

Her lips seared his skin, like he'd been branded with her

mark. "Oh, she knows." And he was grateful she'd taken on the role of Cupid. At least for today. "You have my cell phone number. Call if you need anything. I'll stop by later, once I get Bea settled back at home for her afternoon game shows."

After a quick wave, Nina disappeared inside the house.

He heard the distinct sound of a dead bolt clicking into place. Colin clenched his fists and started back across the street. If Erich thought he could terrorize her again, he would find Nina well protected. Colin would make sure of that.

~ ، ~

The first thing Nina did after she locked her front door was call Gabs. Once she mentioned Erich's letter, Gabs ended the call and drove straight to Nina's house. She arrived in under five minutes wearing her police uniform and a pair of aviator shades that made her look like a star on a cop TV show.

Nina handed the letter to Gabs, then sat at the kitchen table.

When Gabs was finished reading, she held the paper between her fingers, away from her body. "He's delusional if he thinks you'll respond to this crap."

"My sister showed up at my house. Meg saw Colin leave my house and gave the note to him to pass along to me." Nina ground her teeth. How could Meg have accepted a letter from a man who'd kidnapped Nina, then bring it here —to her safe haven? There had to be an explanation that didn't involve her sister morphing into a cruel monster. "She's staying at the North Star Resort, or at least she was."

"How could she do this to you?" She shook her head. "Never mind. I know firsthand people who supposedly love you are capable of some pretty awful things." Gabs spun her key ring around her index finger. "I'll drive you over to the resort. You're not going alone."

"Thanks. I don't know what I'd do without you." A minute later, she climbed into the passenger seat of Gabs's car. During the ride, she attempted to concentrate on anything besides her churning stomach. At any moment, she could throw up. Gazing out the window, she focused on the beautiful landscape passing by. As they weaved their way around the base of the mountain, she watched for wildlife. Up ahead, she saw the red fur of a fox. It darted under the brush before they drove passed. A squirrel darted across the road, then stopped at the centerline, turned around, and ran back in the direction it came from.

Groves of trees lined the road. Aspen, oak, and maple were close to peak and topped with vibrant colors of red, gold, and orange, along with a scattering of green leaves saving themselves for an autumn encore.

When they arrived at the North Star Resort, she exited the car with Gabs right behind her. What room number had Meg said she was staying in? Nina rummaged through her purse until she found Meg's business card. Room five hundred thirty.

Gabs studied the people in the large lobby. "If you do see Erich, let me know. I want to be the one to take him down."

Despite her anxiety, she laughed. "Have I ever told you that you're the best?"

"Maybe once or twice." Gabs's lips twitched. Her fingers drummed on the pocket housing her Taser.

A Taser was how Erich had subdued Seth. No matter how many years had passed since that awful day, she still remembered the overwhelming sickness she felt when looking at the photographs of Seth's lifeless body tied to the trunk of a massive oak tree. The police report stated he'd struggled for a long time to get free from the rope with no luck. If she could go back in time, she never would have accepted Seth's advances.

Nina forced her mind onto more pleasant thoughts—like the beauty of the season. The resort's lobby was decorated for fall, with orange and white pumpkins filling all available spaces. Vines filled with faux autumn leaves were draped across fireplace mantels and swagged across several of the antler chandeliers hanging from the ceiling. The faint aroma of pumpkin spice filled the air.

"Meg's staying on the fifth floor," Nina said, right before spotting Meg exiting an elevator. She was heading toward the coffee shop on the opposite side of the room.

After moving through the crowded lobby, Nina entered the coffee shop. The comforting aromas of roasting coffee beans and sweet bakery softened the edge of her apprehension. Other than the young woman working behind the counter, the small space was empty.

"Where did she go?" Nina pivoted back to face the lobby.

"She's heading out the door." Gabs pointed to Meg as she walked outside.

"I want to talk with her alone." She glanced back at Gabs. "I'll let you know if I need backup."

Gabs stood beside a glass display case overflowing with baked treats. "I'll keep eyes on the lobby...and these doughnuts."

"Get me a chocolate Long John with sprinkles." She smiled. "I'll need something sweet after I'm done with Meg."

Nina found her sister standing across the parking lot, next to a wooden railing that protected guests from a steep drop-off. The view of the mountains from the spot was spectacular, and several benches were lined up along the grassy stretch.

The crunching of leaves underfoot announced Nina's approach.

Meg turned and raised her ashy-blonde eyebrows. Her hand held a package of cigarettes. She tapped the package, top side down, on her palm. "If I was looking for a fresh start, I would have picked a place like this too." Gazing off toward the distant road snaking through the golden land-scape, she pulled out a long white cigarette.

"It's peaceful. I'm happy here." Nina leaned a hip against the fencing.

Meg slipped the cigarette pack into her purse and pulled out a lighter. She lit the tip and took a deep drag before tipping her head back and puffing out a long column of smoke through pursed lips. "Must be nice leaving every-thing and everyone behind."

Keeping a tight rein on her anger, Nina gritted her teeth. "Let's be honest. No one wanted me around." She pointed a finger at herself. "I left Boston, but that didn't mean I left my past behind."

"We all have problems, you know?" Meg shrugged. "You grew up with people fawning over you, telling you how talented you were. Then there was me—the ordinary sister of a musical prodigy. Feeling second-best was crappy for my self-esteem."

"Jealousy is crappy for anyone's self-esteem." She sighed.

With her cigarette hanging between the tight line of her lips, Meg snorted out a laugh. "Let me set the record straight...I am no longer jealous of you. Not after what Erich did."

"He's a sick, murdering monster." Her head swam with too many emotions, causing a light-headed sensation. As much as she wanted to walk away, she pressed forward with their conversation. "Why did you bring the letter from him, Meg? How could you?"

"I didn't have a choice," she said, voice accented with an eastern New England dialect.

"What do you mean *you didn't have a choice*?" Nina stood with her hands on hips. She inhaled deeply in an attempt to calm down. "Have you spoken to Erich since his parole?"

Meg held her half-consumed cigarette between two fingers, a trail of smoke curling from the tip. She lowered her gaze. "He showed up at my house, begging me to deliver an apology letter to you. Of course I said no and closed the door in his face. He kept on knocking and threatened to make a scene if I didn't take his letter." She took another drag of her cigarette and blew. "When I said no again, he told me that if I wouldn't bring the note to you, then he'd figure out where you lived and bring it himself."

Nina's panic spiked. All the old fear, which she'd worked so hard to flush from her life, rushed back. "He can't find me." She pressed her hands against her stomach, pushing back the pain.

"I know," Meg said in a hushed voice. "You probably don't believe me, but I took his letter to protect you."

"Protect me?" Her raised voice matched the volume of the pulse pounding in her head. Were her sister's motivations that pure? "I don't want his apology. As far as I'm concerned, Erich Everett is dead."

"Well, he's not." She dropped the cigarette stub onto the sidewalk and ground it out with the sole of her black fashion boot. "You should take precautions, Nina. I thought I owed it to you to come and tell you that."

"You should have told me about the letter at the hospital."

"You're right, I should have. When I came to your house earlier to give it to you, I panicked. Then I saw your guy friend and thought maybe having him with you when you read it would be better." Meg stilled. The lines bracketing her eyes and mouth softened. "I'm sorry. I should have called the police when he showed at my house. I almost destroyed his note."

"Yes, you should have called the police and then destroyed it." Her anxious body relaxed, confident of no ill intent on Meg's part. Erich, on the other hand, was a manipulating criminal who should never have been granted early release from his punishment. "Go home to your family and stay away from Erich. I'm sure jail hasn't improved him morally or spiritually."

"I wish I could be a better person...a better sister." Meg turned to gaze toward the expanse of mountains dominating the landscape. She brushed away strands of blonde hair from shimmering, tear-filled eyes.

"Me too." With a deep inhale, Nina steadied her emotions. "I can't let him find me. He'll spread his stain on my life all over again."

"Do me a favor and burn that letter." Meg kissed her on the cheek. "Take care, Nina. Let's not wait another ten years to talk again."

CHAPTER 9

ina turned on the TV, if only to fill her quiet house with the sound of voices. She flipped through the channels and stopped on a rerun episode of Friends. Growing up, she hadn't had much time for TV watching. Or dating, or going out with girlfriends, or socializing in general. While she was busy practicing the cello, she'd missed a lot of the events marking adolescence.

Binge-watching *Friends* while laughing along with the casts' antics was one of her favorite ways to spend an evening home alone. But tonight, instead of enjoying the show, Nina wanted to cry.

Her talk with Meg had emotionally drained her. She and Meg had never been close, but age and maturity had smoothed the piercing edges that always poked between them.

While prerecorded audience laughter sounded in the background, she filled Ariel's food bowl. Getting down on her hands and knees, she peeked behind the sofa in search of what the little rascal had stashed away lately. She pulled out a stretchy hair tie, silver hoop earrings she'd sworn were in her jewelry box, the remote control for the DVD player, and a twenty-dollar bill. The cash she slipped into her back pocket, and the rest she gathered into her hand.

As she crawled backward from behind the sofa, a knock sounded from her front door. Her heart leaped into her throat. Since she was already on the ground, she crept across the floor to the large picture window overlooking the porch. Curtains hung along either side, and she used one as cover to peek outside at her visitor.

At the sight of a pair of worn-out black boots, she exhaled in relief. The one person in the world she wanted right now was standing at her door. Her gaze wandered up the muscular form of Colin, finally resting on his yummy face.

Grinning, he glanced down in her direction. "You'd never make it in the CIA." His voice came through the still closed door.

With much chagrin, she laughed and stood. Nina unlocked and opened the door. "How did you know I was down there?"

"I saw the curtain move." He stepped inside, filling her entryway, wearing a leather jacket and snug-fitting jeans. "You need a video monitoring security system." Colin turned his gaze up toward the corners of the entryway ceiling. "Have a camera in here and one outside each door. That way, you won't have to army crawl to make an ID. Just pull up the video feed on your phone."

"I'll think about it." She held out her hand and accepted his jacket. "How was Bea's physical therapy? Is she in much pain?"

"Not too much. She's one tough lady, but tired now after the workout. The female nursing aide is coming in an hour to help her bathe. Right now, though, she shooed me out the door, saying she didn't want any distractions while watching *Wheel of Fortune*."

"She loves that show. Doesn't miss an episode. I showed her how to record them on her satellite receiver, and I swear she acted like I'd gave her directions to the fountain of youth." Nina guided him toward the kitchen. "You want something to drink?" A glass of wine sounded really good right now. Two glasses, actually. One for her and one for Colin. Soft music playing in the background. A prelude to a hot kiss that would surely leave her head spinning.

He shook his head. "No thanks on the drink. I came over to see how you're doing and if you found any more info about the letter."

So much for romance.

"Why on earth would she take a letter from him, then travel across the country to bring it to you?" he continued, his clenched fists hanging at his sides.

"A misguided attempt to protect me and a warning to watch my back." She shook her head. "Erich told her either she brought me the letter or he'd find me and deliver it himself. I wish she would have burned it."

"I want to burn him." Colin leaned back against the countertop. "Do you think this is the end? He'll leave you alone?"

"I guess I'll find out." She poured herself a glass of water and took a sip. "But I refuse to put myself in a bubble. I have to trust my own safeguards as well as law enforcement to keep him away."

"Give me the word, and I'll make a few calls. I still have some connections in Boston who don't mind getting their hands dirty."

Weirdly enough, that was one of the nicest things

anyone had ever offered to do for her. "Hopefully, it won't come to that."

"But if it does, you just let me know." He pointed at her and grinned.

"I will. Promise." She swiped her hand crisscross over her heart.

"Good. In between all the drama today, did you have any music lessons?" He glanced out the kitchen window and then fixed his blue eyes back on her.

Was she foolish to imagine this scene playing out a few years from now? Colin coming home from work and asking about her day. Foolish, for sure. "Only a few today, but I have a full schedule tomorrow. My students have a concert in a little over a month, so we've been working hard on their performance pieces."

"Cool. I never could sit still long enough to learn how to play an instrument, even the piccolo. But I bet you rocked it with your cello."

She laughed. "Not exactly rocked it, but I did enjoy performing. I even enjoyed practicing."

"Shocking." One eyebrow twitched, and the corner of his mouth lifted.

"I know." Nina smiled more in five minutes with Colin than every other minute of the day combined. Her cheeks hurt. "Wait here."

She ran upstairs, then returned carrying her laptop, which contained something very special she wanted to share. A glimpse at a girl who'd held a cello and given birth to music—melodies conceived inside her soul.

When she'd left Boston, she'd also left that girl behind. She might no longer be a musical prodigy, cheered as she took the stage, but she was content with the person she was today. Colin, with his Irish good looks and Boston charm, made her feel comfortable sharing parts of herself she normally kept protected.

She set the laptop on the kitchen table and sat beside Colin. His close proximity made her skin tingle. Could he tell how insanely attracted she was to him? Hope not. Although he might be okay with a short fling, she was not. For her, intimacy came after developing trust and a deep emotional connection. Things that took time and effort to build. Colin, for all his wonderful qualities, had a wanderer's soul. When he left for his next job, she'd likely never see him again.

She clicked on the web search bar and typed in *Nina Montgomery, Kennedy Center*. Then opened the third link from the top—the school's official video of her solo performance.

"During my senior year at Juilliard, I was asked to be a guest soloist with the National Symphony. When I took the stage, I was shaking with nerves." Nina stared at an image of herself on the computer screen—a slip of a young woman in a formal gold gown. Her mother had hired a fashion stylist, makeup artist, and hairstylist because she'd wanted Nina to look perfect. Nina hadn't cared about any of the fluff, she simply wanted to play. "Once the lights dimmed around me, I closed my eyes and opened my heart. The music flowed like an electric current. Or more like lightning."

He tilted his head and gazed at her. "Someday, will you play again, even if only for yourself?"

She looked from Colin back to the picture on the screen. So much had happened since that evening at the Kennedy Center. She'd changed in too many ways to count. Mostly, she'd grown stronger, but still carried slivers of pain—small pieces that dug into her heart.

"Maybe. But not like this." She pointed at the computer.

"Right now, I can't hold my cello without feeling my chest rip open. Erich stole my joy of playing. I really hate him for that."

Colin rubbed a finger over her knuckles in a comforting gesture. "Steal it back. No one, including Erich, can stop you."

At that moment, his presence made her feel wrapped in a blanket of protection. She loved the way his blue eyes were set off by his black lashes and eyebrows. She could sit here and watch him all day. "I sleep better knowing you're just across the street."

He gave her a wicked grin. "I'd rather that knowledge left you too flustered to sleep."

If you only knew. With an inward sigh, she pulled her gaze away from Colin and pressed Play. Soon, the haunting notes of the Prelude to Bach's Suite no. 1. drifted in the air. Each note floated around her like butterflies, fluttering in her heart with overwhelming emotion.

She glanced at Colin, who sat seemingly transfixed. What did he think of the person playing the cello on screen? Along with a talented and passionate young woman, she hoped he saw a reflection of the woman she was today.

~,~

As Colin watched her perform, the rest of the world faded away. Nina was everything that mattered. She cast a spell over him, and he never wanted to be released.

As she glided the bow across the cello strings, she created the most beautiful melody. Her head and upper body swayed with the rhythm, and her hands and fingers moved skillfully on the cello's neck. She appeared so small, almost hidden behind her instrument. In his opinion, she looked like a fairy.

Her blonde hair was pulled back. She wore a formal floor-length dress that sparkled in the spotlight. Nothing else on stage sparkled as much as Nina. She was so stunning, the sight of her made his heart stop.

After seeing this younger version, he realized she'd grown more attractive with age. As she sat next to him and watched herself on the screen while chewing her bottom lip, he had a hard time controlling his growing desire.

The song ended, and the sound of applause filtered through the computer speakers. Nina pressed Stop.

Jolted back to reality, he slid back his chair. He had to regain control, or he'd do something he'd regret. His physical response wasn't the only thing scaring him. He was becoming too emotionally attached to her. The last thing he wanted was to mislead her about his intentions. He wasn't looking for a serious relationship. Or a relationship, period. She knew that, though. *Right?*

Sweat trickled down the back of his neck.

"What did you think?" She twirled a piece of hair around her index finger.

He almost laughed at her question, but stopped himself. She genuinely appeared worried. Who could have watched that video and not been dazzled? "Nina, you're amazing."

"I *was* amazing." Twin circles of pink colored her cheeks. "I haven't heard myself play in a very long time." A wide smile illuminated her face.

"You still are amazing." He rested a forearm on the table and leaned in. His own smile faltered as he became lost in the swirling color of her eyes. "Whether you play again or not." He struggled to take full breaths, like all his common sense had clogged together and wedged inside his throat.

His gaze moved from her eyes to her lips, which were slightly parted in that sexy way women did.

Her breathing was quick and shallow. "I can't become romantically involved with you."

He swallowed hard. "I don't do relationships."

"Then I think it's for the best you leave now." Her voice was just above a whisper.

"Mmmhmm," he mumbled. His thoughts jumbled inside his mushy brain. "I need to get back to—" Who was he working for again?

"Bea." Nina slid forward on her seat until she settled on its edge. "You work for Bea." Her lips were inches away.

He inhaled her feminine scent—a combination of light floral and citrus. She smelled like she belonged on a tropical island, lying on the beach next to him. Colin brushed his thumb across her jaw and over her bottom lip. So delicious. What harm would come from one taste?

She rested her palms on his thighs. Her moan sent him over the edge. Cupping her head in his hands, he closed the space between them. His lips grazed hers, gauging her reaction.

Her eyelids fluttered until they almost closed. Instead of pulling away, she grasped the front of his shirt with both hands and yanked him closer. Her kiss was firm and demanding. Nina was a woman who wasn't afraid to take what she wanted.

And he was ready to be taken. His lips parted as the intensity deepened. With one hand still touching her cheek, he wrapped his other arm around her waist. She wore a sweater, and the thick wool felt soft against his palm.

His logic slipped away like a thief running off with a valuable piece of art, maybe never to be seen again. His sole focus fixated on the pleasure beating through his veins. An electric current pulsed inside him, exposing a life he never knew existed. With one explosive kiss, the course of his future shifted.

Nina slid a hand behind his head and combed her fingers up through his hair. She glided one finger down along his cheekbone before nipping his lower lip. "Hmmm. I've never had my toes curled by just a kiss."

He pulled back a fraction of an inch. "Toe curling, huh?"

She tipped her head back and laughed. "Yes." Leaning back in her chair, she studied him. "A kiss I might live to regret."

"Why?" He would never regret or forget kissing her. How could he when his body still felt lighter than air?

"You're too good-looking, too nice, and too perfect," she said with a sigh.

The corner of his mouth lifted. He could say the same about her. "All fine qualities that should make you want to kiss me more."

Nina pressed her lips together. "Normally, I would agree, except you and I will never work. We both admitted it."

"Never say never, darling." He ran gentle kisses along her neck, starting right below her ear, and inhaled her seductive scent.

"You're a cad." She laughed. "Stop, that tickles."

"Fine. Have it your way." He reclined in the chair, needing separation to clear his head. With their kiss, Nina had flipped him like a karate black belt. Now, he was spread flat on his back, trying to catch his breath. "With lips like yours, how in the world are you still single?"

She took hold of his hand, which rested palm up on the kitchen table, and entwined her fingers with his. "I can't let someone I care about get hurt."

"No one will hurt me if I kiss you." He circled his thumb lightly across her palm. "Trust me."

"Before he kidnapped me, Erich hurt—" She paused and took a breath. "No, he murdered the man I was dating."

"Leave the past in the past." He stood and pulled her onto her feet before wrapping her in his arms. "Whether you date or not, fall in love or not, let those be your decisions. Don't push me away because you're afraid." But his own judgments about himself were enough to know he was disqualified. She needed not only strong but steady, and he was anything but.

"I'm not afraid," she whispered. "I won't allow myself to be afraid."

Holding her head gently against his chest, he stroked her hair. "I've seen my share of evil, and I've learned the best way to fight back is to look it in the eyes and don't blink."

"Fighting metaphors?"

"A life metaphor." He kissed the top of her head. "I need to get back to Bea's house." He paused. "Don't hesitate to call if you need anything. Okay? Anything."

She nodded. "Thank you."

He left her house, wishing he could be the man she needed and knowing he never could. His restless nature and inability to fall in love made him unworthy. Ignoring the ache in his chest, he returned across the street to his patient —his only purpose for coming to Polaris. His only reason for staying.

CHAPTER 10

*O**ne week passed* without another attempt by Erich to contact her. At the end of each day, she breathed easier. Meg had left for Boston, taking Nina's greetings back to their family. She wasn't ready to reestablish relationships, but opening dialogue was a start.

Since their steamy kiss, she'd only seen Colin a few times. Although he was busy caring for Bea, he'd made it clear he was always available if she ever felt unsafe or afraid. Once a day, she walked over to check in and chat with Bea, as well as catch a glimpse of Colin, but glimpses were all she thought was best for her heart.

Bea had proclaimed him a miracle worker, and Nina's heart squeezed at her conclusion he wasn't the miracle man she yearned for. Today, she would attempt her own miracle. Down in her basement storage room, she stared at the cello case on the shelf. Ever since she'd watched her performance with Colin, she couldn't stop the nagging in her brain to try again. Did she have enough courage to pick up the instrument? Could she touch the smooth wood and not be filled with repulsion? Would she be able to pluck a string and not panic at the sound?

She took the large black case down and knelt beside it. With trembling hands, she flicked open the latches. While lifting the top, she focused on taking deep, controlled breaths. A dusty, stale smell wafted up, tickling her nose.

Her cello lay lifeless inside the case, set in a red velvet embrace. Panic pulsed in her chest, alive and kicking.

Ignoring her negative visceral reaction, she gently gripped the neck of the cello and lifted it out of the case. Next, she picked up the bow. There'd been a time when a cello bow was a natural extension of her arm. Now, it felt awkward in her hand.

She thought about Colin and his reaction to seeing her play. He'd said she shouldn't let someone else take away her passion for music. But how could she play one note, let alone a song, without conjuring up painful memories.

Erich's face flickered in her mind. Panic filled her chest as she remembered the feeling of complete helplessness when he'd held her hostage. Nina shivered and placed the cello and bow back into the case. Simply handling the instrument was a big step. Maybe another day soon, she'd slide the bow across the strings and attempt to recapture the magic that had once flowed through her.

With a grunt, she heaved the case back onto the shelf. Once back upstairs, she went to work preparing for her music students' recital. The children were excited to show off their skills, and she felt privileged to bring music into their lives.

After spending an hour fine-tuning the recital program on the computer, she decided to go outside for a walk. The cool air would help refresh her body and mind and hope-fully blow off any lingering anxiety. She slipped a sweatshirt over her head and managed to avoid tripping over Ariel, who scurried past her feet with a gold chain necklace clenched in her mouth. *Silly ferret.*

Nina stopped by the front window in her living room and watched Colin stroll down the driveway next to Bea, toward the waiting handicap accessible van.

Bea's progress was going well, and the fact Colin was so vigilant about her recovery calmed her worry. Another month or so and Colin's employment would end. For Nina, he was a dream too good to be true.

Frustrated with her "woe is me" attitude, she shoved her hands into the front pocket of her pullover sweatshirt. What she needed was to bask in the glow of someone who radiated happiness.

A visit with Celia Batista should do the trick. Her good friend's wedding date was fast approaching, meaning Nina needed to make an appointment at the dress shop for the final fitting of her bridesmaid's dress.

After a short walk down the street, she bounded up the steps to the back door of Celia's house, knocked, and waited.

"Come in." A voice sounded from the other side of the door. "Unless you're Luke."

Nina turned the handle and entered Celia's kitchen. "What did he do now?"

Celia sat at her kitchen table, which was covered with an open textbook and homework papers. She glanced over the black glasses perched on the tip of her nose. "Oh, nothing serious. We had a disagreement over potential names for Alex and Kenna's baby. He's pushing for George. Luke insists the baby is a boy. I say the name of our first grandchild should be less traditional."

Laughing, Nina took a seat at the table. "Well, luckily,

naming the baby is Alex and Kenna's job, not yours or Luke's. How's Kenna feeling?"

"Better now. She's past the phase where she feels nauseous all the time." Celia grabbed her cell phone and opened the stored photos. She found the one she wanted, enlarged it on the screen, and handed the phone to Nina. "Look at her baby bump. I still can't believe I'll be an *abuelita* and a bride in the same year."

"You've been blessed with a lot of love." She felt a flicker of jealousy and quickly doused it. Celia was her dear friend, and the only feeling allowed was joy. "I just saw Bea leaving for physical therapy. Colin has her walking a lot. I think she'll be dancing again soon."

"She told me her goal is to own the dance floor at my wedding reception." Celia took off her glasses and rubbed her eyes. "You want some coffee? I have another two hours of grading to do this afternoon, and Luke's working late."

"Yes, please." Nina hadn't known coffee could taste so wonderful until she tasted Celia's Cafè Cubano. When her lips had connected with the sweet contents inside a little white espresso cup, she'd become an addict. She wasn't ashamed of the many times she'd come over to Celia's house in hopes of being gifted with a cup.

Celia scooped coffee grounds from a yellow tin can and poured them into a small strainer, then set it inside a silver moka pot. The pot was placed on the stove to brew, and Celia went to work whipping up the sugar mixture. "Have you heard anything more from the man who should still be in jail?"

The high-browed look on Celia's face made Nina smile. "Thankfully, no. I haven't had any contact since the letter Meg brought. My mind tells me I'm safe because he's all the way back in Boston." She wrapped her arms around herself, trying to control the chill flowing in her veins. "But I still watch for him everywhere I go. I see him in the faces of other men and fight not to scream."

Celia took the pot off the stove and poured the coffee into the glass mixing cup that held the sugar mixture. She then set out two tiny white saucers and placed cups on each before filling them.

With eager hands, Nina accepted the cup and saucer, inhaling the sweet coffee aroma. The dark liquid was topped with a toasty brown froth. She lifted the brim of the cup to her lips and sipped. *Ahhhh.* Perfection.

"Luke's on the phone with Erich's probation officer and the Boston PD several times a week," Celia said. "He's monitoring the situation closely."

"I appreciate his vigilance. Gabs has been great too. I have the best friends."

"We love you." Celia patted her hand. "Oh, I almost forgot to tell you...I brought home my wedding dress yesterday. I hid it in the closet of the guest room because Luke's insisting he should get a sneak preview before the wedding."

"He should know better." Nina smiled over the rim of her cup and took another drink. "Will you let me see your dress again? It's been so long since I was with you at the bridal boutique."

With a clink, Celia set her cup onto the saucer. "I'll do one better. I've been looking for an excuse to try it on again."

She followed Celia upstairs, both women giggling like a couple of teenage girls. No better way to lift Nina's mood than wedding talk and fawning over a pretty dress. Better to focus on the happiness of others than mourn the fact she might not ever be a bride herself.

~,~

Colin had the afternoon off and meant to fully enjoy every second. He'd left Bea in the capable hands of the nurse's aide who came once a day. Health Shield always hired a local aide to give their private duty nurse extra help if needed and release time, as well as allow the patient to socialize with a fresh face.

He considered calling Nina to see if she was free to hang out, but the memory of their hot-as-fire kiss stilled his hand. She'd been through enough emotional turmoil without getting burned by him. After spending a short amount of time together, he understood his connection with her ran deeper than a surface attraction, meaning he had a legitimate fear of being burned as well.

He spent an hour driving through the mountain roads around Polaris. Then he stopped at a local gym and spent some time knocking around a punching bag. The release of pent-up desires felt good, and he ended his workout sparring with a local mixed martial arts fighter. His partner, Alfonso, was a hard hitter who didn't miss an opening, leaving Colin with sore ribs, a split lip, and the pride of knowing he could still hold his own in the ring against a young, eager fighter.

Not bad, old man. Not too bad.

Instead of getting in his Jeep and driving back to Bea's place, he left his vehicle in the gym's parking lot and took off for a short run. He started at a brisk pace, but quickly realized if he didn't slow down, he'd pass out from lack of oxygen. His body still hadn't assimilated to the high elevation.

Having just turned the corner onto Main Street, he collided with a man on the sidewalk. The coffee cup in the man's hand went flying, and Colin jumped backward to avoid being showered with hot liquid.

"Sorry." Colin picked up the now-empty paper cup from the sidewalk. "Let me go buy you another."

They were standing outside Downhill Delectables, the little bakery where he'd first seen Nina. That day, she'd had a shockingly strong effect on him. When he'd caught a glimpse of her long, sexy legs and large golden eyes, he'd lost part of his heart.

"You don't need to do that." The man brushed beads of coffee from his wool coat. "I was distracted by the scenery and wasn't paying attention to where I was going."

"I can relate. When I first arrived, I needed my head on a swivel to take it all in." Colin's gaze settled on the man, and uneasiness twisted in his gut. Something about this guy gave him the creeps. Judging from his shiny leather shoes, pressed slacks, and neatly trimmed and styled dark hair, he was likely one of the affluent vacationers who frequented Polaris. The lower portion of his face was covered in a beard, and deep lines radiated from the corners of his eyes.

"Do you live in Polaris?" The man looked Colin up and down, and then stiffly smiled.

"Only temporarily." Colin stepped back, putting another foot of distance between them. Not that he was afraid of this guy. His gut warned something was off, and he always followed his gut. He moved to restart his run. "Hope you enjoy your stay."

The man lifted his arm, and he wagged a finger at Colin. "Hey, I know you." He laughed. "Colin Moynahan—the Irish Fist. I lost a lot of money betting against you."

Colin swore under his breath. He should have recognized the man's polished East Coast accent. "Can't say I'm sorry about that." Reaching out, he shook the man's offered hand and gave it a crushing shake. "If I didn't win, I didn't get paid."

"Might have been true in the beginning, but surely not after you went pro. I attended some of those later fights and saw the size of those crowds. You had a killer instinct and didn't hesitate when you saw weakness in your opponent. I admired that about you."

This guy seemed to know a lot about him. Or at least the Colin Moynahan who'd fought his way off the streets of Boston and into some of the area's largest arenas. The person he'd buried the day of his college graduation, when he committed to using his hands only for healing instead of hurting. "In my opinion, those qualities aren't something to be admired."

The man motioned toward the door of the bakery. "Since I have to go in for another coffee, let me buy you one too. If you have the time, we can get a table. I have a few questions about the area, and you might be able to help."

Colin would rather sprint up the side of a mountain than sip coffee and relive his past. "Thanks for the offer, but I have to finish my run and get back to work." Just as he moved past him, a nudge in his brain made him stop. "What questions?"

"I'm searching for someone...an old friend I want to reconnect with since I'm here on business. She's from the same part of the country we hail from." He sniffled and took a fabric handkerchief out of his pocket, then wiped his nose.

Colin struggled for breath as his lungs burned with lack of oxygen. Shock and anger flooded in. The killer instinct he'd denied a moment ago burst back to life. "Erich Everett."

The man's eyes widened under arched eyebrows. "I'm sorry?"

"What's your name?" he asked.

With a grunt, the man pushed past him. But he didn't

move fast enough. Colin struck out and grabbed his arm. "Answer me."

His weak attempt to rip away from Colin's grasp was useless. "Let go."

A crowd of people walked past them. After a momentary glance, the group continued by, chatting loudly.

Instead of easing his grip, Colin tightened, squeezing hard. He pulled who he thought was Erich toward him, close enough to see his pupils dilate and the unmistakable glint of fear. Good, he should be afraid. "I'll ask you again. What's your name?"

"Michael O'Neil. I'm here on a business trip, looking to invest in the North Star Resort." He shrugged his arm out of Colin's hold and then brushed his hands down his coat. "Now, if you'll excuse me."

His certainty wavered. Against his better judgment, Colin watched the man stride quickly down the street. The police station sign was visible from where he stood, only a block away. Time to call in backup.

CHAPTER 11

Colin sat in the office of Captain Luke Veldkamp, debating if he'd made the right decision in coming here. Dread hit his gut, sending him to his feet.

"I need to get over to Nina's house." Colin stepped towards the closed door.

"Stop." Luke glanced up from his computer screen. "Nina's at the grade school giving a music lesson right now, and I have an officer parked outside her house. She's safe, Colin."

He sank back into the padded office chair on the other side of the desk. "For how much longer?"

"I have a call into one of the detectives in Boston familiar with Nina's case, as well as Erich's parole officer." Luke took off his glasses and set them on the desk. "Why do you think the man you saw on the street was Erich Everett?"

"He was from Boston and said he was looking for an old friend."

"That's kind of a leap to identify him as Erich."

"It's a gut feeling. I've learned the hard way not to ignore my instincts." Colin balled his hands into fists, furious with himself. "I should've done something when I had the chance."

Luke set his arms on the desk and leaned in. "Then you'd be sitting in one of my jail cells right now instead of working with me."

"Working with you? Is that what I'm doing? I'd gladly spend time in jail to keep him away from Nina."

"Again, we don't know it was him." Luke ran a hand down his face and sighed. "Have you seen a photograph of Erich so you can make a more positive ID?"

"No. Show me."

Luke typed and, after a minute, motioned for Colin to come around the desk. He pointed to a color photo on the screen. "This was taken right before his release."

Colin's stomach rolled. The man in the photograph was older and haggard looking, with shoulder-length graying hair and an ashy complexion. "The man I saw had dark hair and a dark beard. I think it's the beard that's throwing me off. I don't know for certain." If only he could be.

"I'll make another call to Boston." Luke picked up the phone receiver.

Trying to distract his mind, Colin glanced at the pictures displayed on the bookshelf behind Captain Veldkamp's desk. One photo especially caught his attention. It featured Luke and Celia, along their adult children from previous marriages.

He felt a small twinge of longing for a family of his own. One that was connected by blood as well as love. His buddy James, who'd started Health Shield, had a great wife and a couple of cool kids. James often joked that the day Colin settled down and married was the day he'd finally buy that red Corvette he'd been eying. With the odds highly unlikely, if not improbable, James would be driving his family-friendly SUV for a long time to come. Colin got the impression that underneath the joking was a challenge.

No denying he wasn't as young as he used to be. In a few years, he'd celebrate his fortieth birthday. Colin shook the number out of his head. He had plenty of time before reaching the top of the hill.

Luke returned the phone to its cradle and turned his attention back to Colin. "Thanks for coming to me with this information. Boston PD is sending a unit over to Erich's registered address. I'll get working on things on my end and keep you informed of any developments."

Luke didn't need to get up and walk him to the door for Colin to understand the police captain had just issued a dismissal. One that he wouldn't accept. "I want to help. Bea's house is directly across the street from Nina's, so I have a good spot to keep watch."

"You've done your part. Let law enforcement do our job." Luke stood and walked to the window, then twisted the window shade handle and closed the blinds. "In fall and early winter, the sun shines directly into my office and lands on my desk in the late afternoon."

He didn't care about Luke's battle with the sun or his window shades. He needed Nina kept safe. "The police can't be everywhere."

Luke's eyebrows arched up his forehead. His formerly pleasant expression turned into a perturbed scowl. "I don't appreciate you implying my department isn't capable of the job."

"I'm not doubting the competence of the Polaris PD." He rubbed the back of his neck. "I can play a role in Nina's protection. While you have to follow the narrow path of the law, I'm not as restricted." He swallowed, not expanding further on his remark.

"Why do you want to get involved?" Luke reclined in his large office chair and pressed his fingertips together, forming a tent with his hands. "You have no history with Nina, and from what I hear, you'll leave shortly after your employment with Bea ends. Why are you willing to risk your safety, along with taking attention away from your patient, to play bodyguard for a woman you hardly know?"

Colin refused to rise to the bait. He understood that behind Luke's question was a test, and he respected the cop for his candor. "I've gotten to know Nina well over the past two weeks and have grown to care about her."

"Are you two romantically involved?"

Squirming in his seat, he forced his gaze to meet Luke's blue eyes. "No romance. Only friendship and respect."

This time, only one eyebrow arched. "Surprising, giving how passionately you feel about protecting her. You and Nina are about the same age, both single. And Nina is a wonderful person. She was good friends with my late wife as well as with Celia, my bride-to-be. I want to make sure you won't hurt Nina when you leave town. A broken heart is painful. I can attest to that."

"I appreciate your concern about my relationship with Nina, but I assure you it's not needed." He leaned forward in his seat and rested his forearm on top his thighs. "Both of us have been very honest about our needs when it comes to starting a relationship, not that it's any of your business. She knows I'm not looking to settle down, and I know she's not open to a relationship."

"She's not open to a relationship with the wrong man. When the right one comes along, that will be a different story."

Their conversation was reminiscent of ones he'd had with a few overprotective fathers of some of the girls he'd dated as a teenager. And now, as a grown man, he didn't like the veiled threats. "Say what you have to say, Captain." Crossing his arms across his chest, he stared back at Luke. "Let's get everything out in the open."

Resting the palms of his hands on the edge of the desk, Luke stood. He walked around and came to stand next to Colin, towering over him. "You're a playboy, and I'm sure part of the appeal of your job is traveling from place to place. You've built in the perfect excuse to avoid a serious relationship because as soon as things might turn serious, you leave."

"You have no right to judge." Colin stood and faced Luke. "I've never been anything but honest with a woman about my intentions, and that includes Nina. Just because I don't want a serious romantic relationship does not mean I don't genuinely care about her. She's a smart woman who doesn't need you acting like her father. And I won't sit here and be judged by a man who doesn't know me or where I come from."

For several seconds, Luke stood quietly watching. Then he slapped Colin's shoulder. "I heard you were a fighter, but I wanted to make sure. Brawling in the ring is one thing. You only had yourself to defend. Guarding another person, especially someone you care about, takes more guts."

"I chose a profession in which I care for others who can't care for themselves. I'm not afraid to do what's required to keep Nina safe." He shook Luke's offered hand. After a firm exchange, he stepped back. "So...what do you need me to do?"

~ ˛ ~

"You sound better with every lesson. I can tell you've

been practicing at home." Nina smiled at the little boy sitting at her side. Violin lessons with Garrett, age eight, were always filled with moments when she beamed with pride at his determination and enthusiasm. He'd only begun lessons at the beginning of the school year, and during the last two months, he'd amazed her with his natural musical abilities.

Garrett lowered his violin and rested it on his lap. "I practice every night after school and twice on weekends. Mom says if she hears me play *Morning Is Broken* one more time, she's checking herself into the loony bin." His words held a lisp, the result of two missing front teeth.

"Then let me find you a new song to practice this week. We don't want to drive your mom crazy." Nina had become friends with Garrett's mom, Carrie Ann, several years ago. Garrett struggled with behavioral problems and poor grades, and Carrie Ann, a single mother who worked as the office manager for the police department, did the best she could. When Nina had suggested Garrett try music lessons, she'd been pessimistic her son learning to play an instrument would change his attitude. So when Garrett's behavior and grades began improving only a few weeks after starting violin lessons, Carrie Ann was surprised.

"Can I play something harder? Like *Thriller* by Michael Jackson. I'll have enough time to learn it by Halloween." Garrett's brown eyes widened. With the violin bow placed across his lap, he combed his fingers through his moppy blond hair.

She considered his request. No harm in an extra challenge. When she was a student, she'd pushed her teachers to assign more challenging pieces. "Okay. I'll find the sheet music for *Thriller*, and we'll run through the song at our next lesson. But until then, you have to concentrate on practicing your recital songs. Do we have a deal?"

"Deal." He nodded, and his face split in a wide grin. "How much more time do we have left?"

Nina glanced up at the round clock hanging on the wall. "Just enough for you to go over your G major scale one more time, two octaves. Play half-notes this time, go slow and really draw out the sound."

Garrett moved up and down his scale with a slow control almost unheard of from most boys his age. Once completed, he packed his violin, gave Nina a quick hug, and left the school music room. Likely in search of physical activity to burn off some of the excess energy built up after sitting for an hour.

Alone in the room, she enjoyed the silence. She gathered her sheet music and filed them inside her bag, and then set the chairs and music stand back in their normal spots. Even after eight years of teaching, she hadn't tired of time spent with her students. Actually, she valued those hours more than any others. She loved seeing children discover a love of music. Every one of her students left their lessons with a deeper understanding of music's ability to evoke emotion—fear, happiness, sorrow, excitement. All could be summoned by the power of song.

When she'd been a young student, she'd marveled at the feelings stirred inside her when she played. She'd been amazed that the sounds produced caused a visceral reaction, not only in her, but in her audience.

Her teachers had trained her in the technical aspects of playing the cello as well as learning how to coax out the emotion tucked inside every piece. To peel back the layers of notes and look for the subtle clues left by the composer.

She'd been an eager student, wanting not only to please

her teachers but also her parents. Some of Nina's practice sessions had ended with blood dripping from her fingers, onto her precious cello. Her dream was to attend Juilliard and perform on the national stage, and she'd given up friendships, boyfriends, and other normal teenage stuff to ensure her dreams became reality.

Erich had understood her drive and passion, which was one of the things she'd initially found attractive. After her performance, they'd sit for hours and discuss the nuances of every piece of music. Over time, he created a dependency. If she wanted to succeed in a world of cutthroat competition, she needed him. Only him.

She remembered the evening his gentle instruction had turned to violent domination. He'd traveled with her to California while she performed as a guest artist with the Los Angeles Philharmonic. After her final concert, they ordered champagne and dessert back at her hotel room.

She'd invited a few musicians to her room to join them. Everyone had a great time, laughing, telling stories, and drinking too much champagne. When they left around one in the morning, she giddily went to get ready for bed. And Erich let slip his mask of cool self-control, giving her a glimpse of the monster underneath.

"You should have told me you'd invited guests." Erich stepped into the bathroom, watching from behind as she brushed her teeth.

Nina spit into the sink, rinsed her brush, and turned to face him. Despite the late hour, he remained looking smooth and put together. His medium brown hair was combed neatly, and he was still dressed in the tuxedo pants and starched white dress shirt he'd worn to the Philharmonic performance. The top buttons were undone, giving her a glimpse of his well-defined chest and dark hair.

Nine months ago, when he'd asked her out after her Juilliard graduation performance, she'd been starstruck. Erich Everett was not only drop-dead gorgeous, he was a big player in the classic music world. He'd been one of the top cellists in the country before turning his time and wealth toward supporting promising talent.

Despite the twenty-year age difference, she found him elegantly attractive. Plus, he understood and supported her goals. Nina's success was all that mattered to him.

She smiled, trying to restore her humor. "I'm sorry. I mentioned something backstage about celebrating a successful run of performances, and several of the musicians asked about joining in." She touched his arm and felt him stiffen. "I thought it would be fun."

"I'd made different plans for us. Ones that didn't involve a group of drunken hack musicians." He looped an arm around her waist. "You're better than them, Nina."

"I don't compare my musical abilities with anyone I share the stage with." Her festive mood soured, and she pulled back, but Erich held firm.

"You should if you want to be the best. Those people are talented musicians, but they have nothing on you." He yanked her close. "I saw the way that other cellist sat beside you on the sofa, constantly touching you."

"Leonard Friedman? Get a grip. He wasn't flirting." With a tight throat, she let out a strained laugh.

"He wanted you. I could see it in his eyes."

The dark expression settled on his face like a cloud covering the moon, setting off warning alarms in her body. His fingers dug into the tender flesh of her upper arm. "Erich, stop. You're hurting me."

One side of his mouth lifted in a sadistic grin. "Do you want him too, Nina? Is that why you invited him back to your room? So you could flirt with another man in front of me?"

"No." Tears spilled from her eyes.

"How many other men have you bewitched with your music and brought to your bed?" He raised his hand, then slapped it across her face.

Reeling, Nina cried out and covered her stinging skin with her hands.

"I want you to be the best cellist in the world, and if I didn't think you had the potential, I wouldn't waste my time with you. After everything I've done, you owe me."

Her stomach heaved, and she fought the urge to throw up. Fear sent a rush of adrenaline through her system. "I don't owe you, and you don't own me. The music I create is mine."

"And no one helped you along the way? No teachers, or family, or a wealthy donor willing to fund your dreams?"

She pushed against his chest with her free hand. In the past, he'd been slightly controlling, but she'd blamed his behavior on the fact he was older and worldlier. But tonight was different. He'd become physically abusive. "Keep your money if that's why you think I'm with you. We're over."

"Over?" His face screwed up like a rotten Halloween pumpkin. With his fingers clasping her chin, he raised her face to meet his gaze. "No. What we have together is special. It will never be over."

Her fear spun to panic. "Trust me, it's over." She shoved him away and ran.

Her cell phone rested on the coffee table. She grabbed it as she rushed by. Standing by the door to her hotel suite, she raised the phone with a trembling hand. "Stay away from me, or I'll call the police."

Erich's face went pale, besides two angry patches of

crimson staining his cheeks. "Put down the phone and let's talk." He held out his hand.

"I think we've both said enough. I want you to leave, now."

He stepped forward but stopped as her finger hovered over the dial touchpad.

She didn't want to call the police, which would make bad press. *Please just leave.*

"Have it your way." He straightened his posture and rolled back his shoulders. "I'll get my suitcase out of the bedroom."

Nina nodded and watched Erich disappear into the bedroom. A few minutes later, he came out with his suitcase and garment bag.

"Tomorrow morning, when you wake up and realize your mistake, call me. If I accept your apology, then we can catch a cab together to the airport."

"Don't wait for my call." She moved to the side to give Erich access to the door.

As he exited the hotel room, she felt her body tremble. Nina closed the door behind him, and then clicked the dead bolt in place as well as secured the chain lock.

For the remaining hours of darkness, she tossed and turned in a restless sleep. In the morning, she contacted the airline and changed her flight. Not only would she avoid a cab ride with Erich, she refused to be on the same flight back to Boston.

Once back home in her small flat in Beacon Hill, she officially ended her relationship with Erich Everett, despite his threats.

Little had she known how difficult removing Erich from her life would prove to be.

CHAPTER 12

*A*s *Nina closed the door to the music room*, she heard the sound of footsteps approaching. Her heart skipped a beat at the sight of Celia walking down the hall. Memories of Erich made her jumpy. If only she could permanently scrub him from her mind.

"Nina, I'm glad I caught you before you left." Celia's mouth was set in a firm line. "Luke's on his way. He needs to talk with you."

She adjusted the straps of her laptop bag, which dug into her shoulder. "Why? What did he say?"

"I'll let him explain. I told him to meet us in my classroom."

Nerves danced inside her stomach. Luke, a police captain, wouldn't coming here unless something was wrong. Warning bells rang out in every cell of her body. She followed Celia to her classroom. Once inside, she started pacing. "When will he be here?"

Celia placed a hand on Nina's shoulder and guided her to sit in the office chair behind her desk. "Soon. Keep calm."

She slouched in the seat and exhaled. "He has news

about Erich." Judging from the loss of color on Celia's face, she knew she was right.

"Would you like something to drink?" Celia opened a dorm-room-sized refrigerator placed beside her desk. "I have water, regular, and sparkling."

"Do you have any of those little bottles of wine in there?" She spun the chair to peek inside.

Celia snickered. "No, but I've been tempted to. Especially the week right before Christmas break."

She accepted a bottle of water and waited. When Luke and Gabs entered the classroom with serious expressions on their faces and tense body language, she knew her gut feelings were confirmed.

"Don't get up." Luke motioned to Nina as she started to rise. After taking off his Stetson, he pulled up one of the few adult-sized chairs in the room and sat alongside the desk. "Colin came to the police station a few hours ago. He was running along Main Street and bumped into a man. After a brief conversation, Colin questioned whether the man he spoke with was Erich Everett."

Her heartbeat escalated, sharp and unsteady, building to a crescendo.

Gabs knelt beside her and took her hand. "Steady, girl. Don't pass out on me."

"I won't." But she might hyperventilate, which could lead to oxygen deprivation, which could lead to passing out. *Shoot.*

Breathe, Nina. Breathe. "Was it really him?"

"Colin looked at several of Erich's mug shots from his time in jail, and he can't say for sure. I placed a call to the Boston PD, and they sent officers over to Erich's apartment. The officers reported that a man fitting Erich's description answered the door when they knocked. He identified himself as Erich Everett and insisted he hadn't left the city since his release."

Gabs squeezed her hand. "There's no way he could have gotten back to Boston within only a few hours of Colin spotting him in Polaris. Most likely the man Colin saw here was not Erich. The man actually identified himself as Michael O'Neil, an investor interested in the North Star Resort."

"How do we know for sure?" Nina's heart slowed at the news Erich had answered the door to his apartment that afternoon. He might be sneaky, but he was still human, and couldn't be in two places at once.

"I have officers checking at North Star and the other local hotels and resorts." Luke's grip tightened on the brim of his hat. "Once we locate this Michael O'Neil, I'll pay him a visit, and then we'll know for sure."

"I think until then, Nina should stay with me." Celia put an arm around Nina's shoulders. "No taking chances with your safety."

"Thank you, Celia, but for the sake of my mental well-being, I need to keep things as normal as possible. I don't believe he's here, not after the Boston PD's house call." Nina stood and rested her back against the whiteboard at the front of the classroom. "After ten years in jail, I'm sure he wouldn't skip out on parole and risk being sent back."

"What about the letter?" Gabs asked. "Shows that you're still on his mind."

"He wanted to apologize and used my sister to deliver his message. He doesn't know where I live now or my last name."

"True." Luke scratched at the blond stubble covering the lower portion on his face. "But Celia's right. We can't leave your safety to assumptions and chance, but I understand your need to keep a normal schedule. Colin volunteered to stay with you whenever you're home during the day. And Gabs will be there at night."

She pushed off the whiteboard. "Colin's job is to care for Bea. He doesn't have time to babysit me."

"He said Bea's recovery is going great. He's arranging for a temporary replacement." Luke cleared his throat. "Colin's actually the perfect person to babysit you."

Heat rose and flushed her face. "He is actually the worst person to babysit me." She rounded on Luke. "And why are you suddenly promoting him? You hardly know him. We all hardly know him."

"Not you," Gabs murmured.

"I heard that." She pointed a finger at her best friend. "Just because I kissed the man doesn't mean I know him any better than the rest of you."

Luke's face softened. "I've worked in law enforcement long enough to develop a very strong internal lie detector. Colin Moynahan is a good man who wants to help."

"You kissed Colin and didn't tell me?" Celia lowered herself to sit on the corner of her desk. "I can't believe you didn't tell me."

"It was just a kiss." She shrugged. "Well, maybe more than just a kiss, circling back to why him staying with me is a very bad idea."

"I vote he stays with her at night too." Gabs winked.

"Or you could sleep at Bea's place," Celia suggested.

"No." She stomped her foot. Something she hadn't done since primary school. "Colin continues to care for Bea, end of story. And once his job is over, he's going to Hawaii for his next patient."

"He's temporary." Celia glanced at Luke, and then back to Nina. "I understand your apprehension."

Even Gabs sobered. "Fine. I'll take the night shift, but we

still need to figure out who will stay with you during the day."

"No one." Nina walked to the large window in the classroom, which overlooked a small garden. The flowers had faded, now only shades of brown. Brittle stalks rose from the dirt like a skeleton army. Soon, the ground would be covered in white. Winter would overtake fall and spread snow and cold. Nature would hide its gift of color, storing it away for safekeeping until spring. Then death would give way to life, and nature's glory would once again be displayed in its full spectrum.

She turned back to face Luke, Celia, and Gabs. "You, along with Bea, are my family. I love you, and I love the way you watch over me. I won't have unsubstantiated fear disrupting our lives. If we get proof that he's nearby, then we call in the twenty-four-hour protection." Nina walked up to her small group of friends and held Celia's hand with her right and Gabs with her left. She smiled up at Luke, whose eyes were suspiciously glossy. Was the tough lawman getting emotional? No wonder Celia called him her tenderhearted man.

"We'll do it your way...for now." Luke put his Stetson on his head. "I'll be in touch." After giving his fiancée a peck on the cheek, he strode out of the classroom.

Gabs and Celia flanked her, both hugging her so strongly, she was afraid she'd get crushed between the two of them.

"Just remember you're not alone," Celia said. "You need anything, I'm only a few houses away."

"And I carry a gun." Gabs patted the holster on her hip. "Although mine's not as big as Colin's, and he has two."

"Colin has two guns?" Nina crinkled her brow.

"Yeah." Gabs flexed her arms and kissed each bicep. "I'd buy tickets to that gun show."

Celia giggled. "I have seen him in a tight T-shirt and highly recommend paying extra for the good seats."

Nina rolled her eyes. "Good grief. This conversation is over. I need to get home and put dinner in the oven." She patted her tummy. "Baked polenta with mushrooms and gorgonzola."

"Yum." Celia walked with them to the front door of the school. "Give me a call tomorrow, and let's make plans to get together this weekend."

"I'd love that." With the straps of her laptop bag securely over her shoulder, Nina walked across the parking lot to her car. She gave Gabs a quick hug before getting inside and starting the engine.

Now alone, she took several seconds to wrap her head around what Luke had shared. Could Erich really be in Polaris, maybe watching her right now? "Stop," she growled to herself. *Boston PD checked on him and he's at home, far away.* She refused to be drawn back into the paranoia that had controlled her life in the months Erich stalked her in Boston. Always afraid to step outside her apartment. Looking over her shoulder and expecting to see him lurking behind. Never feeling safe, no matter where she was or who she was with.

He'd found ways to get to her when she least expected. A bouquet of flowers delivered during rehearsal. Notes left inside a book she was reading. He warned her against dating, but she hadn't known ignoring his threats would end in an innocent man's death.

Nina started towards home. A place Erich had never seen, never visited, and didn't know existed. When she'd moved away, she hadn't left a trail. Besides her immediate family, no one else knew how to contact her. She'd wanted to disappear, and for the past ten years, she'd done just that.

As she drove through the active downtown area, her gaze searched the sidewalks. Maybe for Colin. Maybe for Erich. Maybe for a distraction. Certainly, though, because she loved Polaris and every heartwarming element that made it home.

Polaris was hers, and no monster from her past would corrupt her hard-won sense of peace.

CHAPTER 13

After a short debate that ended with him deciding he was an idiot for even questioning his instincts, Colin texted Nina, saying *I'm coming over.*

Moments later, he knocked on her front door. When she opened it, he saw a cheerful woman—surprising given the emotional turmoil he'd put her through once again.

"Hey, come in. I was just cleaning up from dinner." She waited for him to enter before closing and locking the door behind him.

"Is Gabs or Celia staying with you?" He handed over his coat. Although he wanted someone here with her, part of him hoped for time alone.

"No, for now. I don't believe Erich's left Boston."

He followed her into the living room. As he sat beside her on the sofa, he fought the desire to touch her and hold her close. He embraced the burn as penance for not being everything she needed. "I'm kicking myself for not dragging that guy down to the police station. Then you'd know for sure."

"You did the right thing by letting him go and then

talking to Luke." She rested her hand over his. Her long, elegant fingers draped across his lumpy knuckles. "Luke's communicating with the Boston PD, who are keeping watch on Erich's apartment."

Colin also had eyes on Erich's apartment. Earlier, after leaving the police station, he'd called a few buddies from back in South Boston. Those guys knew a few other guys who were willing to do some street-level investigating for cash.

He had no problem paying a few hundred dollars for information. Those guys could get people to talk. From the address Colin had been given, he knew the part of town Erich had settled in was middle-income blue collar. Most around that neighborhood weren't the type who'd say more than two words to a cop. Not exactly the downtown swank he'd lived in before his stint in the big house.

So far, his source in Boston had come up with little. The man living in Erich's apartment kept to himself, rarely leaving or speaking to any other tenants. Knocks on the apartment door had gone unanswered.

"What if I made a mistake and worried you for nothing?" His voice cracked. Racking his fingers through his hair, he became frustrated at his own helplessness.

"Enough of the what-ifs. Luke often reminds me to deal only in facts, so that's what I'm trying to do." On the sofa, she sat propped on her hip with her feet tucked under, her body facing him. "I lived for years chasing the dream of being a famous cellist. During the weeks Erich held me in the cabin, I came to the realization I might not make it out alive. He'd killed Seth, and he might have killed me if I didn't hand over my soul." Nina took a shuddering breath. "And all the success I'd been chasing meant absolutely nothing. I had no real friends and a strained relationship with my family. Toxic, really. If I had died, people would've remembered me for my music but little else."

Colin leaned in and brushed his hand down her smooth hair. "I don't believe that."

"Because you didn't know me in Boston. I'm different now because I promised myself that if I did survive, I'd remake my life." Nina's hands trembled.

He held them in a warm embrace. The physical contact calmed him.

"Reclaim it, really," she said. "Once the stress of the trial was over, I knew moving away from Boston was what I needed to do. And when I got here, I worked every day to become a better person."

"What Erich did was not your fault, even if you were a self-centered princess, which I'm not saying you were." He reflected her small smile. "You're the kindest and most genuinely beautiful person I know. And this time, you have an army of people who care about you."

She straightened her back. "I trust the system will keep him away from me."

He wouldn't tell her about his efforts working outside the system. That would be his secret. Or at least the specifics. Luke had been wise enough not to ask for details. "Are you okay here tonight by yourself?"

Her face grew pink. "I wish I had the guts to say no."

"Say no." His lips brushed her cheek, and he inhaled. Why did she have to smell so good?

"Yes." Nina pulled away and shook her head. "Yes, I'll be fine alone tonight."

Pushing down a groan, Colin grinned. "Then I should leave." *Leave before you push your luck and she kicks you out.* All he wanted was to taste her again and feel her melt under his touch.

She walked him to the door, then gave him a strong hug before he headed out. "Your patient needs you more than I do. Good night, Colin."

After giving her a gentle kiss on top of her head, he left with the deep sense of longing. He needed Nina—more than anyone else in the world.

˜ ˛ ˜

"I'm very pleased with your progress." Dr. Brown lowered the blanket covering Beatrice's waist and lap. "Your incision is healing well, with no sign of infection. No small feat for a geriatric patient with diabetes."

"Young man, you better be careful who you call geriatric." Bea laughed. "But I suppose it's better than being called old."

"I would never classify you as old, Mrs. Maxwell. Your long life has honored you." Dr. Brown pushed up his glasses to the bridge of his nose. "After reading over the reports from your physical therapist and Mr. Moynahan, here, I have confidence that within the next month, you will notice a substantial decrease in pain level." He glanced at the open folder in his hands and flipped over several papers. "I trust Mr. Moynahan will keep you from overdoing your activity, even as you begin feeling better."

"Doctor, don't worry. Colin sticks to his rehab plan like honey to a bear."

"Good to hear," Dr. Brown said.

"I would have been confined to a long-term care facility if it wasn't for him and the wonderful company he works for."

Colin stood, growing uncomfortable. Back in his boxing days, he'd been showered with compliments. Showered in bull crap, really. None had ever come from a place of sincerity. Only greed. Now, their compliments held no ill intent, but he still struggled against his natural instinct to balk. "Beatrice is an excellent patient who's determined to reach full recovery ahead of schedule. To be honest, I think she just wants to get rid of me." His easy smile was evidence of his teasing humor.

Bea waved her hand through the air. "Now, why would I be anxious to be rid of such a nice man who's also a very good cook, I might add? Between Colin and the nurse's aide he's got coming in, I'm being treated like royalty."

"As you should be." Dr. Brown gently patted her knee.

"Queen Bea." For the first time since his grandmother had died, he felt a deep connection with someone he cared for. Normally, he kept a professional distance. But with Bea, she reminded him so strongly of his own dearly loved grandmother. No doubt he'd struggle when the time came to say goodbye.

"I'll step outside the room and review your insulin level history with Mr. Moynahan, along with his rehab plan for the upcoming weeks. Mrs. Maxwell, are you all right dressing by yourself, or would you like assistance?" Dr. Brown snapped closed the medical folder and stood.

"I've dressed on my own the last few days without much trouble, but if you wouldn't mind having one of your nurses stand outside the door, just in case. Then she can walk me back to the waiting room." The skin around her eyes and mouth wrinkled as she smiled. "You have any of those sugar-free suckers up there, Doc? I could sure use something sweet."

Dr. Brown chuckled. "Cadence, our receptionist, bought a bag just for you. I'm fairly certain you have my entire office staff wrapped around your finger." He opened the door and stepped into the hall.

Colin followed. "Along with the staffs at the physical therapy office and every restaurant we go to."

"Oh, shush, now" Bea waved them out. "You two go on now and let this geriatric patient get dressed."

Grinning at her playful charm, Colin closed the door, then met Dr. Brown at a high work counter down the hall.

A nurse whose petite height and fresh face made her appear not much older than twenty came to stand outside the door of Bea's room. She glanced quickly at Colin and smiled.

Not wanting his concern for Bea to come off as an attempt to flirt with the nurse, Colin directed his attention back to Dr. Brown.

"Beatrice is thriving in your care," the doctor said. "Because her diabetes complicates her recovery and her surgery complicates her diabetes, she needs access to round-the-clock medical care. I've practiced long enough to know you've gone above and beyond for her."

"It's nothing less than she deserves. What anyone in her position deserves." Colin shoved his hands into the front pockets of his jeans and rocked back on his heels.

"Beatrice and her late husband moved to Polaris back when it was still a struggling mining town with a few ski runs. They were both instrumental in helping the town grow and adapt to change." Dr. Brown reached toward the back of the workstation and pumped a few squirts of sanitizer onto his hands, then rubbed them together. "Over the past decade, she's spent many hours at the school and library giving talks on the civil rights movement and her experiences in Milwaukee, as well as more current issues and ways our community can embrace and celebrate diversity. I, as a Black doctor, am deeply grateful for all the work she's done."

"She's shared a few stories of her protest marches. It took a lot of guts to show up and speak out, knowing others would be waiting to do you harm." Colin inhaled the strong smell of alcohol-based hand sanitizer and wondered how many times during the course of a day did the good doctor disinfect his hands. His grandmother used to say, *"Wash your hands and fingers for any germs that lingers."* He smiled at the memory.

"It took guts and a large number of voices all refusing to be silenced." Dr. Brown opened Bea's file folder. "Now, while I have you here, I'd like to go over Beatrice's rehab schedule and see if we need to make any adjustments, given her progress is moving better than expected."

Twenty minutes later, Colin escorted Bea outside to the waiting handicap accessible van. She'd insisted on finishing her sucker before leaving the doctor's office, saying she couldn't grip the walker with both hands and enjoy her treat at the same time. She was even given more candy for the road. Colin had seen the receptionist slip several colorful suckers into the pocket of Bea's coat.

He was beginning to crave a sweet treat too. But his candy came in human form and went by the name Nina. Every day, his longing grew. Scary feelings. He loved his job and enjoyed the freedom and adventure that came along with it. Days, weeks, and years spent meeting new people and visiting new places. His future was laid out in a twisting line that encircled the globe, without the restraints of another person's desires.

As well as no companion to share the journey. While Colin helped Bea get settled into her seat in the van, he was hit with a sense of solitude. Someday, he'd have to decide how he wanted to spend the second half of his life. Would his wanderer's soul ever find a place to rest?

He climbed into the passenger seat up front next to the driver. "Do you have time for a stop up at the North Star Resort?"

"We can have lunch there," Bea announced from behind. "The café has a grilled cheese sandwich and tomato soup combo that's to die for. Not literally, though. Can't joke about those kind of things at my age."

Laughing, their driver turned the van out of the parking lot and onto the road. "My next scheduled pickup isn't for another two hours. That soup and sandwich sounds good to me. I'll take you up there and have lunch, then bring you back home." He pressed a button on the radio, and the sounds of classical music filled the van.

Colin listened, trying to peel apart the layers of the symphony to locate the sound of the cello. He closed his eyes and imagined Nina on stage, sitting with the large instrument pressed between her knees. Her own eyes closed in concentration. Her hand gripping the bow, soaring across the strings.

The blast of a car horn shook him out of his fantasy. A silver sports car flew past the van, and he didn't miss the driver's one-finger salute.

"Jerk," the van driver said. "Sorry, ma'am. It's just these tourists come up here with some bucks and act like they own the place. I'm not speedin' and putting my passengers in danger so some yuppie can get to his manicure appointment on time."

The driver of their van looked somewhere between fifty and sixty. His long silver-gray hair was pulled back into a ponytail, which ended at the middle of his back. He had a slight Southern accent. Texas maybe?

The longer Colin was in Polaris, the more he realized the city was filled with transplants from all over the country. Nina came from Boston. Bea came from Milwaukee. Celia Batista had moved from Miami and Luke Veldkamp from the Sacramento area. He liked the diverse culture and styles. If he ever got the urge to settle in one place, he'd want a town like Polaris.

After a few twists and turns along the road, the van pulled up to the covered entrance of the resort. Placed on either side of the wide doorway was an artful display of purple mums, and pumpkins and gourds of all sizes. To the right was a large pumpkin, the front carved with a snowboarder-in-flight design. His attention focused on a sign advertisement for a hot air balloon ride company.

The only way to beat the sight of the autumn-colored mountains from the ground was to view it from above. Peak color would be over soon. Had Nina ever gone up in a hot air balloon here? Maybe a ride floating through the air would give them time alone to work out a way to continue a relationship even after he left town. Or to come to terms with the fact their lives were too different to be compatible. But most importantly, it would take Nina away from the stress she was under while her feet touched the earth.

Colin helped Bea exit the van and guided her to the lobby. The fall decorations inside slanted more towards Halloween, reminding him to pick up a few bags of candy for the trick-or-treaters that would show up on Bea's doorstep at the end of the month.

"You go on and do what you need to do." Bea halted her slow march across the lobby. She stood beside a stuffed beaver dressed up like a pirate—eye patch and all. Bea gave it a side-eyed glance before shaking her head and turning back to Colin. "I'll wait for you in the café. You want me to order something for you for lunch?"

"Order another of whatever you're having." Colin continued escorting her to the café.

"Does your task here have to do with Nina?" she asked once they arrived at the entrance.

"Yes. The police were already here, asking about Erich, and they came up empty. I want to have a look around myself."

"You're really taken with my Nina." Her smile grew wider.

"She's a good person. How could I not be?" He couldn't hold her gaze and looked toward the stacked-stone fireplace at the other side of the room.

Bea clucked her tongue and shook her head. "Young people. Back in my day, if we had feelings for someone, we spent time together. Got to know one another."

"Nina and I are friends." *Keep on telling yourself that, man, and maybe you'll start to believe it.*

She clucked her tongue again, even louder. "I'm old, but not senile. You light up when you're around her, like someone's turned you on."

Colin snorted. "Good one."

"What did I say?" Bea gazed up at him for several seconds then smiled. "Oh my, you do have a dirty mind for a good Irish boy."

"Never said I was good."

"You don't have to." She stared at him with warm brown eyes. "You came to Polaris to care for me, and you've done a wonderful job. But I love Nina as if she's my own child. Protect her, Colin. She is your true purpose here. I believe that with all my heart."

CHAPTER 14

"*This is a surprise.*" Nina moved aside to let Colin enter. His large frame filled her small foyer, surrounding her in a strong masculine aura. It felt safe and comforting, as well as gave her courage. Like a superhero's armor. Nothing would get through its shield.

Her skin tingled at the sight of him. Colin's tousled dark hair now curled at the back of his neck. The lower portion of his face was shrouded in a light growth of stubble—very sexy.

Every time she was with him, her body buzzed with attraction. Would she ever become desensitized to his charming good looks? Since he'd leave here someday soon, she'd probably never get to that point. Then again, Nina was certain she could see him every day, all day, and never lose her fascination.

"I want to take advantage of the nice weather and go for a drive. You want to join me?" He shoved his hands into the pockets of his charcoal-gray coat. "I heard the views from on top of Mount Holiday are killer, especially this time of year."

"I'd avoid using the word killer when you're standing next to a five-hundred-foot drop-off...but a scenic ride does sound nice." She glanced toward the back of her house and the mess. Housecleaning could wait. Not like there was anyone else around to care. Well, there was Ariel. Too bad she hadn't trained her ferret to dust and mop, skills that would offset stealing jewelry and hiding important household items.

"Go grab your coat and let's get shakin'."

The sound of Ariel's tiny claws tapping across the hardwood floors proclaimed her arrival. Her long, white-furred body skidded to a halt and came to rest at the toes of Colin's boots. After a brief hesitation, she leaped for the ends of his laces, using her paws and mouth in a voracious attempt to untie them.

"What does your rat think it's doing?" He glanced down at his feet, then at Nina, one brow cocked. "A gutsy move, but one doomed to fail. No way am I letting her run off with my boot."

Giggling, she scooped up Ariel and snuggled the little fur ball. "She does have big ambitions. I've never seen her go after a shoe before."

"Must be the smell." One corner of his mouth twitched with a grin. "My grandmother used to make me leave my shoes outside when I came home. She called me skunk paws until I discovered Odor Eaters."

The smile on her face grew. "Okay, you stay here...with your shoes on, and I'll get my coat. Be right back." She placed Ariel on the floor of the family room and pointed toward her nest behind the sofa. Once she was sure Colin's boots were safe from another ferret attack, she picked her coat off the rack by the back door. After deciding she'd wear hiking boots in case they left the car for a walk through the woods, she met him back by the front door.

"Ready." She balled up a knit cap and stuffed it into a coat pocket. She'd learned the hard way pleasant weather in the mountains could change fast.

He held the door for her, and she locked up behind him. When he opened the passenger side door of his Jeep, she thanked him. Nice manners. Ones that likely would have made his grandmother proud.

Once inside, he turned the ignition and backed out of her driveway. "Since I admitted to having notoriously stinky feet, it's only fair you make an embarrassing confession."

She scoffed. "You totally did that on your own. Plus, I have no embarrassing confessions." Glancing over, she saw a smirk on his handsome face.

"Doubtful. Everyone has something they won't tell people. Something that only comes out after you've spent a lot of time together or had too many beers. Take farting in your sleep, for example."

"Oh, good grief." She covered her eyes with her hand and snorted with laughter. "I'd never admit to that, even drunk. Okay, let me think."

Gripping the wheel with one hand, Colin played with the radio dial with the other. He moved through stations until he found one playing country music. "Passing gas is a natural bodily function. Even more so after a meal heavy on beans, which you should know, being a vegetarian."

"Would you stop." She swatted his arm. How could she think of a non-embarrassing embarrassing fact about herself if he kept joking?

"Take your time. We have a while before we reach our destination." He sent her a quick glance.

She caught sight of his blue eyes long enough to send

her heart pounding as hard as if she'd stepped onstage with her cello. The adrenaline rush she'd received right before a performance was only matched by Colin Moynahan and his alluring blue-eyed stare.

For several minutes, they rode without talking. The only sounds came from the purr of the engine and the energetic fiddle from a country song. Nina gazed out the window and visually absorbed the landscape passing by. Thick groves of birch lined the road, their white trunks and golden leaves creating a masterpiece of mother nature. After a switchback turn, the valley came into view, with the town of Polaris resting snug in the center. From above, the miniature houses, resorts, and shops appeared like a scenic layout built around a model train set.

"Okay, I have something, but you have to swear not to laugh." She bit her lower lip, questioning her sanity. Because of her past, Nina treasured privacy. She didn't like to talk about herself to begin with, and then to admit something embarrassing was a level of openness she'd only experienced as a small child. Obviously, Colin hadn't outgrown that stage.

"Are you going to tell me now or make me wait until Halloween? Which really isn't that far away."

"No, it's not. Do you have a costume?

"Stop right there." He wagged a finger at her. "Spill, poppet. We're almost there."

She breathed deeply, pushing back the giddiness bubbling up. How did this man manage to make her feel like a carefree girl and forget about her troubles? The answer—his good humor, something he never seemed to lack. Turning to face him, she pressed her lips together in a very serious expression. "I have a karaoke machine."

He turned the steering wheel to round a bend in the

road. "So do a lot of other people. You'll have to do better than that."

"And I use it a lot...at home...by myself." Nina turned slightly in her seat to face him. "I put on little shows, though no one's there to watch. I could never stand up and sing with an audience." The rush of her admission cleared away any lingering anxiety. "Well, Ariel sometimes hops on the sofa and listens. She loves Backstreet Boys songs."

"Backstreet Boys?" He took his eyes off the road long enough to give her a quizzical look.

"Yes. Don't tell me you didn't listen to the Backstreet Boys growing up?"

"*Ahhh*...the musicians I listened to wore flannel, not sequins."

Was that a dig on her favorite boy band? "Figures you're a grunge rock type of guy. Anyway, when I was a teenager, I liked to watch their music videos. It was one of the only normal teenager things I did. Even after so many years, I can still slide and spin like Nick Carter."

"Who?" Colin scratched at his scruffy chin.

"Only the cutest boy in the band. I had the biggest crush on him."

Arriving at a parking lot next to an empty field that did not fit the scenic destination he'd advertised, he put the vehicle in Park and turned to face her.

"Let me see if I got this." He cleared his throat. "Your embarrassing secret is you put on karaoke concerts for your rat? And while you're singing, you dance memorized chore-ography to music videos you watched twenty years ago?"

"Yes, that's right." Crossing her arms, she stared him down. "It's a great way to burn off stress. Maybe you should try it."

Suddenly, his face beamed with a wide smile. "Maybe I will. But only if you demonstrate first...and I get to choose the song."

"I don't think so." She grinned back. "The reason I don't sing in public is because I can't carry a tune. Go figure. I played the cello like an angel, but my singing sounds like a cat in heat."

He laughed. "Now I really want to hear you sing. I'll even pay."

"Let me think about it." She rubbed her hands together. "Okay, still no."

He reached over and put a hand behind her neck, then leaned in. "Nina...singing or playing, I have no doubt you are perfection."

~ ˎ ~

Colin couldn't get enough of her. The sight of her beautiful face. The warm floral scent of her skin. The musical sound of her voice. Being with her produced a chemical reaction in his blood and brain. He needed to touch her, to hold her. But he knew he shouldn't. Because as much as he longed for her, he'd rather deal with the ache than cause her heartbreak.

"I'm far from perfect." She glanced up at him with large eyes. "But you, on the other hand." Her fingers danced across his chest.

"Am flawed beyond redemption." Suddenly, he wished for warmer weather that would make their bulky coats unnecessary.

"You are a good man." Nina placed a hand against his cheek.

"The thoughts going through my mind right now prove I'm still a bad boy at heart." His pulse pounded hard and fast. If she continued to gaze at him so doe-eyed and inno-cent, he'd fling his self-control off the side of the mountain and kiss her. And keep kissing her until she totally ravaged him, body and soul.

Which would be wrong. He needed distance to clear the yearning from his system, and that wouldn't happen while they sat close together in his Jeep. His breathing sounded seconds from hyperventilating.

"Since you gave such a great confession, I have a bonus one for you." He peered over, worried her opinion of him would change with the background he'd share. "I was a professional boxer in Boston. I started on the streets and back alley matches, then a promoter discovered me. He set me up with a real trainer and real fights. I did okay for myself. Okay enough to pay for college."

"Wow." She brushed a finger over the knuckles on his right hand. "Do you still fight?"

He shook his head. "Only in the gym for a good workout. My last fight was the night before I took my final college class. I won, of course." Colin winked. "And then told my promoter I was retiring."

"How did he take that?"

"He knew it was coming. If I wasn't training, I was study-ing. Fighting was something I was good at, not something I enjoyed."

"I'm glad you found your true calling. Thanks for sharing that with me. I like getting glimpses into the person you used to be...what shaped you into the man you are today." Nina paused. She turned to face the wide expanse of the valley. "Why did you stop here?"

"One of the benefits of moving around as much as I do is

that the world stays fresh and new." He watched the slight flicker of her eyelashes and the dip in the corners of her mouth. "And I know you've lived here awhile now, so I thought you'd like a different look at your hometown."

She brushed strands of golden hair from off her face. "So you brought me to a valley? It's pretty, don't get me wrong, but not exactly breathtaking."

Sitting next to Nina, he considered his view beyond breathtaking. Nothing he'd seen or ever would see could be as beautiful as her. "This isn't our destination. Actually, we have a little farther to go."

"Okay." She drew out the word and narrowed her eyes. "What are you up to?"

"Up to." He laughed. "That's funny. Just wait and see."

After a short drive, he rounded a curve to the sight of a rainbow. Not just any rainbow, but a colorful hot air balloon set on a grassy field. He parked and glanced over at Nina.

Her eyes were the size of a full moon. "Is that for us?"

The smile on her face was contagious. "Yes. Do you want to go up with me?"

Colin exited and went around to open the passenger side door. He took her hand and slowly helped her out.

She didn't take her gaze off the balloon. "I do. I do so very much."

"Good." He guided her across the field to meet the balloon operator. After a short safety briefing, Colin stepped inside the basket, keeping hold of her hand.

"I've always wanted to do this. How did you know?" She looked up at the huge, colorful balloon hovering above.

"I didn't." He brushed his fingers over her silky hair and inwardly sighed. "I thought you could use a distraction."

"This is quite the distraction." She squealed when the balloon lifted off the ground.

As they floated above valleys and beside grand mountains, his focus rarely left Nina. He loved the expressiveness of her face. When she saw a herd of elk running across a field below, her tawny eyes glowed with excitement. Her laughter filled his heart with warmth. Her face held a smile that affected his soul.

I'm in so much trouble.

The balloon operator, showing his experience at taking couples up for romantic rides, kept his back to them.

Their view from the balloon was amazing. With the aspen and maple trees at peak color, gold, red, and orange swirled below. The snowcapped mountain range look different from this perspective. No less impressive, but vaster. A long stretch of tall stone peaks formed a defensive wall. How had people crossed these mountain ranges for the first time? The sheer scope and size would have had him turning around and heading home.

"I feel so free up here." She tugged down her hat to cover her ears. "For the first time in weeks, I have no anxiety. I'm not worried about Erich because..." She paused and faced him. "Because I'm like a bird soaring in the air. So high that I can see for miles, and no one can touch me."

"That was the idea." Colin set his finger under her chin and lifted her face, his lips inches away from hers.

"Except for you," Nina whispered. "Your touch makes my skin tingle."

"Tingle is good. What about when I kiss you?" He leaned closer and felt the warmth of her breath on his face.

"Sparks. Fireworks. Like the huge flame above our head." She pointed up to the burner, roaring with sound and heat. "Very dangerous and hard to control."

He kissed her then, gently on the mouth.

She pressed in harder and looped her arms around his neck.

No escape. Exactly where he wanted to be. He nipped at her bottom lip. "Don't control the flame. Let it burn."

"Not smart to joke about the very thing that could send us falling to our deaths." She smiled against his lips.

He indulged in another kiss before pulling back. "I know it won't be easy, but let's find a way to make this work. You and I." Colin tapped his heart, then hers. "You got me. I'm a complete goner."

"Really?" Her eyes widened.

"Really." *Okay, one more.* This time, he settled for a kiss on her smooth brow. He felt the drop of the balloon in altitude, as well as his disappointment their ride was coming to an end.

"You want to find a way to make a relationship work between us?" Her smile faded. "I don't believe that's possible. Not long-term."

"Anything's possible if you just believe." He pinched the tip of her nose in an effort to bring back her smile.

The balloon operator faced them. "We'll be on the ground in fifteen minutes. Keep a hold on the basket as we go down."

Nina transferred one hand from him to the basket. "I wish we could stay up here until the sun goes down."

"But as the saying goes, all good things must come to an end."

"I think you just answered your own question."

She'd landed a hard blow, but she'd have to bring him to his knees, blood dripping from his mouth, to make him drop out of this fight. "We don't have to end. Sure, I travel, but in between patients, I'll stay here. And you can join me wherever I'm working if your schedule allows. See how easy it is?"

"For how long? Long-distance relationships don't lead anywhere unless they stop being long-distance."

"Okay." He blew out a breath. "Not easy. But worth the challenges." Forgetting the operator's instructions, he held on to her with both hands.

"Honestly, Colin, I have a lot of emotional baggage, some you already know and some I find too painful to share. I won't risk opening my heart to a man who isn't around most days of the year."

He wanted to argue but couldn't. Would he give up his career someday to build a life with Nina in Polaris? Maybe. "Then what can I say to convince you to give me a chance?"

Her gaze flickered down to his lips, and she licked her own. "I don't know. I'm at an age where I should understand how this works but I don't."

"I'm right there with you. Let's find out together."

The basket of the balloon now hovered only several feet off the ground. Colin had enough brain cells functioning to let go of Nina with one hand and grasp the basket. Good thing. The bumpy landing would have landed him on his rear.

Once the hot air balloon was secured, Colin held Nina's hand while she exited the basket, and then he climbed over.

They walked to his Jeep in silence. Not one clever comment or joke came to mind. After he opened the car door for her, he moved around to block her path to her seat.

He had no words. Only action. Cupping the back of her head with his large hand, he held her gaze. "I'm going to kiss you. This time, I won't be gentle. Tell me now if that's not what you want."

She raised herself up on her tiptoes and grabbed his

jacket, pulling him closer. She crushed her mouth against his.

Heat built between them like the friction created by two sticks sliding across one another. Colin's lips burned. Instead of pulling away, he sank in, enjoying both the pleasure and pain. Could he walk away from his career and his dream of seeing the entire world for the gift of kissing Nina every day for the rest of his life? The option grew more appealing by the second.

Parting her lips, she sighed. Their tongues tangled.

He hooked one arm around her waist. The other became lost in her hair. For a second, he remembered the balloon operator, whom they'd left not far away. Then Nina's hand slipped under the hem of his coat, under the hem of his shirt, and connected with his skin. All rational thought fled his brain.

"You got me, Nina." He trailed his lips across her cheek, then gave her earlobe a quick nip. "I want you in my life."

Slowly, she opened her eyes—honey-colored orbs that regained their focus. She grazed his cheek with the back of her hand. "I care about you, but once you leave, I'm afraid the heat holding us together will cool and there will be nothing left but good memories.

A very real fear he held as well. "I don't believe it's only heat holding us together." He shifted his body to allow her access to her seat. "You've become very important to me."

"But so is your job and your love of travel. Let's just wait and see if we still feel strongly about starting a relationship at the end of your stay here in Polaris." She hopped inside the Jeep, still breathing heavily.

Resting his forearm on the doorframe, he bowed forward and gave her an innocent peck on the cheek. "I'll accept that answer...for now." He stepped back and closed the door, her sweet scent still filling his nose.

While she weighed the risks of offering her heart to him, Colin would continue to guard her closely. Because earlier, when he'd held her while they floated across the blue mountain sky, he'd felt himself fall hard and fast. His heart now resided with Nina. Scary for a confirmed bachelor with no desire to settle down. Especially when he had no idea how to make those two pieces of his life fit together.

CHAPTER 15

"*You can go on back*," Carrie Ann said from the other side of the open sliding glass partition. "Captain Veldkamp is expecting you."

"Thanks." Nina waited for the sound of the buzzer and then turned the door handle. She left the lobby and entered the secure area of the police station. Before she went back to Luke's office, she paused next to Carrie Ann's desk. "I wanted to tell you Garrett's been doing so well in violin lessons. He asked about learning a more challenging song. I'm very impressed with his progress."

A large smile beamed on Carrie Ann's face. "Learning the violin has been so good for him. He's like a new child... focused, obedient, and he doesn't fight me about his homework anymore. You know, when Garrett told me he wanted to learn to play an instrument, I initially told him no. I didn't think he'd stick with it."

"You never know which fish music will hook." Music had hooked her at an early age too. Even though she no longer played, she didn't regret the good things the cello had brought into her life. Just the bad.

"Well, Garrett is hooked. Thanks, Nina." Carrie Ann stood and wrapped her in a hug. "And if you ever need anything...someone to talk to, a shoulder to cry on, or even an emergency chocolate delivery, let me know. Okay?"

She squeezed her hand. "Thanks." After a short walk down the hall, she approached Captain Luke Veldkamp's office. Nina stopped by his open door and raised her hand to knock on the frame, but the sound of salsa music made her hesitate.

A giggle bubbled up in her throat at the sight of Luke. Dressed in his police uniform, he had his arms raised like he held an invisible dance partner. His hips stiffly swayed in time with the beat.

She loudly cleared her throat.

Luke froze and turned his head in her direction. After a second's hesitation, he jumped to his computer and silenced the music. "Nina. I wasn't expecting you already."

"Clearly." She entered his office and closed the door behind her. "Sorry to interrupt."

With his cheeks flushed red, he took a seat behind his desk. "It's fine." Luke looked at his computer screen and then at her. "Don't tell Celia."

"That I saw you dancing with air?"

He exhaled a long breath. "She wants to dance the salsa for our first dance at the wedding reception. I'm an awful dancer. I don't have two left feet, I have three. So she signed us up for lessons at the dance studio downtown. Our poor teacher has already given up on me, and I thought if I practiced on my own, maybe I'll catch on before the big day."

"That's very sweet." She sat on one of the upholstered chairs facing the desk. "I'm sure Celia won't care if you step on her toes a few times during your first dance. She'll be too happy as your wife."

"It's not only her opinion I'm worried about. Her entire Cuban family will be watching and questioning why she married a man who moves his hips like a robot."

"A good dancer doesn't make a good husband. But if you want some extra practice, let me know. I took ballroom dance lessons when I was a teenager. All part of growing up as a girl from a wealthy family." She rolled her eyes.

"I'll keep that in mind." He folded his hands and rested them on his desk. "Discussing my lack of dance skills was not why you wanted to see me."

"No." She steadied her breath in an effort to slow her pounding heart. "Have you heard any more news from Boston about Erich?"

"He meets with his parole officer tomorrow." Luke leaned forward. "If he shows, then we rest easy."

"And if he doesn't?"

"You have no reason to believe he knows where you live. You've changed your last name."

"But he could find me." She balled her hands into fists, an automatic gesture whenever thoughts of Erich entered her mind. "Plus, we have Colin's sighting a few days ago."

"I deal in facts, Nina. We don't know the man Colin saw was Erich. I've had officers go to every resort in the area and show Erich's picture to the staff. No one has seen him. Add the fact he answered the door when Boston PD made a house call. We have no credible evidence that you should fear for your safety."

"I understand what you're saying in my head." She swallowed hard. "But I can't shake the constant feeling of dread. I dreamt last night I was back in the cabin with Erich, being forced to play the cello for him and fearing for my life."

"His actions traumatized you. Since you were rescued, you've made big changes in your life to help you cope. I can't imagine what Erich's release stirred up inside you. Please know my department and I are vigilantly monitoring the situation."

"I do know." She rested a hand over his. "And thank you."

"I'm also aware Erich is smart and cunning, and I've been in law enforcement long enough to understand how dangerous those people are." Luke reclined in his chair and brushed his hand down his face. "This is the point in our conversation that I insist either you move in with someone else or someone moves in with you. Temporarily, of course."

"I don't feel that's necessary."

"I do. At least until we get some reassurances from Boston that he's were he should be."

"Luke, I sleep with a Sig Sauer next to my bed and I know how to use it. Trust me, I'm ready if he shows up uninvited."

He grinned. "I'm sure you could put a few holes in him if need be, but your friends want to help. LT Joyce has already volunteered to sleep overnight at your place."

Maybe having Gabs over wouldn't be so bad. Just for a few nights, though. She'd think of it like she was back in college. "Fine. Tell Gabs to pack an overnight bag."

"She already has." He swiveled in his chair. "I'll call you as soon as I hear from Erich's parole officer."

"Thanks." She squirmed in her seat. "Hey, can I ask you a personal question?"

"Depends." He grinned. "Is it about Colin?"

Her cheeks burned. "He took me on a hot air balloon ride yesterday, and we had some time to talk. He asked me to give him a chance, relationship-wise." She sighed. "He's a great guy but he travels all over the world doing a job he loves. Why would I get involved with a man who I know has no long-term potential?" Tell that to her heart, which was slowly falling for him—very, very hard.

"Because he may decide that Polaris has more to offer than anywhere else in the world." His serious expression softened, and his blue eyes grew lighter.

A lump expanded in her throat. "I haven't dated since what happened in Boston. A man died because he showed romantic interest in me, and I'm scared the same thing will happen to Colin. I couldn't live with myself if Erich hurt him."

"Don't tell that to Colin." Luke clenched his jaw. "You have just as much right as anyone else to find love. Probably more so. If you feel a connection with Colin, then don't you dare let Erich steal what could be a wonderful future together. Colin's more than capable of defending himself."

She could no longer hold back her tears. "I can't go through it again. Erich killed Seth because of me."

Luke stood and wrapped her in a strong embrace. "You can't keep your heart closed off forever."

Sobs racked her body. She felt her soul reaching out for Colin like the roots of a scorched plant in search of water. After a taste of his refreshing sweetness, how could she not want to do anything, including open herself up to potential heartbreak, to keep him in her life? "When will it stop?"

He stepped back and held her at arm's length, holding her gaze. "It will stop. I guarantee it."

~ ⸱ ~

Colin weaved through the aisles of Tuck's Corner Market, grabbing a box here and a can there. His mind was not on his task—buying the items on Bea's grocery list and getting back to her house in time to make dinner.

Actually, she'd be cooking tonight with his assistance. The act of preparing a meal would be physically and mentally beneficial. Every step toward regaining her independence was a win. It was the reason he was here. He only wished time would stand still for a little while, giving him a real chance to start a relationship with Nina. He feared he'd leave town before their roots could grow deep enough to sustain a love affair.

Colin relived their hot air balloon ride in his mind. Now if that romantic gesture hadn't convinced her to give him a shot, he might be out of luck.

During a pass through the meat department, he snatched a package of chicken breasts Bea needed for her pot pie. He read over the list, noticing several things he had yet to locate. Back in the produce section for a head of cabbage, Colin spotted Nina's friend Gabrielle. She held a peach in one hand, turning the fruit while intensely studying it. After poking the flesh several times, she sniffed it, then added it to the clear plastic bag in her shopping basket.

"You do that with each one?" Colin approached and stopped his cart next to the bin of peaches.

Gabs arched an eyebrow. "I'm picky about my fruit."

He lifted one and spun it in his hand. "Picky can be good. But you might pass on the sweetest ones."

"True." She flicked him a smile before grabbing another peach. "Could say the same thing about people."

Laughing, he placed his peach back on top of the pile in the bin. "Damage done in the past doesn't mean you're not worth choosing...or your own choices are limited."

Gabs placed another peach in the bag and then tied the top with a green twist-tie. "I like that you understand Nina. Just so you know, I'm rooting for you. Even if you two don't work out, I think her opening up to a relationship is a step forward. She's lived in fear for so long, she's become frozen."

It was his pleasure to help thaw her out. "She seems happy with her life here."

"She was happy. I mean she still is, overall. Until stupid Erich and his stupid letter, and now the possibility that he's stupidly jumped parole to find her. Ugh," she grunted. "I'd like ten minutes alone with the creep."

Gabs was tall and athletic and possessed an assertive nature. Colin could imagine the damage she could do in a short period of time. "Nina's lucky to have so many good friends. Although, she could use a big dog at her house for extra security. Her little rat isn't much of a deterrent."

"You mean Ariel?" Gabs laughed. "She's more likely to sink her teeth into your jewelry than your flesh. Starting tonight, I'm staying at her house. I can't be there during the day because of work, but at least she won't be alone at night." She began walking toward the banana display. "You should make arrangements to come over to her house during the day. Kill two birds with one stone—keep her safe and spend more time together. Really get the sparks flying."

"I like the idea, but I still have Bea to consider. She's my first responsibility, and I put requesting a replacement on hold. Even though she's healing well, she can't be left alone for long periods of time."

She lifted a bunch of ripe bananas and placed them inside the basket hooked on her arm. "Too bad." With a shrug of her shoulders, she strode over to the tomatoes. "So what happens if you get sick yourself and can't care for a patient?"

"Well, luckily, that hasn't happened to me yet." He pushed his shopping cart to meet her by the vegetable cooler. As he reached in for the head of cabbage he still needed, the sprayers activated, sending cool water misting over his hand and arm. He grabbed the closest cabbage, placed it in his cart, and wiped off his wet arm on the leg of his jeans. "Health Shield's policy is that if a private duty nurse feels too ill to render the necessary care, he or she calls the main office for a replacement. Same goes for if you're only mildly ill but caring for a patient with a compromised immune system."

"So get sick. You'll have a valid excuse to get another nurse for Bea, plus you'll need a place to stay while you get better." She smirked. "I'm a genius."

"How do you suppose I get sick?"

She scratched her chin. "You could fake it."

"I'm not lying." He moved his cart to the side to let an elderly gentleman pass. "Plus, Nina made it clear she doesn't want me camped out at her house."

"Yes. But if you were sick—"

"As much as I care for Nina, I take my job seriously." He leaned on the push bar of the cart and rested a foot on the metal bar underneath. "I do have a nurse's aide scheduled to come in once a day, giving me some free time."

"Then use that little free time to court Nina. I'll figure out a way to keep eyes on her during the day when you're not around. She's out at the library and school for hours almost every weekday. And she has music students at her home for lessons."

"Sounds like a plan." He pushed off with his cart and started walking away. "See you later."

"Colin."

The tone of her voice made him halt. He turned to face her.

"Don't break her heart," Gabs said. "If things don't work

out between you, don't leave her more damaged than before you came to town."

He opened his mouth to speak, but she raised her hand, causing him to swallow his reply. He'd never hurt her, and he trusted she would never hurt him...at least not on purpose. Though, his growing feelings for her put him in a dangerous spot—one he'd never stood in before. He wasn't sure he'd be able to walk away unscathed.

"Don't break her heart." After a pointed look, she moved away in the opposite direction, toward the front of the store.

A fair warning from a good friend. One he'd take seriously. Not due to the threat of likely bodily harm from a very capable police lieutenant. If he tried a relationship with Nina and it didn't work, he'd make sure they parted on good terms. He'd protect her heart. His, on the other hand, would most likely be destroyed.

CHAPTER 16

"*This is like a slumber party.*" Gabs stepped out of the bathroom, clothed in fuzzy pink pajama pants and a cotton T-shirt. "Can we do each other's makeup?"

Nina covered her face with her hands. "Aren't we a little old for that."

"You're never too old for blue eyeshadow and overdone blush. From what you said, you didn't have slumber parties growing up. Thought you'd like to see what you were missing."

"Maybe some other night." Nina let loose a deep yawn and stretched her arms over her head.

"Then let's go downstairs and watch a movie. Not one of those sappy ones. Do you have *Die Hard*?"

"Gabs, we both need to get to bed. You have an eight a.m. shift tomorrow, and I have music class at the library at nine." She moved around Gabs to switch off the bathroom light.

"Oh, come on." Gabs nudged her in the ribs. "You're teaching music to toddlers. How much sleep do you need?" She grinned. "Just kidding. I'll be a good girl and go to bed."

Nina was halfway down the hall to her room when Gabs

called out. "Hey, I forgot to tell you, I saw tall, Irish, and handsome at Tuck's Market today."

"Who?" She could tease too. Only one man in Polaris fit that description.

"Oh, come on." Gabs strode toward her. "Don't play coy with me."

"Okay, fine." She held up her hands in surrender. "I suppose you want to recount your entire conversation."

"You bet I do." Gabs nodded and followed Nina into her bedroom.

Nina flicked on the light and did a quick check to make sure no one was lurking in the shadowed corners of her room. Would she feel the compulsion to check her surroundings for the rest of her life? Always expecting to see Erich jump out from the darkness?

Nina sat on her bed cross-legged, and so did Gabs. "Okay. Tell me all about it."

"I was in the produce section, trying to find a few good peaches, when Colin stopped to say hi. Don't you think a man pushing a shopping cart is super sexy?"

"I guess." Nina laughed. "Men doing anything domestic is sexy."

Gabs's smile faded, and her gaze dropped to her lap.

"Hey." Nina jiggled Gabs's knee. "What's the matter? Is it Troy?"

She nodded and sighed. "Ever since he closed his store, he's turned into a different person. He's home almost all day, but refuses to help me out with anything. And then he brings up my career and how he thinks I'm wasting my time and I should find a safer line of work."

Nina bit her bottom lip. Knowing her friend, she knew that comment flew like a lead balloon. "Your job. Your choice." Her feelings for Gabs's boyfriend had always been lukewarm. In her eyes, he came off as one of those macho guys who needed to constantly prove just how macho he was. Add losing your business and being unemployed, and his attitude had turned from bad to worse.

"I need a break." She sniffled and wiped a tear from her eyes.

She scooted over and wrapped Gabs in a warm hug. "I'm sorry. He's an idiot if he lets you go."

Gabs snorted. "That may be true, but he's my idiot."

"I'll always have your back." She gave her friend one more squeeze before moving back.

"Enough about Troy." Her smile returned, though not as wide as before. "Back to my peaches."

"You mean Colin?"

"Yeah, and Colin. But I did get some really good peaches. I'm thinking about making a pie."

"Pie's good." She smacked her leg. "What did Colin say?"

"Oh, nothing much." Gabs shrugged. "He told me I was being too picky about the peaches, and I warned him not to break your heart."

She folded her arms across her body. "You shouldn't have said that." What must he think? That she'd gone straight to her friend with all the nitty-gritty details of their hot air balloon ride? Besides, given her reluctance to start a relationship, she might be the one who'd end up hurting him.

"Don't worry. I was nice about it. He needed to know that if you open your heart again, after everything you've been through, he should treat you with care."

"I appreciate your protectiveness, but he's been perfect in the caring department. Colin asked me to give him a chance." As strongly as she wanted to jump into the deep end with him, she couldn't totally remove the vines of apprehension twisting around her body, holding her back.

"What did you tell him?"

"That I wanted to wait and see." She blew out a breath. "I won't be able to think straight until I'm certain Erich is in Boston. Right now, I'm unnerved, and unnerved people don't always make the best decisions."

"True." Gabs tossed a small bolster pillow at Nina. "You want my advice?"

Nina lay on her side, snuggled the pillow to her body, and propped her head up on her hand. "You'll tell me regardless."

"You know me so well." Gabs stretched out her long legs and crossed her ankles. "You told me a while ago that you don't date because you're not interested. I think Colin checks all your boxes. He's funny, smart, good-looking, and kind. Take a chance, Nina. There aren't many men out there like him."

She blew out a breath. "You make it sound so easy."

"Love isn't easy. It's hard and can be painful, but when you get it right, it's so worth it."

"Are you sure, given everything you're going through with Troy?"

"Most definitely." Gabs yawned. She stood and walked to the door. "Good night." Pointing to the gun on the bedside table, she raised her eyebrows. "Remember I'm sleeping right down the hall, so if you hear a bump in the night, don't grab your gun and shoot."

Nina's gaze flickered over to her black Sig Sauer. "Promise. Good night."

After Gabs closed the door, she hopped into bed and read a chapter of the book she'd started. As much as she'd resisted having someone stay with her, she eased into a wonderful relaxation knowing Gabs was right down the hall. Soon, her eyes grew heavy, and she turned off the table lamp by her bed. Within seconds, she was asleep.

A crash from outside startled her out of a very good dream. Through bleary eyes, she saw the time glowing on the clock—2:00. She lay still and listened. Only silence. Maybe she dreamt the noise. But she really should get out of bed and make sure.

The screeching sound of a car alarm made her jump. With trembling hands, she put on a sweatshirt, grabbed her gun, and opened the door.

Down the hall stood Gabs, her gun firmly grasped in her hand. She jerked her head to the stairs and then started descending.

Nina was right behind her, keeping the barrel of her gun pointed down. She'd trained for hours at the shooting range, becoming comfortable with a gun and learning how to safely handle a weapon. But she'd never carried a gun when she was so scared. The intense pounding of her heart might crack a few ribs.

"Stay back." Gabs grabbed the handle of the door to her attached garage and turned. With gun raised, she slowly pushed the door with her foot. Once the door was fully opened, she reached around and flicked on the light switch.

In the middle of her garage, her car blinked and honked in wild harmony. But thankfully, she didn't see any signs of forced entry, either to her car or the garage. She took her key fob off the hook in the kitchen and hit the button to stop the alarm.

"Thank you," Gabs said. "Your car ever go off like that before?"

"By itself?" She shook her head. "No. It's a first."

Gabs strode around the vehicle, studying it. She checked the door on the garage that led outside. "Still locked."

"Guess an animal got in." She shivered in the cold air. Outside, the temperature was predicted to drop into the thirties. Felt about the same inside her garage.

"Maybe a large animal, but where is it now?" Gabs tilted her head and looked up at the rafters.

"I don't know, but I'm freezing. Let's get back in the house." Once inside, she turned off the garage's interior light and locked the door, then double-checked to make sure she really locked the door.

She went around the house, turning on lights and checking each room. Once she found it clear of disturbance, she reluctantly turned off the light. By the time she met Gabs upstairs, she'd grown more uneasy by the second.

"I walked around outside and didn't see anything out of the ordinary." Gabs cupped her hands to her mouth and blew. "It's frickin' cold out there...and windy. A garbage can might have been blown over and made the crashing sound."

"Probably." She hated feeling paranoid, but her gut told her the sound was from a source more sinister than garbage cans and raccoons. "I guess we can go back to bed."

"Don't worry." Gabs pointed at her. "Get back into bed and dream about Colin. It will be morning before you know it."

"Will do, Lieutenant." With a forced smile, Nina slipped back into her room. She placed her gun on the nightstand and said a prayer Gabs was right. She had nothing to fear.

Fear found her anyway. In her dreams, she was trapped in the cabin—Erich talking like they were lovers on a holiday, not a deranged man who kidnapped the woman he was obsessed with.

She saw Erich's desperation and need to control. Over

their days together, he disintegrated from pretend adoration to honest craziness. And when the cops kicked down the cabin door, taking both of them by surprise, she cried tears of relief.

Nightmares haunted her until the light of early dawn filtered through her bedroom curtains. And when she got out of bed, she couldn't clear the memory of Erich's vengeful rantings echoing inside her head.

CHAPTER 17

*C*olin woke up with a splitting headache, body aches, and sinuses as congested as the Chicago Loop at rush hour. Blame his illness on the power of suggestion. Now, he was stuck with the decision to call in a nurse's aide and hope he felt better by the end of the day, or notify Health Shield so they could find another private duty nurse to replace him short-term.

In all the years he'd worked for Health Shield, he'd never gotten so sick he needed someone to fill in. Maybe fate had intervened and handed him the perfect excuse to stay at Nina's place. Surely, she wouldn't deny him a spot on her sofa and some pampering.

He eased out of bed, setting his feet on the floor. A low groan sounded in his throat as the blood rushed to his head. When he walked to the dresser to get his cell, his joints cried out in misery. He fell back into bed and made a call to the company he'd contracted for the nurse's aide service for Bea. Then he called James.

"Colin," James answered after several rings. "How are things going in Utah?"

He coughed. "Great until I came down with the world's worst cold."

"You sound terrible, man. Are you taking the day off?"

Lying back in bed, he closed his eyes. "Yeah. Have someone coming in to cover for me today but this feels like more than a twenty-four-hour deal. I might need a temporary replacement until I can shake this thing."

"Sure. I have several people available. How about you call me around noon and give me an update? If you're still feeling bad, I'll send someone down."

"Thanks." Colin coughed again, causing his chest to burn. "Don't want to get my patient sick."

"You have somewhere to stay?" The hum of a car engine sounded over the phone. "Sorry about the background noise. I'm heading into the office."

"I met a great girl, and I'm hoping she'll let me crash over by her."

"With you, there's always a girl." James laughed. "How many broken hearts have you left scattered all over the world?"

"None." No way for Colin to know for sure, but he'd tried his best to avoid hurting anyone. "Nina's different. She's special."

A moment of silence punctuated Colin's statement. "Oh, well, that's great. Should I start shopping for my new Corvette?"

Colin laughed, which initiated a coughing fit. "No, not yet. We're still working things out. She might not want a bum like me."

"Highly doubtful. But, hey, let me know what your plans are after your contract is up in Polaris. You have six weeks before you're needed in Hawaii, and I have a new job available in Japan for the time in between. You'd be a perfect fit, and I know you've always wanted to go over there."

"Let me think about it." He'd planned on staying in Polaris through the holidays, but a trip to Japan was tempting. Though now, even a dream destination dimmed when compared to being with Nina.

"Sounds good. Now go over to your girlfriend's house and crash for a few hours. Don't forget to call with a status update."

"Sure thing, boss."

He chuckled. "Go rest. That's an order."

Once he ended the call with James, he forced himself to dress and take the long walk downstairs.

Bea was already awake and started a pot of coffee. She turned, and her face instantly grew serious. "You look like a corpse brought back to life." She tsked. "Get back in bed."

"I don't want to share this black death hanging over me." He stood in the doorway, keeping a good distance from his patient. "I have a nurse's aide coming in fifteen minutes. She'll stay with you for the day, help you with your exercises, and check your insulin levels. I texted Nina to see if I could go over to her house and sleep this thing off."

"Staying at Nina's is a good idea. Not that I don't want you around." She gave him a motherly smile. "But you need some caring for, and that girl is the kindest person I know. Next to you, of course."

"I hate to impose."

Bea released one hand from her walker and waved a finger. "Trust me, you won't be imposing. I'll be glad she has someone over there, you know, just in case. Even if you're sicker than a kid the day after Halloween."

He laughed, resulting in another coughing fit.

Bea went to pour him a glass of water, but he waved it away.

"I'll be upstairs until I hear from Nina." He covered his mouth with the crook of his arm. "Wait for the nurse's aide before you start breakfast."

"Oh, all right." She sighed and lowered into a kitchen chair. "Can't wait till the day I rule my kitchen again."

"Soon," he said over his shoulder as he made for the stairs. "A few more weeks, and you should feel as spry as a teenager."

"Ha. Then you better watch out."

Her laughter followed him up the stairs. When he got back to his room, he checked his phone. There was a text from Nina saying he should come on over.

Thanks. Have to wait for Bea's nurse to arrive. I'll try to keep my germs to myself, he typed back.

What fun would that be? :) came her quick reply.

At the thought of her lips tangled with his, his body warmed. Instead of the flush of infection, a sweltering heat caused sweat to roll off his forehead.

Colin rested in bed until a knock on the front door roused him from a light slumber. Before heading down, he grabbed his coat and shoes.

Bea beat him to the front door. "Good morning, sunshine. Thanks for helping poor Colin out."

The nurse's aide stepped inside. "Morning, Mrs. Maxwell. How's my favorite gin rummy partner doing today?"

He guessed the nurse's aide was somewhere between forty and fifty years old, with dark hair and dark eyes. Hillary had worked with Bea several times during Colin's stay. She and Bea acted like long-lost friends. He could rest easy and hopefully kick his cold, knowing Bea was in good hands.

"Got my cards out, just in case we want to play a few hands after breakfast."

As the two women walked to the kitchen, Colin made his exit. The weather grew colder by the day. Light snowflakes rode the brisk wind. No doubt they would change over to fat, moisture-rich flakes soon. The mountaintops were already covered in white. He could almost feel the pulse of excitement around Polaris for the start of ski and snowboard season.

His throat burned as a series of coughs racked his body. He climbed up to Nina's front porch and knocked. The front door opened, and Gabs stood on the other side of the screen door, a huge smile on her face.

"Come on in, Colin. I heard you're not feeling well." She winked and held the door open. "Funny how these fall colds come on so suddenly."

"I am sick," he whispered with a raspy voice. "I'm not faking."

"Yeah, right." Gabs took his coat, snickering.

He shook his head, too weak to argue. Someday, he'd pay her back for the teasing. Someday, when he wasn't feeling like his head was the size of Nina's cello.

"I'm leaving for the station. See you later," she called back to Nina, who was still hidden somewhere else in the house.

"Bye, and thanks for staying over last night." Nina's voice sounded from the direction of the kitchen.

When she entered the foyer, his mood improved. She was like a rainbow after a storm. Colorful and bursting with hope.

"You can use the guest room upstairs at the end of the

hall, or stay down here and doze on the sofa." Nina gave him a quick hug and peck on the cheek. "Sorry you're sick. I have music class this morning at the library, but I'll be home for lunch. Should I pick up some soup from Dutch's Sandwich Shop? He makes the best chicken noodle."

He slipped off his shoes and wandered to the sofa. "Soup sounds wonderful. Maybe I'll have my appetite back by lunch." Lying back, he groaned. "Or I could be dead."

"You won't die from a cold." She spread a thick green blanket over his body. "Rest now. Eat later. I'll leave out some cold medicine in the kitchen. I use the tablets that dissolve in water. The effervescence always helps clear my head."

"Thank you, Nina." His body and brain were relaxing, and his eyelids closed. In the distance, he heard Nina's activity around the house. Then the sound of the door closing told him she'd left for her class.

He swallowed, causing his throat to burn. Letting his body relax, he slipped into sleep. A little while later, the faint noise of nails tapping over wood roused him. Wonder what Nina's rat was up to? *Hopefully not trying to steal my shoes.* He lifted his lids a fraction and saw Ariel sitting on the area rug in the middle of the floor, looking up at him. "Hello to you too."

A few seconds into their staring contest, she scampered away.

Though every part of his poor body hurt, he stood and shuffled to the kitchen. The medicine Nina left might help him feel better. He took out one of the packets and read the directions. Place two tablets in a small glass of water and let dissolve. Then drink. Easy enough.

While he waited for the tablets to dissolve, he used the bathroom. He came back into the kitchen and saw his glass of water was now orange. As he slammed down the liquid, little bubbles tickled his sinuses.

The floor creaked behind him, and his heart leapt. Probably just the rat scurrying about. Who knew a person could get so attached to a thieving ferret?

As Colin rinsed out the glass and placed it in the dishwasher, he wondered if his contacts in Boston had found out any new information on Erich. The guys were sometimes hard to get a hold of, but he trusted them for this job. Back in the day, they'd run with Whitey Bulger's boys. If the need arose, they were the kind of people who'd take care of business.

While slowly making his way back to the sofa, he couldn't wait to lie down again and fall back to sleep. His head throbbed with sinus pain, and he gripped the back of a chair for balance. With his gaze focused on the floor, Colin shuffled to the sofa before collapsing, but the sound of deep laughter jerked his body into high alert. He propped himself up on his elbows and noticed he wasn't alone.

"No need to rise on my account." The man he'd run into on the street days ago now sat in the wingback chair in the corner of the living room. "I'd like to say I'm sorry to see you ill, but your poor health plays nicely in my favor."

Erich Everett. His instincts had been right. Colin bolted upright, and his headache threatened to split open the front of his head. He patted around on the sofa for his cell. No luck. Had he left it in his coat pocket?

"Don't bother." Erich raised the gun and took aim at Colin's chest. "Though I'd rather not use it, at least in the house. Messy business, you know."

He did know, having witnessed a drive-by shooting when he was sixteen. So much blood pouring out of tiny wounds. If he felt sick before, he was close to vomiting now. "You'll be caught and sent back to jail."

Erich shrugged. "The idiots back in Boston will figure out I've violated parole in a few hours when I don't show up for my appointment. Do you know how demeaning it is to have to report twice a week after spending ten years in confinement?"

"Nothing less than you deserve. Why are you here?" he asked, even though he knew the answer. Anger fired on all cylinders.

"The same reason you are, I suppose." He gave a short laugh. "Nina has that effect on men, wouldn't you say? She bewitches you until all you can think about is her. Then, when she tires of you, she expels you from her life." Erich stood, a scowl on his face. "I gave her everything, but it wasn't good enough. I spent years in hell because of Nina Montgomery. Or is it Pettit now?"

"Leave her alone." A hacking cough had him doubled over.

"The Irish Fist isn't so tough now." Erich waved the gun at Colin. "You're in no position to make demands."

He moved toward Erich until the gun was inches from his chest. "You don't scare me."

"No?" Erich shook his head. "That's a shame. You care about Nina. Too much for your own good. Let's go."

Colin weighed his options in his very fuzzy mind. If he refused to go with Erich, he'd no doubt be killed. Which meant Nina would find herself alone with her kidnapper. Going with Erich would buy him time to come up with a plan.

He walked to the front door and put on his boots. Dread produced nausea.

"You made a mistake by falling in love with her and

thinking she loves you. Nina uses and discards men." Erich motioned with the gun towards the back of the house.

"Then why are you using me to get to her? If you don't think she cares for me, she won't come." Minus his coat, Colin opened the back door.

Erich's face burned red. "Because even if she doesn't come, I'll make sure you never touch her again with your filthy hands." He shoved Colin in the back, causing him to stumble. "You're not good enough for her. I don't know why Nina's attracted to men who are so unworthy. Base lust, I suppose."

As he walked outside, the cold air pricked the exposed skin on his face and hands, like he was stuck with hundreds of tiny pins. The overheating he'd experienced inside the house washed away, leaving a bone-deep chill.

"My car is parked on the street behind her house. Cut through the neighbor's backyard and make sure not to draw attention to yourself." Erich held the gun inside his unzipped coat.

Every step rattled his joints. Colin needed his strength. But the virus had ravaged his body, leaving him weak. Would Nina come home and wonder why he was gone? How long would it take for the Boston PD to contact Luke with the news Erich had fled?

He took comfort in the fact that Nina had both Luke and Gabrielle to protect her. Surely she'd go to them if she suspected Erich had paid a visit to her house. Even better, Luke would intercept Nina before she returned home.

As Colin climbed into a nondescript late-model car, he glanced at the rear of Nina's purple house, and his heart ached, knowing this might be the last time he'd see anything connected with her.

CHAPTER 18

*a*s Nina pulled up her playlist for her class, Move to the Beat for Preschoolers, one of the librarians who worked the front desk entered the room.

"Looks like you have an admirer, Ms. Pettit." The gray-haired woman carried a large bouquet of flowers. So large, the blooms covered her face. "Where would you like me to set them?"

"Oh." How had Colin managed to order her flowers when he was so sick? At least, she assumed they were from Colin. He was currently her one and only admirer. She glanced around the room, not finding a safe spot from the ten or so preschoolers who'd be moving and grooving in a few minutes. "I'll take them. Thanks." Nina held out her hands and received the glass vase.

The room next door was empty, making it the best and safest place to store the gift until she left for home. She entered the smaller meeting room and flipped on the light, then set the vase down on an empty table.

Lifting a white envelope from its plastic holder, she saw her name written in cursive on the front. Her stomach danced with nervous flutters as she pulled out the card. A red heart dotted the upper right corner. Underneath read:

Nina, you mean everything to me. I can't imagine a life without you. I'll wait patiently until you come to me.

She saw no name written below the message. The flowers must be from Colin—his way of reaching out and stating his intentions without pressuring her. She reread the line *I can't imagine a life without you.* Hadn't he said something similar after their romantic balloon ride? When she sniffed the blooms, the sweet fragrance of roses filled her nose. He'd sent roses in a variety of soft pastel colors. Without counting, she guessed there were about two dozen in the arrangement.

Voices sounded from the room next door. With one last glance at Colin's gift, she turned off the light and went to meet her preschoolers and their parents. Time to move to the beat.

After forty-five minutes of leading a group of super-energetic three- and four-year-olds, she had a backache like she'd just finished an eight-hour construction shift. She loaded her boxes of instruments into the trunk of her car, then went back for her flowers.

How would she get them home without either tipping over the vase or crushing the flowers? She placed them riding shotgun in the passenger seat. Luckily, she found a blanket in the trunk and wrapped it around the vase. Then she strapped the lap belt over the mass, holding it secure.

Just don't take any sharp turns or hard brakes. She normally drove like a grandma, so a little extra caution shouldn't be a problem.

Her nervous excitement kicked into overdrive as she pulled into her driveway. Would Colin be awake or asleep? She kind of hoped he was asleep so she could enjoy watching him for a little while. Earlier, while she'd been getting ready to leave, she'd walked past the room and saw him dozing, sprawled out on her sofa. He'd looked so unguarded and peaceful. Nina imagined him as a little boy, and then pictured the children he might father someday.

But could she imagine building a family with Colin? A man who claimed he wanted her in his life, but resisted settling down? Despite the warnings from her head, her heart decided it wanted him. She'd take a chance for the possibility of a great reward. Maybe, a few years from now, she'd tuck into bed a little boy with black hair and blue eyes.

Once at home, Nina set the vase on her kitchen table. No floor creaks from footsteps or Colin's deep voice greeted her. When she entered her living room, she was surprised to see the sofa empty. The green blanket she'd placed over Colin lay in a pile on the floor.

Must have decided he'd be more comfortable sleeping up in the guest room. She tiptoed up the stairs and down the hall. The door to the bedroom was open, so she peeked inside, expecting to see Colin's large form on the bed.

The room was dark, and her eyes took several seconds to adjust. An empty bed sat undisturbed, its floral comforter pulled up and the pillow shams still neatly in place.

Her stomach fluttered with a different set of nerves. Ones produced by an alarming realization that Colin wasn't here. Had he gone back over to Bea's? He wouldn't have if he was still sick.

She glanced out the window and noticed his Jeep still parked in Bea's driveway. So he hadn't gone too far. Where was he?

This morning, he'd been very sick. So much so, he'd struggled to walk across the street. In the few hours she'd been gone, she doubted he'd had a miraculous recovery.

Uneasiness pooled in her gut. The image of Seth's body tied to a tree flashed in her mind. Without hesitation, she ran to her room and grabbed the gun box from the drawer of her bedside table. Maybe she was overreacting, but she couldn't shake the dread crawling up her spine. She took out the key from inside her dresser drawer, unlocked the gun box, and removed the weapon. In her closet, she found her shoulder holster and put it on. She checked the ammunition magazine, making sure it was filled, then snapped it into the gun. With unsteady hands, she slid the gun into the holster, then covered up the bulk with a thick, zip-front sweatshirt.

She didn't have to see Erich to feel his presence, which hung inside her house like a poisonous fog, making her gag.

Before she called Luke, she went back downstairs. Colin's boots were missing from the mat by the front door. She checked the closet, and her fear was confirmed. His coat still hung inside. On her way through the entryway, she grabbed the little decorative knife displayed on the table. It was small but sharp, and she might need a second line of defense.

Her panic spiked. History wouldn't repeat. She would not let Erich harm another man because of his connection to her. Nina took her cell out of her purse and saw she had a missed call from Colin. Okay. This was good. Had he gone out for a walk to get some fresh air? *Maybe I overreacted.*

Her finger hovered over the cell phone screen. After a second's hesitation, she hit Dial. While she listened to ring after ring, the rush of her heartbeat pulsed in her ears. Finally, the ringing stopped, and she heard an exhaled breath.

"Colin?" *Please be on the other end of this call.*

"He's a little tied up at the moment." Deep laughter sounded. "Nina, my love. It's been too long."

She pushed down the bile rising in her throat. "Go to hell, Erich." His laughter grinded her already worn-down nerves.

"All in good time. I have a few things left to do here on earth before I say goodbye."

No doubt those few things were unfinished business with her. "What do you want?"

"I've always only wanted you. Imagine if we would have found a way to work out the disagreements between us back in Boston. Instead, one man is dead and another's life hangs on a delicate chain."

Her fear spun into fury. "Seth's death was not a result of my kicking you out of my life. He died because you are an evil monster." She took a deep breath. "And you're proving that all over again by taking Colin, a man who has nothing to do with you and me."

"He desires you, and now we'll see how much you desire him. Will you come to me in order to save him? Or can I do with him what I did to Seth?"

She growled—an animallike noise originating deep in her soul. "You hurt Colin, and I will make you pay. Jail will seem like a vacation compared to what I'll do."

"Calm, Nina. He's a little woozy but all right...for now."

Her vision blurred, framed with red. "Let him go, and then I'll come to you."

Erich chuckled. "When you're with me, I'll let him go. That's the way this work. I need a guarantee you'll follow through."

"Fine." She patted the gun strapped to her side and grabbed her car keys. "Where do I go?"

"So eager. Good."

Nina wished he were standing before her so she could slap his smug face. Over a decade ago, she'd been a young woman, fresh out of college, easily taken in by an older, sophisticated man. She'd been weak and eager to please. Even after she'd broken off their relationship and he'd begun stalking her, she'd been afraid to confront him.

No longer. Her fear had given her strength. She'd learned self-defense, both hand-to-hand and with a firearm. Erich was dangerous, no doubt, but she would not cower.

Through the speakers of her cell, she heard a muffled shout. Colin? She was wasting time playing games. "Erich, where are you?"

"First rule...you stay on the line with me until I see you. No calling your hick town police friends. Wouldn't want anyone else to get hurt." He cleared his throat. "Drive to the Stille Nacht scenic pull-off on Highway Eighty. I'll be waiting in a blue sedan. Park your car. You'll ride with me to our destination."

While he talked, she scribbled down "Met Erich at Stille Nacht. He has Colin" on the back of a piece of junk mail. She left it sitting in the center of her kitchen table. Pointing the police in the direction of the scenic pull-off would at least help jump-start their search.

"I'm in the garage now and getting into my car." She slammed her car door shut, pushed the garage door remote, and turned the key. The grip of her gun dug into her side, a wonderful feeling of reassurance that she wasn't going into this defenseless. Thank goodness she'd grabbed the gun when she did.

As she pulled out of her driveway, she glanced at Bea's house. The nurse's aide's car was still there. Good. She wouldn't want Bea to be left alone in Colin's absence, which hopefully wouldn't be too much longer. Once she arrived, he'd let Colin go. Nina was the prize. Colin was only a tool. He held no significance to Erich.

"I'm on my way."

"Which makes me so happy. I've waited so long to have you again."

And she'd lived in dread for those same years. A recurring nightmare that had finally come to claim her waking hours.

Her drive to the overlook seemed to take forever. She continued the call with Erich the entire way, giving him a play-by-play of every turn. Part of her was strangely relieved at the upcoming confrontation. Instead of shrinking in fear, she'd take action.

She didn't regret her decision to go straight to Erich without calling for help. Not with Colin's life at stake. She could handle Erich on her own. She had no other choice.

When she pulled off into the overlook's parking lot, her stomach heaved at the sight of Erich standing next to his car. She parked and exited, the entire time refusing to break eye contact.

The last time she'd seen him, he was being escorted out of the courtroom after his sentencing hearing. His face had been screwed up in rage. Now, he appeared calm, though the years in prison had aged him considerably. Erich was still handsome, but his face was lined and his eyes sunken. His nice clothing did little to draw her attention from the fact his frame was thinner. He'd dyed his hair dark brown and grown a beard that must have been dyed as well. His incarceration had not been kind. So why would he do anything to jeopardize his freedom?

Nina knew the answer—he was a psychopath. She had to remember what type of person she was dealing with. "I'm here. Now take me to Colin."

Grinning, Erich opened the passenger door. "Always in such a hurry. I remember that about you."

"You don't know anything about me. Not anymore." With nerves buzzing, she climbed inside his car.

"Don't worry. We'll have plenty of time to get reacquainted."

As he pushed the door closed, she took long, deep breaths.

I can do this.

Erich got seated and turned to face her. "I've missed you, sweetheart. I've missed your music. We'll get it right this time between us. I promise."

She bit the inside of her mouth in an attempt to halt the angry words filling her throat. Engaging him would be pointless. Soon, her actions would effectively deliver what she wanted to say.

~ ˎ ~

Colin pulled against the nylon cord tying his hands together behind the back of the chair. The cord dug into his already tender flesh, causing him to grimace. Despite the fact he'd been working to loosen the knot since Erich had left the cabin, his bonds held firm. *Damn.* He wanted to be free before the monster returned with Nina.

If not for his cold, he'd have more fight. The medicine he'd taken earlier had helped clear his head and dull the pain in his joints, but he still felt sluggish. Frustrating, because at this moment, more than any other in his life, he needed the strength to take down Erich before he could touch Nina.

He wanted her to stay home and call Luke, not follow Erich's instructions and come to this cabin in the middle of who knows where. His heart hitched. Would she put herself at risk to protect him? Colin would rather die than see her walk through the cabin's door.

From his short time with Erich, he'd profiled him as extremely smart, arrogant, and obsessive. And he no longer cared about the consequences of his actions, making him extremely dangerous.

Colin sat bound to a kitchen chair, placed in a corner of the cabin's small living room. He stared out the window, wondering just how deep in the mountain's backcountry he was. The landscape was covered with a thick grove of snow-covered trees.

He'd think the setting pretty—remote cabin in the woods with a large fireplace in the living room. All the privacy one would need for a romantic getaway—or a vile abduction. A small kitchen was tucked off toward the rear. If he strained his neck, he could glance down the short hall-way. He assumed the two doors belonged to a bedroom and bathroom.

The interior decor looked original. No TV or phone that he could see. Likely this place was a hunting lodge, and, judging from the musty smell, one that hadn't been used in a long time.

Most of the high-end rental cabins hugged the outskirts of Polaris. The wealthy visitors wanted to be close to the restaurants, shops, and skiing in town. He'd looked into booking one for a few weeks after his job with Bea ended.

As he listened to the antique clock on the wall slowly ticking away the seconds, he thought he'd go mad. Trying to distract himself, Colin studied the clock made out of a circular cut of a tree trunk, glossed with lacquer to bring out the many rings marking the tree's years.

Ninety minutes passed before he heard the sound of a

car approach. They were about a forty-five-minute drive outside Polaris. Not too far, but far enough to leave a large search area.

Desperation made him rock in the chair, hoping to break enough of the wooden spokes to free the cord looping around his lap, legs, and feet. Nothing.

The front door of the cabin flew open. Nina, along with a cold blast of wind, rushed inside. "Colin," she cried out. "I'm so sorry." Kneeling beside him, she sobbed while working on untying the cord holding him down.

"Why did you come?" He lowered his head to kiss the top of her head.

"Leave him." Erich entered the cabin. His body cast an ominous shadow. He slid his gun into a holster resting on his hip. "What happens to him is for me to decide."

Nina stood and stared at Erich. "You said you'd let Colin go. I'm here and expect you to honor your word."

The tall man shrugged off his wool overcoat. "Give me your sweatshirt. I'll hang it in the closet."

"No. I'll keep it on." She wrapped her arms around her body. "It's cold in here."

"I'll start a fire." Erich strolled to the river rock faced fireplace. "Not only will it keep you warm, it will set the mood." He smiled, and his gaze flickered over her body. "I must say, Nina, age has only made you more beautiful."

"Keep away from her," Colin growled, then began coughing. He ignored the aches in his joints as he strained to get free.

Laughing, Erich approached Nina and stroked her cheek. "You've never heard her play, correct? She's the most talented cellist I've ever heard, and all I've ever wanted was for Nina Montgomery to get the fame she deserves. It's not too late, my love."

She rounded on him. "This isn't love. You poisoned my music."

Colin's cough became overwhelming. Why had she come instead of going for help? She'd walked into an animal's trap.

"Then let Colin go." Nina stepped closer to Erich.

"Really? You're okay with sending your lover on a death march through the wilderness in freezing temperatures?" Erich asked. "Ironic that history will repeat itself."

Without warning, Nina lifted her arm and slapped Erich across the cheek with a loud crack. "You sick animal."

CHAPTER 19

*N*ina raised her hand for another go at Erich, but he intercepted her arm, holding it in a bone-crushing grip. She struggled, and he squeezed harder. "You're hurting me."

Laughing, Erich dropped her arm. He rubbed at the red spot on his cheek. "Don't push me." He glanced at Colin. "Or would hurting him be a larger deterrent? Let's try."

"No." She stopped him with the touch of her body to his, despite the sickness his nearness caused. Should she pull out the gun and shot him now? With his attention so focused on Nina's every move, she doubted she'd success-fully get off a shot before he grabbed her. "It's freezing in here. Will you make me a fire?" Nina tipped her head to meet his gaze. His dark eyes appeared as cold, hard, and shiny as obsidian.

She ignored Colin's low pleading to stop. *Please under-stand I'm doing this for you.* Did he understand how much he meant to her? Unfortunately not, since the stubborn guard around her heart had stopped her from accepting what he'd offered. Perhaps the realization now came too late. If—no, when—they both survived this, she'd tell him how deeply she desired to keep him a part of her life. She adored Colin Moynahan—loved him—and refused to be denied a true and pure romance by the actions of an evil man.

Erich touched her arm and moved close. His breathing grew shallow and quick. "I've spent years dreaming about this moment...when can I touch you, feel you, smell you, and hear your voice."

With care, she eased back. She didn't want him feeling the gun strapped to her body. "I don't know if I can still play the cello. Not like I used to."

"Give yourself time." Erich knelt in front of the firebox. While keeping part of his attention set on Nina, he placed some paper and kindling down on the rack, then several large logs on top. With a flick of the fire starter, he ignited the paper and kindling. Soon, a warm glow bathed the room. "Come here and warm yourself." He waved her over.

She avoided Colin's gaze as she lowered herself to the area rug by the fireplace. If she looked at him, tied up and helpless, she'd break. Then both of them would be at Erich's mercy. Heat radiated from the fire. Nina stared at the dancing flames. "Thank you." She had a gun but absolute terror kept her hand from reaching into her sweatshirt and making the move. *Help him relax and lower his guard.* Only then would she be able to catch him off guard and fire a shot that would hit its mark.

She'd been hopelessly attracted to Erich during their first months of dating. When she looked at him now, repulsion filled her. The person he was inside distorted his outward appearance. He was no more attractive than a monster in a horror movie.

"I'll spend the rest of my life ensuring your comfort." Erich rubbed a strand of her hair between his fingers.

"You'll spend the rest of your life in jail," Colin shouted.

"Looks like our guest requires a gag." Erich stood and reached for a long piece of flannel that had been ripped off a blanket.

"No." She placed a stilling hand on his arm. "Ignore him. The truth is I didn't come here for Colin." Clearing her throat, she prepared herself mentally for what she'd say next. "I'm here for you. You've endured so much and still stayed faithful. We have a bond that can't be broken by disagreements or time apart."

He turned from Colin and knelt onto the floor. "I have stayed faithful." Erich cupped her face in his hands. "But you have not."

"He doesn't mean anything to me." *Colin means everything.* Her throat blazed with repressed tears. "He's not good enough. You, Erich, were the only one who really understood my worth. You treasured me like no other man."

"You are a treasure." His eyes brightened, and his pupils dilated. "I will help you play again. But this time, only for me. No one understands your talent and worth like I do."

His nearness repulsed her. If she didn't act soon, she'd become violently ill. "I'm so sorry for ever doubting you."

"I forgive you." He stroked her cheek. "But even so, there are consequences to your actions."

Despite the fire, she chilled. "Consequences?"

Erich blew out a long breath. "I lost my freedom and endured the indignity of incarceration because of your stubborn pride. There's a price for what you did. I require payment before we can move on."

She stood and walked toward the large window looking out over the front porch. With shaking hands, she unzipped her sweatshirt and opened the strap securing the gun. Securing the flaps of her sweatshirt to cover the gun, she slowly turned to face Erich. "And what payment do you think is fair?"

His easygoing smile warned her that she was running out of time. She'd seen that same feral smile the last time he'd held her captive. An expression of arrogance mixed with madness.

"A life." He flicked a glance at Colin, still bound to the chair. "His life in payment for what you took from me."

"Murder will not set things right between us." She looked at Colin, who appeared surprisingly calm given the subject of the conversation. She'd come so close to realizing a dream. Her spine stiffened. There was no way she'd allow that to be taken away.

"Think of it as a test. How else can I know for certain your loyalty is with me and only me?" He stepped towards her.

Reaching underneath the open flap of her sweatshirt, she grabbed her gun. In a flash, she pointed the weapon at Erich's chest. "Colin is not a brief diversion, and I will never be happy with you."

Surprised flashed in his eyes, and he quickly masked his reaction. One corner of his lips lifted in a crooked smirk. "Nina, darling, you get my hopes up only to break my heart all over again."

"You don't have a heart." She nodded her head in Colin's direction. "Untie him."

Erich shrugged and headed toward Colin. "Are you sure? This is a path you can't come back from."

"As long as the path leads far away from you, I'm positive." Her temper burned. Erich would pay for what he'd done. Poor Colin looked ready to pass out, slumped in the chair. He'd been sick before he was kidnapped. He must be feeling worse now.

Bending at the waist, Erich fumbled with untying the cord binding Colin's hands. He reached lower and paused. In an instant, he rose. Held in one hand was a long hunting knife, its blade pressed to Colin's throat.

"Don't," Nina cried out, still pointing the gun at Erich. "I'll shoot you if you hurt him."

~ ، ~

Colin recoiled at the sting of the cold metal pressed to his neck. He'd hated every minute of Nina's performance for Erich. He was willing to die in order to protect her. But in this situation, his death would only serve to keep her in danger.

Gabs likely would return to Nina's house when her shift ended—around five or six. He assumed at that point she'd alert Captain Veldkamp that Nina was missing. Luke would move the mountains around Polaris to find them once he knew she was in danger. But who knew how long that would take? By then, he might be dead and Nina taken to a different location.

"Put down the gun, Nina." Erich's cool voice sounded from behind. "Bleeding out from a slice to the jugular is not a pleasant way to go."

Colin steadied his breathing, afraid to move. The blade had pierced his skin. Warm blood rolled down his neck and pooled in the jut of his collarbone.

With trembling hands, Nina lowered the gun.

"Put the gun on the coffee table, grab a kitchen chair, and set it near the fireplace." Erich eased back the knife blade.

She followed his directions.

Colin's heart ached as he watched her once again serve

as a pawn under Erich's control. Her eyes pooled with tears. *Just run. Run, and don't look back.*

"Now, sit down like a good girl," Erich said after she set down the chair.

Seated, she shivered. "I hate you."

"Hate and love are closely related." He removed the knife from Colin's throat and stepped over to grab Nina's gun. "There were times when I hated you so much, I dreamt of strangling you with my bare hands. Then, I'd wake to the sound of your music in my head and remember how deeply I loved you."

With the threat of imminent throat-slitting removed, Colin inhaled a large gulp of air. Adrenaline flushed out some of his earlier cold symptoms. His sinuses were stuffy, but his splitting headache had faded to a dull pain between his eyes.

"No matter how this ends, I will never love you." Nina craned her head away as Erich approached.

He pinched her face between his long fingers and turned it back so she was forced to look at him. "Don't test me. I don't want to hurt you." Another length of nylon rope appeared, and he began looping it around Nina's body.

The sight stoked Colin's anger. He worked feverishly to loosen the knot tying up his hands. "Leave now, Nina. Let him do what he wants to me. Just run."

Erich ignored his raspy protest. "Pretty as a present." He secured her feet to the legs of the chair. "We'll have more time to discuss our future in a bit. First, I have to deal with him." With Nina's gun tucked inside the waistband of his pants and his own secured inside his holster, Erich approached Colin. He took the hunting knife and slit the rope in several places.

The pressure holding his wrists and ankles eased, and

Colin moved to get the blood flowing through his extremities.

"Get up." Erich motioned upward with his hand. "And behave, or I'll shoot you and Nina can watch you die."

Nina flexed against her bonds and screamed. Tears streamed down her flushed face.

Colin stepped toward her, but Erich gripped his arm and pulled him back. "Let me say goodbye." Shrugging his arm free, he continued walking. When he got to Nina, he knelt before her.

"Don't cry." His thumb gently wiped across both cheeks. "I'll see you again. I promise."

"Enough." Erich yanked Colin up by the collar of his shirt and shoved him toward the door.

The sound of Nina's sobbing followed him outside. Before the door closed behind him, Nina called his name.

"I'm so sorry." Her muffled words were barely audible. "I love you."

As the door clicked shut, her voice was silenced.

Her words hit him like a sword blade to the heart. He had no illusions Erich would let him live. His chest ached with all the what-ifs.

After binding Colin's hands again, Erich pushed him into the car. He strode around the hood and entered, settling into the driver's seat. "I'm give you the same gift I gave Nina's other lover: a chance. A small chance." He turned the ignition.

Colin checked the time—one forty-five. The car lurched forward, and so did Colin's stomach. He thought of what Nina had told him about Seth. The man had been tied to a tree and left to die of exposure. The temperature now was cold enough to be a real threat.

After a drive that seemed to last forever, Erich stopped

the car on the narrow road and removed the cord around Colin's wrists. The trees were sparser here, mostly evergreens. They'd gone up in elevation.

"Get out," Erich barked with the gun pointed at Colin.

So this was the game—leave him to wander around the backcountry until dead. A small chance indeed. Before he opened the car door, he glanced at the digital clock set into the dashboard. The time was now two thirty. Sunset was around seven p.m.

He stepped outside, closed the door, and watched the blue car disappear around a bend in the road. The cry of a bird overhead startled him out of a stress-induced haze. If he were to survive, he had to move.

The countdown started now.

CHAPTER 20

After about twenty minutes of struggling to get free, Nina stopped to regroup. She could use this time to strategize. Erich would no longer believe she wanted to be with him. Not after she'd just declared her love for Colin.

Her chest squeezed at the memory of Colin being shoved out of the cabin. He'd looked back at her with those sapphire-blue eyes, and her life condensed down to that moment. She loved him, though she'd fought the feeling, and he needed to know. She might not get another chance.

Nina would kill in order to save him. She'd come here under her own free will with the promise he'd let Colin go. Not that she trusted Erich, but at that moment, what other choice did she have?

The last time Erich had kidnapped her, she'd been taken from her apartment, gagged, blindfolded, and tossed in the backseat of a car. Where he'd kept her then was similar to now, a cabin set back in the woods. A place where he wouldn't have to worry about a neighbor walking over or a lost motorist stopping for directions.

Back then, he'd spent a long time preparing for her stay

—buying enough food and supplies to last months, installing multiple dead bolt locks on the doors to which only he held the key, nailing every window shut. The only way she could have escaped was to break a window and climb out. But even that would have been impossible. She would have been caught well before she made it past the frame. Fortunately, she'd been spared physical violation. One of the only mercies he'd shown her during the nightmare.

Now, from her spot by the fireplace, she saw the door had only a standard dead bolt lock. The windows were too far away to see if they'd been nailed shut, but instinct told her they weren't. Judging by the almost bare kitchen, he wasn't planning on staying here long.

The fire had died down to embers, causing her to shiver. Staying here was imperative to her rescue. Gabs would eventually find her note, which would lead the police to her car. Not a guarantee she'd be found, but at least the police would get a general direction of where she'd been taken.

Nina glanced down to her feet and saw the handle of her dagger sticking above her sock. With Erich in possession of her gun, her little knife was her last line of defense.

The sound of tires crunching over gravel accelerated her already rapidly beating heart. Seconds later, a car door shut, and heavy footfalls boomed on the rickety front porch. The door opened, and Erich appeared, backlit by the afternoon sun.

He slammed the door behind him. "Finally, we're alone." After locking the dead bolt, he slipped the key into the front pocket of his pants.

"What did you do to him?" Raising her chin, she met his gaze full-on. *I will not cower.*

"So predictable." Erich picked up the hunting knife,

which he'd set on a side table when escorting Colin outside. He twirled the thick handle in his hand. "They say a woman always wants what she can't have."

"Unlike men?" She snorted a laugh. "Or should I say, like you?"

He touched the tip of the blade to his index finger, drawing a dot of red blood. "The difference with me is I take what I want. I'm patient and willing to sacrifice, and in the end, I always win."

"Not this time, Erich." Not now or ever again.

When he moved behind her, she tensed every muscle in preparation. She held her breath and waited for the sting of the blade slicing into her back. Instead, she heard a brief sawing sound, and the rope loosened around her wrists. With another slice, he removed the rope around her legs and feet. Soon, the bonds holding her upper body to the chair slackened.

Erich grabbed her under the arms and pulled her to stand. "I gave your boyfriend the possibility of survival. Don't make me regret it."

Nina's legs trembled, not only from fear but the lack of blood flow while she'd been bound. "He's alive?"

"Alive when I left him." Erich studied his fingernails. "No guarantee for how long."

Relief rushed out in a long breath before panic swelled. Colin had a limited amount of time before the cold and possibly wild animals endangered his life.

Erich sighed. "What can I say to convince you that we're meant to be together?" He wrapped an arm around her waist. "You're mine, Nina, whether you accept it or not."

Her gaze flickered down to the gun tucked in the waistband of his pants. Could she get to it in time? Probably not. Especially when he seemed to read her mind.

When they'd dated, she'd come to the conclusion Erich always thought he was the smartest person in the room. Women were inferior. And he hated being corrected, especially in a public forum.

If she couldn't overpower him, she'd use psychology. "I haven't play the cello, or any instrument, in a really long time. I don't even know if I can anymore."

"Of course you can. Your music is a natural gift, and given practice, you can be even better than you were before." He guided her to a red plaid sofa.

She sat, offering him a feeling of control. Blowing into her hands, she shivered. "I'm cold. Is there more wood for the fire?"

Erich glanced at the fireplace and grinned. "Remember the evenings we spent at my apartment, sitting by the fire and talking about music for hours?"

If only she could scour the memories from her mind. "As I seem to recall, you did most of the talking."

As he stacked several large logs into the firebox, he laughed. "Guilty as charged. I had so much I wanted to teach you...about music, history, and life."

How could one person be so full of himself? His ego mixed a toxic blend with his lack of conscience. "Thank you for the fire." She leaned forward, stretching out her hands to the heat. Thinking of Colin outside in the cold with no coat, she blinked away fresh tears. Along with renewed anger, and determination to get free and save him.

"Don't want those precious fingers growing cold." He sat beside her on the sofa. "I know what you're doing...playing nice so I let down my guard. We'll leave soon."

"I won't go with you."

He tapped his fingers on the grip of her gun, and then

pulled it out of his waistband. "You will. I don't want to hurt you, so don't force me to."

Panicked, she knew leaving meant the chances of anyone finding her shrank to almost nothing. She had to stall. Had to think. *Should have taken the shot the moment you saw him.* Why had she let fear cause her to hesitate? Nina gritted her teeth. Nothing short of a time machine would change the past. *Push ahead. Plan your next move.*

Because if she didn't, her photo would be one of thousands of missing persons photographs tacked to police boards all across the country. And Colin might never make it out of the mountains alive.

~ ॰ ~

During the drive, Colin had memorized every turn, chanting the sequence over and over again in his mind. His best guess was Erich had driven between twenty-five and thirty miles per hour, so they'd likely traveled about seven or eight miles.

With a healthy body, the trip back to the cabin would take a few hours. Instead, he struggled for breath, between the racking cough and the high altitude. Would his body hold out for hours of hiking? Did he have a choice? He would make it back to Nina or die trying. Of course, he'd vote for the first option.

He made slow progress, putting one foot in front of the other. He channeled every ounce of fury, pumping adrenaline through his veins. Because when he stood at the door to the cabin, he'd kick his way inside and knock Erich to the ground.

He arrived at a fork in the gravel road, giving him the option to either turn left or curve to the right. After a moment's thought, he went right. The sound of gravel crunching under his boots was the only steady sound. Cold wind bit his hands and face. The tips of his ears had gone numb. His thin shirt was little protection. The sun provided a small hit of warmth when he wasn't in the shade. Thinking of the darkness to come, he quickened his pace. Night temperatures had been dropping to the lower thirties in town. Up here, the temperature went even lower. His skin prickled with the knowledge he would likely not survive a night outdoors with no protection.

Before his legs gave out, he stopped for a break at a clearing in the trees. Before him spread a wide expanse of mountains. A colorful valley rested at their feet. Sitting on a boulder, he searched for signs of life—a cabin, cars, smoke spiraling from a chimney. He listened for anything other than the echoes of nature. Never in all his life had he craved the rumble of a car motor more badly.

Once he'd caught his breath, he stood and continued his journey. He halted at another fork in the road and replayed the memorized directions in his head. Somewhere along the way, he'd lost count of turns. Instead of containing his frustration, he screamed into the October wind. Why not? No one was around to hear.

Deciding to turn left, he walked with shrinking confidence. This road seemed to be leading him farther up the mountain. Instead of the thick forest of juniper and spruce trees that surrounded the cabin, the vegetation around him thinned.

He came upon a path perpendicular to the road, which looked like a driveway. Another cabin? His throat burned with tears. He could be only moments away from finding help. As Colin approached the cabin, he noticed the absence of a vehicle. The front door was locked with a hinge and dead bolt. He went to the side of the cabin and glanced through a low window. The interior was dark and empty. On the wall, he saw an old-fashioned rotary phone. Did it still work? Only one way to find out.

He picked up a dinner-plate-sized rock from the yard and tossed it into the glass, shattering the window. Once the pane was cleared of glass shards, he climbed inside. Taking long strides, he reached the phone, then lifted the receiver before placing it to his ear. Silence. His heart sank. There was a very real possibility he might never see Nina again. A woman who meant more to him every day. A woman who'd declared her love—her last words to him. Ones locked away in his heart.

I will prove myself worthy.

Glancing around the dusty, dark cabin, he coughed. Now what? Stay here, build a fire, and hang out until the next morning? Meanwhile, Nina was trapped with a monster.

He found an old men's coat inside one of the closets, then climbed back out through the window. Time to move. His best bet was to search for clearings that gave him a good view of the mountainside and valley below. Maybe he'd see the city of Polaris resting in one of the surrounding valleys. Then he'd have a clear direction to navigate.

A long coughing spell made him hunch over. Queasiness overtook him. Once he caught his breath, he stood and continued his march. He wouldn't stop fighting for her until his last breath.

CHAPTER 21

"*We could have had a wonderful life together.*" Erich sat on a plaid-fabric-covered wingback chair, his legs crossed. He picked lint off his pants. "You needed me, Nina. But instead, you kicked me out of your life."

"I didn't need you." Nina's mind was far from Erich's nonsense, but she needed to keep him talking in order to stall while she came up with a plan to escape.

He snorted out a laugh. "You left music."

"I left music because of you." She inhaled. *Control your temper. Play along.* "Why me, Erich? You were...still are...an attractive man. You had money and power. Why waste your time and resources on a woman who didn't want you?"

Standing, Erich strode to the window. He moved back the curtain to glance outside. "I wanted to help you become the best cellist in the world. When I heard you and saw your beauty, I knew you were the one I was destined to spend the rest of my life with."

"What I wanted didn't matter to you."

He turned to face her. "Of course you matter to me. Why do you think I'm here?"

Instead of jumping up and smacking the faux sorrowful expression off his face, she folded her hands. Channeling her anger, she dug her fingernails into her flesh. "Kidnapping me and hurting someone I care about is not showing love."

"Love," he spat. "Women use it to manipulate men, just like you did earlier with the trash I deposited on the side of the road. You tease us, Nina, with your coy words and actions. You led me to think you wanted only me."

Nina's head throbbed with tension. Trying to make him see reason was useless. His mind was twisted and self-centered. All she was to him was a doll to use for his own needs. And if she refused, he'd dispose of her.

The air inside the cabin was warm from the fire, scented with the aromas of smoke and wood. The flames frolicked over the wood like red and orange fairies. Gray smoke curled up and disappeared up the chimney flue.

She remembered a big news story last summer about wildfires in Wyoming, which had burned hundreds of acres of forests and destroyed a few homes and cabins in the process. Since the area around Polaris had seen a wet autumn, forest fires here would be unlikely. But a single cabin, especially an old one, could still catch fire. How tall would the smoke column rise? How far away would it be seen?

Fire and smoke. Her salvation from hell.

She got up off the sofa and stretched. "Can I put one more log on? My hands are so cold." To prove her point, she set her palms on top his hands.

He shook them off. "Your fingers feel like ice. Yes, but only one log. It will be night soon, and then we'll leave."

Nina rummaged through the wood pieces stacked in the rack next to the fireplace. She selected a long section of branch and added it to the fire, leaving one end jutting out. Instead of closing the metal chain curtain meant to contain sparks, she left it opened.

Dropping to her knees on the braided rug set before the hearth, she rested her head in her hands. With focus, she summoned all the emotions built up over the last hours and released a flood of tears. From what she remembered about Erich, he hated crying. Especially female tears.

Erich grunted. "Why do women have to sob over every little thing?"

Like fearing your boyfriend's dead and being held hostage is just a little thing. "I have a life here, and friends. Are you really taking me away from everything I've built?" She sniffled and glanced up at him. His face and body appeared distorted through her tear-filled eyes. A more fitting mirror of his personality.

"What have you built here, Nina? You have a small house and teach music to children. That's the future you want?" He chuckled. "The woman I knew back in Boston had big hopes and dreams. She wanted to tour as a solo performer. A headliner at some of the world's best performing arts centers."

"Is that what this is, then? You putting me back in the spotlight after you've taken me against my will?" Still kneeling, she straightened her back. Anger burned inside her hotter than the fire. If only she could ignite a blaze with her fury alone—summon fireballs into her hands, then launch one at Erich, more around the room, until the cabin burned with her fury.

Erich approached. His eyes narrowed, and deep lines furrowed between his eyes. He lowered to his knees and pinched her chin with his cold fingers. "So ungrateful." His grip tightened. "Would you rather be outside, freezing, like the man you claim to love?"

"Yes." She struggled against his hold, which grew stronger. Would he continue until her jaw snapped? If he couldn't break her spirit, he'd break her body. "I love Colin. He's a good man who accepts me for who I am."

"Then he accepts a quitter. A has-been. A failure." He released his hold and jerked her head to the side. "Pathetic. I endured three thousand six hundred fifty days in a jail cell because of you. One day didn't go by that you weren't on my mind. I knew when I got out, I'd either spend the rest of my life with you or kill you."

Nina faced the fire, gathering the courage to strike. One end of the log she placed inside was engulfed with flames. The other was still untouched by fire, poking out slightly from the firebox. She memorized its placement before turning her attention to Erich. "You won't kill me." Her lips lifted in a smile. "You're not man enough."

A crimson flush stained his face. He set his elegant hands around her throat and squeezed. With his eyes burning into hers, she moved her arm toward the log. For a second, her hand fumbled through the air. Panic hit her heart. She struggled to take in a breath. Finally, she made contact with the hard, round log. Her fingers wrapped around it, gripping tight. The bark dug into her palm. Heat scorched her skin.

She didn't feel any pain except the sting of hatred. As she fought for breath, she gathered her remaining strength and swung her arm. The burning end of the log struck the side of Erich's head with a thump.

In an instant, his hands left her throat. She gasped, and the rush of air created its own fire down her esophagus.

Stumbling back, Nina rose to her feet. Below, Erich lay writhing on the floor, clutching his head.

She reached inside her sock and pulled out her small knife. Without hesitation, she took the rickety wooden chair she'd been tied to and pushed it into the fireplace. The old, dry wood ignited. Not wanting to leave anything to chance, she grabbed several books off a nearby shelf and tossed them in for added fuel. With the log still in her hand, she ran to the nearest window and lit the curtains on fire, and then dropped the log on the floor.

"What are you doing?" Still holding the side of his head, Erich lifted to a seated position on the floor. "You'll kill us both."

"Unlock the door and let us out." She stood over him, pointing the tip of her knife down at his chest.

When he glanced up, she saw a flash of fear as well as hatred. His cheek, ear, and temple were an angry red, and she got some slight satisfaction from knowing she'd put that burn on his skin.

With a shaking hand, he groped for the gun in the holster.

She reached for it too, hoping to take the weapon before he could use it against her. *If you get the gun, you can force him to open the door.*

He scooted backward, out of reach. The murderous expression on his face sent a chill up her spine, despite the growing heat of flames surrounding her.

She didn't take her gaze off him, but out of her peripheral vision saw the flames were spreading. They didn't have long before they were both burned alive inside the cabin. Nina leaped forward, making for the gun again, but Erich rolled away.

His fingers wrapped around the gun grip and drew it out.

A monster of her own creation roared inside her. She angled her body and kicked, aiming her foot at his hand. The gun flew in an arc across the room and skated across the floor, finally coming to a rest against the wall at the far side of the room.

He pushed to his feet and growled. "You're dead, Nina."

By now, the small fires she'd set had grown intense. The curtains she'd ignited were fully engulfed, spreading fire to the window frames and log walls. Smoke pooled at the high ceiling of the cabin. Soon, it would fill the interior, leaving her unable to breathe.

Erich took one step backward then pivoted, going for the gun.

With the knife still in hand, she charged. Her body slammed into his, knocking them both to the ground. The knife plunged into his arm before it slipped out of her grasp.

Heat licked any exposed skin. Sweat dripped down her face and back.

On the floor lying facedown, Erich groaned. She took advantage of the moment of shock and jumped to her feet, then sprinted toward the gun. Lifting it, she held tightly— couldn't allow him to overpower her and get the gun back. Her gaze trained on Erich, who was now standing, she fired. The bullet struck his thigh. Her instinct to shoot to kill ran deep, but she'd rather not have his death on her conscience, no matter how vile he'd lived his life.

"Give me the key to the door. We need to get out. It's over, Erich." She sent another bullet flying over his shoulder, piecing the window behind him. The added oxygen fed the flames.

The burned side of his face was bumpy and red. His left eye had swollen almost completely shut. A patch of his neatly styled hair had burned away, leaving a shadow of stubble. Blood oozed out of the wound in his thigh. Erich Everett's appearance finally matched the ugliness he harbored inside.

"This is over when you're dead." He raised his right hand, a gun clutched inside.

My gun. Nina didn't wait to hear the pop of it firing. She dove to the ground.

Panic-stricken, she crawled on all fours for cover behind a small table set in the corner of the room. The kitchen was the only spot inside the cabin she could see that was not overrun by flames. She pushed the table onto its side, setting the thick wooden top between Erich and herself.

Rising up to peer over the edge of the table, she took aim with the gun in her hand. The click of an empty chamber sent her heart sinking. This was Erich's gun. Had he only loaded two bullets? Nina released the magazine and checked inside—empty. Unfortunately, she'd come better prepared with a fully loaded weapon. And even more unfortunate, Erich had her gun.

The sound of his loud footfalls, heavy breathing, and the crackling of the fire burning around her combined into a sickening roar. Her heart pounded like a jackhammer inside her chest.

Erich was coming. Fire surrounded her. She had no weapon—and nowhere to hide.

~ᵧ~

Colin marched on. He never appreciated the vastness of the backcountry until wandering its trails for hours with no sign of human life. Now, he found himself on a narrow, downward sloping trail. Eventually, he should intersect a main road. Or at least one that saw regular traffic.

His frustration level was matched only by his despair. By now, Nina could be in Erich's car, miles away. Or worse, injured or dead. A psychopath like Erich was capable of anything, even with the woman he supposedly cared for.

Colin moved around a thick spruce and into a clearing. A two-foot section of rock jutted out from the mountainside. He stepped onto its smooth surface and searched the valley below. The sun was partially hidden behind the mountain. He desperately searched for a cabin or road. A flash to his left caught his eye. Turning his attention, he saw an eagle soaring above golden treetops.

Another sight made his heart stop—smoke. Thick gray smoke spiraled up from a cluster of trees, maybe about a half mile to the east. A naturally started forest fire was unlikely. Not without a lightning storm, and the sky was clear of rain clouds.

The smoke appeared to be more than the output from an average cabin chimney. An entire cabin must be on fire to produce that much. A shot of adrenaline hit him like a Wade Boggs home run swing. *Nina.*

He coughed to clear his lungs and throat. With renewed purpose, he left the trail and sidestepped down the steep terrain. Twigs from low brush snagged his jeans. He pulled away and continued, careful not to lose his footing. If he tumbled down the mountainside and broke a dozen bones, he'd be no help.

The smoke marked Nina's location. That singular thought drove him on. Loose rocks underfoot tumbled away, and Colin slid downward about five feet. He grasped on to a sapling. The thin tree bent with his weight but held. Once he was sure of his footing, he released his hold and continued, every footstep a chance taken.

A boom echoed across the landscape, sounding very much like the discharge of a gun. Not a rifle, whose sound would be deeper. The image of Erich's pistol flashed in his mind. And then Nina setting her own weapon on the table to save Colin's life.

Disregarding all concern for himself, he broke out into a run. The smoke column was growing closer. He could see it twist and twirl as it spun upward into the air currents. An orange glow fire shone like a lighthouse beacon. At moments, tall trees blocked his view, but his body moved with an instinctual drive.

Descending at a rapid pace, Colin's feet scrambled to keep up with the momentum of his upper body. When he reached a plateau, he breathed a sigh of relief. Ignoring the pain in his legs, chest, and head, he pushed on in a full-out sprint.

As he zigged and zagged around rocks and trees, he pictured Nina's sweet face. She'd said she loved him. Had she told him the truth, or were her words only a reaction to a desperate situation?

The sight of a blue car parked ahead pushed that question to the back of his mind. A cabin appeared, flames surging from several windows. Smoke streamed out from under the front door and from various points on the roof. How much longer before the roof collapsed?

He heard her muffled cry, which originated from inside.

The green paint of the closed front door bubbled from the heat. Colin stepped onto the small porch and stretched the hem of his shirt to cover the doorknob. The metal scorched his palm. He twisted and pushed, but the door held firm. Trying again, he rammed his shoulder into it with more force. Nothing. His shoulder throbbed from contact with the hot door.

Erich had locked the door from the inside, and Nina was trapped in a burning building with a madman.

Get inside to her—now.

CHAPTER 22

From her spot behind the overturned table, Nina curled into a tight ball. A bullet punctured through the tabletop a few inches to her left, barely missing her, and hit the log wall behind her with a crack. The heat became overwhelming, as well as the smoke. The fire had spread at an amazing rate, eating up old dry wood and furniture like a Thanksgiving meal.

If Erich didn't kill her with his gun, she'd die soon from smoke inhalation. Even if she died before help arrived, at least her friends and family would know what happened to her.

More than anything, for these last moments of her life, she wished to be wrapped in Colin's arms. So much so, she imagined him calling her name. Hopefully, he'd found safety. If the fire drew attention to the area, surely someone would find Colin. Or he'd see the activity and walk toward help.

A banging startled her back into fight mode. Erich approached. Soon, she'd be exposed, like a wild animal stuck in a trap. Nina could snarl and nip, but she remained caught at the hunter's mercy, or lack thereof.

Erich's head appeared over the edge of the table. With her knees tucked into her chest, she whispered a prayer. Then, with every ounce of strength she had left, she kicked out with both feet. The impact pushed the table forward and into Erich's legs.

Nina didn't wait. She bolted upright and saw he'd stumbled backward. Inhaling to catch her breath, she choked on the toxic smoke swirling through the air and coughed. Erich had dropped her gun, and she scrambled to reach it but the heat of the fire had her retreating. She hunched low and scrambled toward the kitchen—the only space not ablaze. Soon the area where the gun rested had been overtaken by flames. The bullet inside the chamber fired, sending it into the wall.

Stopping by the goldenrod-colored refrigerator, she lowered to the ground. A loud banging began, sounding in the direction of the front of the cabin. Had help arrived? If the front door opened, the fresh rush of air would fuel the fire even further. In that moment, she prepared for the end. Her life had been good, especially the last years spent in Polaris. She thought of her family and her friends and of all the things she'd miss—Celia and Luke's wedding, her students' music recital. Who'd take care of Ariel? Then the memory of Colin filled her with peace. He'd been an unexpected gift, and she was so thankful she'd told him that she loved him. In her mind's eye, she pictured them walking hand in hand, hair turned gray after many years together. Her eyes grew heavy, and she coughed. Gathering her will, she'd attempt escape, running to a window and breaking it to climb through. She wouldn't let her life end here—not now.

~ ˌ ~

Colin's shoulder burned with the trauma of ramming into the door over and over again. The old door and frame held firm. He searched Erich's car for tools to help break into the cabin, but found only more nylon cord and a few books.

He wouldn't give up, no matter how deeply he injured his body. Deciding to give the door one more try before moving to one of the windows, he ground his feet into the grass like a sprinter on starting blocks. After a few deep breaths, he shot forward and bounded up the stairs. With all the force of a linebacker, he rushed the door. The wood frame cracked, then split, and the door gave way. He fell forward into an inferno. Heat washed over him. Flames burst with renewed energy from the rush of air.

"Nina!" Thick smoke blocked his view of the interior of the cabin. He could barely see four feet ahead. "Nina!" he called out again. With Erich lurking in the smoky shadows, he braced for the sting of a bullet piercing his skin.

"Colin!"

Her voice drifted from the cloud of smoke like a whisper from an angel. Between the crackling and popping of wood, and the breaking of glass from the heat, he struggled to make out her words. "I'm here! Follow the sound of my voice." He coughed.

"Get out! You're in danger."

So was she—and right now, her safety took top priority. "Move toward my voice. I'm not leaving without you."

He stepped forward, keeping clear of the flames to his right. Squinting, he gazed into the smoky fog. "Crawl, Nina. I need to get you out of here." Above him, fire licked the ceiling beams. One of the support logs running the span of the cabin's roof fell with a crash, adding more fuel to the blaze on the floor.

As he took another step, he saw the top of her blonde head coming toward him. She was crawling in an effort to keep low. "That's it, honey. You're almost to me."

The moment her wide eyes peered up at him, Colin's breath caught. A few hours ago, he honestly thought he'd never see her again. And now, he was so close to getting her back. *Come to me.* He bent forward and reached out a hand. Appearing out of the smoke like a dragon, Erich rushed forward. He slammed into Colin, knocking them both to the ground. They rolled together, and Colin felt fire searing his skin.

Nina screams blended with the boom of another part of the roof collapsing.

"Go!" Colin yelled. As his shirt caught fire, the skin on his back screamed in pain. He punched Erich in the ribs over and over until he loosened his hold.

Nina stood by the open front door, a wall of fire separating them. Her face glowed orange in the firelight. Tears streaked down her dirt-smeared face. "No." She shook her head. "I'm not leaving you."

The cabin's exterior walls and roof roared with the strain of supporting a disintegrating building. Smoke filled Colin's eyes, and they watered, blurring his vision. Above him, Erich's face swam like a monster's reflection in water. Pressure increased around his throat. Was Erich choking him? His hazy mind struggled to focus.

Oxygen deprivation crushed his chest. Colin sent any remaining energy to his shoulders and neck, and swung up his head, striking Erich on the forehead. The force sent Erich pitching backward. With the release of pressure on his throat, Colin rolled to his side and gasped for air. But the air he inhaled left his throat and lungs convulsing. His back throbbed where his shirt had melted to his skin.

Another crash sounded, frighteningly nearby. He no longer saw Nina, but his view of the door was blocked by tall flames. *Please be safe.*

Beside him, Erich rose to his knees, his entire upper body covered in flames. A scream tore from his mouth.

Colin's gaze searched the interior for a way out. His options for escape were looking very slim.

~˒~

Growing desperate, Nina rushed back to the cabin. The intense heat pushed her back. She stumbled to a spot about ten feet away. How could she just stand here and do nothing? If Colin died, she'd live for the rest of her life with the soul-splitting pain he'd died because of her.

The forest around her was eerily quiet. Even the always-constant chatter of birds had stopped. Her gaze focused on the open door, waiting to see Colin's form appear. She waited until panic built to the point she'd explode. *Enough.* The man she loved was inside. He'd broken down the door and rushed in to rescue her. She had to help him get out.

As she stepped toward the cabin and welcomed the heat, a thunderous crash forced her to retreat. The front portion of the roof collapsed. Flames rose from the newly formed opening.

Nina screamed. *No. This can't be happening. Colin, don't leave me. I need you so much.*

Sobs racked her body. The sound of an approaching car motor barely registered. Nothing mattered if Colin was dead.

A car door slammed. Then another.

"Nina," a voice sounded like shouting through a tunnel. "Nina."

Hands squeezed her shoulders. A face materialized before her.

Luke.

"Colin!" She pointed toward the burning cabin. "He's inside."

"Joyce, stay with Nina," he barked.

Gabs wrapped an arm around her waist, holding her upright.

Nina sagged into her friend and let sorrow overtake her body.

As Luke approached the cabin, he shouted Colin's name. He glanced at the front before taking off at a sprint around to the other side of the cabin.

"Come on." Gabs kept hold of Nina and guided her in the direction Luke had headed.

The fire wasn't as intense on the cabin's back side because the kitchen had been the last to catch, so the roof there still held. A door was placed at the far corner of the wall, which might lead into a back bedroom. A silver latch and lock held it closed.

Luke kicked the door, and the wood groaned. He kicked over and over again until it broke apart from the frame. "Stay back," he shouted to Gabs and Nina and disappeared inside.

She wanted to rush forward, even if that meant dying alongside Colin. Gabs's hold remained strong.

After what seemed like an eternity, Luke appeared, carrying Colin's sagging body over his shoulder.

"Easy, now." Luke gently set him down on a pile of leaves, away from the danger of the cabin.

In a rush of joy and panic, Nina ran to Colin and

dropped to her knees. She searched his face and felt sick at the sight of burns across his skin. His breathing was shallow and uneven.

"I'm going back in for Erich," Luke yelled over the sounds of the fire.

Nina couldn't get out the words to stop him before he disappeared back into the burning cabin. If Luke lost his life in an attempt to save Erich, she'd never be able to face Celia. She whispered a prayer for protection.

After long seconds, Erich stumbled out the door and down the steps. He landed on the ground with a thump.

Luke followed soon after. He hunched over, hands on knees, taking deep breaths.

Thank goodness. Her attention returned to the unconscious man on the ground before her. "Don't leave me. I love you."

"We need to get them to the hospital." Gabs stood over Erich's prone form. "I called for fire and EMS response."

"We don't have time to wait. I'll pull the truck around." Luke took off towards the front of the cabin.

She softly brushed a patch of Colin's black hair untouched by the fire. Her heart now beat outside her body, aching and unprotected. And it would crumble to ashes if Colin didn't survive.

CHAPTER 23

"*That wraps up the official part of my visit.*" Luke snapped closed his notebook. "How are you holding up?"

Nina rested her head back on the hospital's flat pillow. "The nurse put ointment on my burns, so that's eased the pain." Had it really only been a few hours ago since Luke and Gabs found them at the burning cabin and rescued Colin? The whole ride into town was a blur. When they'd arrived at the hospital's ER, Colin had been whisked away, while she was taken to an exam room. After being treated for injuries, she was brought up to her own room, where she'd stay overnight for observation.

After she got settled in, Luke had arrived to take her statement. She cringed at reliving the nightmare with Erich, but understood Luke's need the get the details while they were still fresh in her mind. "I'd feel better if I could see Colin."

Luke patted her hand. "I know. He's in the ICU, and I don't have enough pull to get you in there right now. Be patient. You'll be with him again soon."

If he didn't pull through, she'd never see him again. Her stomach sickened. "Will he be all right?" Colin had to survive. He was too good a man not to.

"There's only so much the hospital staff will share with me. Colin is stable and being well cared for. His friend, James, is flying from Chicago and should be here shortly. Since Colin has no close family, he signed his health care power of attorney over to James. Once James arrives, he'll direct Colin's medical care and hopefully give us updates." He leaned forward in his chair. "Colin has a team of people working on him. I want you to stay focused on your healing. You just survived a very traumatic ordeal."

"What about Erich?" Her mouth soured saying his name. As much as she didn't want to think about him, she had to know if he'd survived. She'd seen him escape the cabin. Now, she wanted to make sure he didn't escape justice.

"He's in rough shape. Guards are posted outside his room, just in case. He's not going anywhere." A knock sounded, and Luke turned his head toward the door.

A nurse entered, carrying a medicine tray. She gave her a small cup filled with three pills, which Nina swallowed down with several gulps of water. Once the nurse left, she returned her attention to Luke. "Were you able to interrogate him?"

He shook his head. "Erich's been unconscious since the cabin. We searched his car, though, and discovered he'd made two trips to Polaris. The first was around the same time you met with your sister, Meg. We don't believe they traveled together, but that he gave Meg the letter in hopes she'd go see you in person. He followed her here, and she was unaware."

Nina rubbed her temples. As tremulous as her and

Meg's relationship had been, she believed her sister would never knowingly lead Erich to her. "After following Meg, he must have gotten back to Boston quickly to not alert his parole officer."

"He was traveling under a fake name. My department is working with the Boston PD to figure out his movements since his release from prison. They got a warrant and searched his place."

"What did they find?" She became chilled and wrapped her arms around herself. "Did he even live in the apartment he listed as his address?"

He scratched at his chin. "They found a few personal belongings. Everything belonged to Erich. A man pretending to be Erich was living in the apartment when the police raided the place. He was arrested."

"Oh." So that was how Erich managed to be in two places at once.

The fine lines between Luke's brows deepened as he scowled. "When the police searched his apartment, they found Erich had been collecting items associated with you. The walls of one of the bedrooms were covered with various photographs of either you alone or the two of you together."

The news, though not surprising, made her want to vomit. "What will the police do with it all?"

"Some they'll save as evidence, and the rest they'll destroy." He took a deep breath. "The only reason I'm telling you this is because you need to understand what a sick person he is. His obsession was not your fault. He could have become fixated on anybody."

"But he became fixated on me." She turned her pointer finger into her chest.

He took her hand and gave it a gentle squeeze. "If Erich

survives, I will make sure he spends the rest of his life in jail. I'll do whatever is necessary to keep him away from you."

"Thank you. For everything." Exhaustion hit her, and she struggled to keep her eyes open. "I need a nap."

Standing, he set his Stetson on his head. "Then I'll leave so you can get some sleep. I'll be back tomorrow morning. Good night."

After he left, she cried until sleep finally pulled her under.

˜ ˎ ˜

Nina saw flames dance before her eyes. She screamed. The sound roused her out of sleep. Lifting her eyelids, she focused on the details of her hospital room. The white blanket covering her body. A vase filled with flowers set next to her bed.

Panic induced from her nightmare lingered, making her heart rate monitor beep rapidly. She inhaled deeply, then exhaled. Again, she focused on her breathing. The beeping stopped as her heartbeat returned to normal.

Her heart ached to be near Colin. Even if he was sleeping, she still needed to be at his side, holding his hand. Guilt held her captive in her hospital room. Colin cared about her —a big mistake. A mistake that had killed Seth.

The door to her room opened, and a nurse entered. She carried a tray topped with a covered plate. "Here's your breakfast, dear." Nurse Danica set the tray on the swinging-arm table by her bed. "You have visitors. Do you feel up for company?"

Nina scooted up to a seated position. "Did you get their names?"

"Mrs. Maxwell and her caregiver, Gretchen Williams."

She swung the table over Nina's lap. "How are you doing this morning? Dr. Murphy said he'll release you today as long as all your vitals look good."

"I'm sore, but otherwise, I feel okay, physically." Tears welled in her eyes, and she sniffled them back.

"Healing the mind will take more time." Nurse Danica patted her hand, the one free of the IV needle. "You've been through something terrible. The love and support of your friends and family will be important during the next few weeks, even months."

Yes, her friends would help her recover. That knowledge gave her peace.

"Please show Beatrice and her nurse in." Nina could use a strong dose of Bea's motherly loving. "Before you leave, I was wondering if I can see Colin Moynahan. He was hurt in the fire at the cabin. He saved my life."

Nurse Danica rubbed Nina's shoulder. "I'll have to check with his doctor. He's still sedated, but no longer in ICU."

Her body sagged with relief. "He's improving."

She nodded. "The man's a fighter. Can't say the same about the other person who was brought in with you."

"Erich?" His name caught in her throat.

Nurse Danica pursed her lips. "He didn't survive the night. Can't say that I'm too sorry either. Not after what he did to you and Mr. Moynahan."

The news he was no longer walking the earth lifted a weight off her chest. He would never hurt her or someone she loved ever again. "I can't say I'm sorry either."

"I'll find out about you seeing Mr. Moynahan after I escort in your guests." The nurse left Nina's room, closing the door softly behind her.

She closed her eyes. A sob sounded from her throat. Erich was dead. His reign of terror was over.

The door to her room swung open, and Bea entered, followed by her new private duty nurse. Holding a cane for support, Bea marched over to Nina's hospital bed.

"Oh my goodness, child." She clutched her hand over her heart. "I needed to see for myself you are all right."

"I'm fine." Nina wiped a tear from her cheek. "I'll likely go home today. But Colin..." She faltered and covered her mouth with her hand to stop the flood of emotion.

Bea lowered herself into a chair placed next to the bed. "Colin's friend from Chicago, Mr. James Brockwell, is here. He flew down last night with this wonderful nurse here. James will take him back to Chicago once he's cleared to travel." She pointed to the woman standing behind the chair. "Ms. Williams will stay with me for my remaining weeks of recovery."

"I'm glad you're being taken care of." Nina held Bea's hand. The human contact soothed her anxiety.

Thank goodness Colin's friend, whom he'd said was as close as a brother, had come to oversee his care. If James was taking him to Chicago for treatment and recovery, Nina wouldn't see him again for a long time. She'd insist on visiting him before he was taken to Chicago. A thank-you and maybe, a goodbye.

He'd be better off in a large hospital with a specialized medical staff. So why did the loose seam in her chest feel like it had just ripped wide open?

Bea rubbed Nina's hand. "When Captain Luke came over to my house yesterday looking for you and Colin, I got so scared. He went over to your house and saw the note you left. They found your car quick enough. Took a little longer to find you."

"I started the fire, thinking the smoke would signal help. And now Colin is badly burned." She swallowed hard, blinking back tears. "I should have never gotten involved with him."

"Child, none of this is your fault," Bea said.

"Tell that to my heart."

Bea brush her hand down Nina's hair, just as if she was a little girl. "I will every single day. You can take that to the bank."

Nina talked with Bea for a little while longer, until Bea's private duty nurse told her they needed to leave for a physical therapy appointment.

"You call me once you're discharged and back home," Bea said from the doorway. "Gabrielle told me she's in charge of you for the next few days."

Chuckling, she waved goodbye to Bea. Nina had no doubt Gabs would stick close for the foreseeable future.

When her nurse came back to take her breakfast tray, she asked again about visiting Colin. Her soul lifted when Nurse Danica gave her a big thumbs-up. Nina got seated in the wheelchair. A hospital volunteer came to take her to the elevator and then pushed her down the hall to Colin's room.

As the door open, her breath stopped. The lights inside his room were dimmed. A slow and steady beeping came from Colin's monitors. A man sat in a chair off to the side, an ankle propped up on the opposite knee. He typed on a computer, which rested on his lap. At the noise of her arrival, he looked up and smiled warmly.

The man flipped closed his laptop and stood. "You must be Nina." He reached over to shake her hand. "James Brockwell."

"Hi. Pleasure to meet you." Her voice was barely a whisper. James was shorter in stature than Colin, but had the same muscular build. His blond hair was messy, and his nice clothes rumpled. She assumed he hadn't left Colin's side since he arrived.

"Wish I could have the pleasure under better circumstances." James glanced over his shoulder at the hospital bed. "They're keeping Colin sedated, for his own comfort and to help the healing process. My friend here has run the table on medical ailments."

Yes, he had suffered a lot of injuries during one event— defending her. With caution, Nina stood and shuffled over to Colin's bed. "Oh." Pain and sorrow choked her. Lying on the bed, he looked so helpless. He rested on his stomach with wide pieces of gauze covering most of his back and neck. His arms were wrapped as well. Several bags filled with clear liquid hung nearby and were connected to his IV.

Colin's head was turned toward her. One cheek relaxed against the mattress. She bent down and kissed the other, then brushed a lock of black hair off his forehead. "I'm so sorry."

"He wouldn't want you feeling guilty." James stood next to her. "The two of us go back a long time. He's the most unselfish person I know...and the best."

"But he was kidnapped by a man who was after me." Nina's eyes burned with tears, and she squeezed her eyelids to keep the dam from breaking. "He went into a burning cabin in search of me."

James put an arm around Nina's shoulders. "Colin told me he met someone special. In all the years I've known him, he's never said that to me."

She gazed down at the man who filled her heart. "Really?"

Nodding, James placed a hand on an unwounded spot on Colin's arm. "He did. I asked how serious things were getting because I've always figured with him, it would be one and done. He's had plenty of casual relationships, but nothing that ever involved the heart. You changed that. You mean more to him than anything else, even his own life."

Unable to hold back any longer, she sobbed into James's chest. She rested her head against him, and he supported her as she released years of pent-up emotional pain. When her well of tears was drained, she stared down at Colin, memorizing everything about him, from the small scar by his ear to each black eyelash.

"I have a private flight arriving this afternoon. There's an excellent burn trauma care facility at one of the hospitals in Chicago. He'll get first-class care. I'll make sure of that."

"Good." She accepted the tissue James offered and dried her face.

"You're welcome to come along, or travel to join him later. I have plenty of guest rooms, and my wife would enjoy some female company around the house. We have three boys." He smiled.

"Thank you for the offer. I'll think about it." Right now, the thought of being anywhere but home left her queasy.

"Of course. After the experience you just survived, I'd understand if you need the safety of familiar surroundings. Here's my business card. My cell's written on the back." He helped her back into the wheelchair. "Call me anytime. And I'll keep you updated on his condition. Please, consider coming to Chicago when you feel up to it. Colin needs all the love he can get."

She glanced once more at Colin lying on the bed, his dark hair a stark contrast to his pale face. What came next for them, she wasn't sure. The only thing she did know was that he'd take part of her with him to Chicago—the best part of her heart.

CHAPTER 24

*B*eing back home was supposed to give Nina a sense of normalcy. Instead, anxiety made her skin crawl. She felt irritated and moody, and Gabs had given her more than one look of concern over the past two days.

Nina closed out the latest email from James updating her on Colin's condition. He was doing well, and his doctor would bring him out of sedation tomorrow. So far, his burns had resisted infection. A skin graft on some of the large burn areas on his back was the next step in his healing process. She was so thankful for the high quality of care James provided. Not that Polaris Hospital wasn't a good facility, but it was small and lacked the specialists Colin needed.

James had ended his email by extending his invitation again—partially the cause of her melancholy. As much as her heart ached for Colin, she couldn't travel to see him. Her fear had crippled her. Even walking out the door left her struggling for breath. Her primary battle was returning to her music students. Their recital was a little over two weeks away. But the memory of the flower delivery at the library made her nauseous. She'd thought once Erich was dead, her fear would be gone. Gabs called it PTSD. Nina called it a roadblock to reclaiming her life and her love.

Nina set her laptop on the coffee table and picked up her mug. The liquid inside was now cold. She stood and groaned at the burst of pain in her torso and legs. The bruises covering her body were too many to count. Right now, she probably had more black-and-blue skin than normal color. As she walked out of the room, Gabs appeared, dressed in yoga pants and a baggy sweatshirt.

"Don't you need to leave for work?" Nina asked.

"Police chief gave me the day off." She flopped onto the sofa and bounced a few times. "So, what do you want to do? We could go downtown and get some lunch. Maybe see if there's anything good playing at the movie theater?"

"You don't need to babysit me."

Gabs held up a hand. "Don't start. I'm your friend, and there's no way I'm leaving you home alone. Not after everything you have, and still are, going through."

"I'm weighed down, like a lead blanket is draped over me. I can barely breathe. My skin chills and then heats. I'm nauseous most of the time." She leaned a shoulder against the doorframe. Yes, Gabs was her best friend, but she still felt alone. No amount of company could drive out the isolation filling her.

Gabs stood. "I wish I could do more to help. Tell me what you need."

"I need to stop feeling afraid." She walked toward the window and gazed outside. The wind whipped the tops of almost-bare trees. Nina shivered despite the warmth inside her house.

"He's gone, Nina. Don't allow him to cause you any more pain."

"Easy to say." She huffed. "I still hear his voice in my head."

"That's on you." Gabs crossed her arms and raised her chin. "You're letting him stay rent-free as a ghost inside you."

"It's not like I can control what the trauma has done to my brain." Anger burned her. How could Gabs act as if her anxiety and depression were a choice?

"No, but you blame yourself for what happened back in Boston and again for what Erich did to Colin." She pointed a finger at Nina. "Erich's actions were responsible for Seth's death. He abused you, stalked you, kidnapped you. Then here in Polaris, he threatened a man you have deep feelings for. Almost killed both you and Colin. Let go of your own guilt. That's what's suffocating you now."

"How do you know?" She whirled around, blood boiling. "You have all the answers, huh? I can snap my fingers and look, everything is sparkles and sunshine."

"I didn't say the process is easy, but I've watched you since you've gotten home from the hospital, and you're frozen."

"Part of me died when Colin was trapped inside." She yanked a hand through her hair, which caused pinpricks of pain across her scalp. "I should be the one in the hospital right now. Not him."

"You're alive." Gabs rested a hand on her shoulder. "And so is Colin."

"I can't do this right now." She turned to leave, but Gabs increased the grip on her shoulder.

"Yes, you can."

Nina shrugged and Gabs dropped her hand. "You really make me mad."

"Good. Get mad. Yell and scream and tell the world how angry you are that someone like Erich Everett was let out of jail after he murdered a man and kidnapped you."

"Since his conviction, I knew he'd come after me once he was released." Her indignation rose with Gabs's prodding. "He didn't obey the law before. Why would he follow the rules while out on parole?"

"He used your sister to find where you live, then fled Boston first chance he got." Gabs balled her hands into fists and rested them on her hips. "And why did he risk being sent back to prison?"

"Because over a decade ago, I had the nerve to break up with him." A low growl formed inside her chest. Pent-up anger flowed like a tidal surge. "He wanted my talent to use for himself. He killed the man who attempted to replace him in my life."

"That's it. Let it out." Gabs set her feet wide and rubbed her hands together, like she was bracing for a storm.

"I gave up the cello, something I loved, because he contaminated my joy of playing." Nina picked up a glass knickknack and launched it at the wall.

"Whoa." Gabs took her hand. "Let's go outside and do this the right way."

After Nina put on her shoes and coat, she went into the backyard. They stood on the brick-paver patio. The dying flower garden behind Gabs reflected her own heart. Was it possible to get the color back? How long would she need before she bloomed again?

Holding a pillow to her chest, Gabs took a fighter's stance. "Hit me." She jerked her head and smiled.

"I can't—"

"I said, hit me." She pounded the pillow with her fist.

"Punch, yell, do whatever you have to. Exorcise that evil man from your body."

Nina balled up her fist and lightly punched the pillow. The ache in her muscles helped remind her she was alive. "He'll never hurt me again."

"I've taken kickboxing class with you. I know you can hit harder than that."

Channeling her anger, she struck out again. This time, Gabs grunted.

"What happened to Seth was not my fault." She reset her arm and punched. "Erich went after Colin to get to me. He didn't care who he hurt in order to get what he wanted."

"You are a survivor."

"I am a survivor," Nina yelled. Her arm grew tired, but she hit the pillow again. "I am a survivor!"

"That a girl." Gabs's eyes shone with tears. "Love is your weapon and shield."

"Erich used my heart against me."

"Your heart will heal."

Nina's anger was losing steam. Her arm grew weak with the release of emotion, and her body relaxed. "I told Colin I love him."

Lowering the pillow, Gabs stared, gaping. "Ah! About time."

She shrugged. "I kinda blurted it out. I was afraid I'd never see him again."

"What did he say?"

"He didn't say anything." The heat Nina had generated during her short fit of rage cooled off, and so did she. Inhaling, she filled her lungs with cold air, and then exhaled, breathing out a cloud. "He could have been avoiding handing Erich one more reason to want him dead. Then there's men's natural allergic reaction to the word *love*. Just because Colin said he cared about me doesn't mean he's fallen in love."

Gabs hooked her arm though Nina's and led her back inside. "There's only one way to find out."

"I know." She shrugged off her coat and hung it on the hook by the door. "Talking would be so much easier if he wasn't in Chicago."

"How do you feel about going there to see him?" Gabs filled a teapot with water and set it on the stove.

Nina took out two tea bags from the ceramic container on the counter. She inhaled the herbal scents of lavender and chamomile. "I'm having a hard time getting up the courage to leave my house."

"Well, the separation might be a good thing."

"Why?" She furrowed her brow in confusion.

"Because even before the incident with Erich, you and Colin were trying to figure out where your relationship was headed. And you, in particular, still hadn't committed to anything beyond friendship. So in my opinion, before you see him again, you need to figure out where your heart's leading you."

"But I told him I loved him." Yes, she did. And she knew that being in love with someone didn't mean a life together was possible. Once Colin fully recovered, he'd begin traveling for work again. Where did that leave her? Where did that leave them?

Gabs was right. As heartbroken as Nina was about being apart from him, she'd use the time to recover emotionally. Whatever the future held, she knew she carried the inner strength and courage to continue her life's journey.

~ ᵥ ~

Thank goodness for pain medication. Colin shifted his body as he attempted to get into a sitting position. Even with the morphine, his back was still sore. Which he considered a good thing. The pain reminded him to move with caution. The last thing he wanted to do was re-damage his skin.

Tomorrow, he'd go into surgery for a skin graft. If all went well, he'd be sent home or, more precisely, to James's house, to finish healing.

During his three-day sedation-induced slumber, his head cold had cleared. One ailment to check off the list. Along with the burns, he'd fractured two ribs, a few fingers on his right hand, and his left clavicle. On strictly the vanity side, the hair on the left portion of his head had mostly burned away, leaving short stubble. He was grateful to still have both eyebrows, although underneath one brow, his eye sported a pretty purple bruise.

The bumps and bruises were no big deal. Neither were the fractured bones. He'd dealt with similar injuries back during his fighting years. And the burns would heal. Maybe leave scars behind as a souvenir. Having a visible reminder of what Erich had done was something he could live without.

As he poured a cup of water from the little plastic pitcher the nurse left, James walked in.

"Hey, sleeping beauty. Who drew the short straw and had to kiss your face in order to wake you up?" He sat in a chair next to the bed and smiled.

"I thought that was you." Colin puckered his lips and made kissy sounds.

"Not with your new hairstyle." He pointed to Colin's head of mangled hair. "You want me to bring in clippers and shave it all off?"

"Even with this mess, I still don't trust you with clippers. Remember the time in high school when you gave me a buzz cut and the guard fell off? Went all the way down to the scalp." He laughed. "I went to the homecoming dance practically bald."

"You looked wicked that night. Let's hold off on the haircut. I'm sure Jenna will do a lot better job at home."

Remembering he was now in Chicago, so far away from Nina, he sobered. "I appreciate everything you've done, Jimmy."

"That's what friends are for, man...and you're my best."

"Have you heard from Nina today?" The fact that he hadn't spoken to her since the cabin left him uneasy. Jimmy kept her updated on his condition, but now that he was awake, he needed to hear the sound of her voice. He'd been told Nina was out of the hospital and doing fine physically. But emotionally, she had to be hurting.

"Talked to her this morning while you were still snoozing." He tossed his cell next to Colin's lap. "Call her yourself. I think she'd rather hear from you."

"Thanks." He picked up the phone. "I should probably order a new one. Not sure where mine ended up."

"If you call your provider, I can grab a new phone from the store on my way home." James stood and walked to the door. "Colin."

He glanced up from the phone screen. "Yeah?"

"She's a wonderful woman."

"I know."

"As much as I value your work, I understand if you feel the time has come to plant some roots."

Colin studied his friend, who looked way too serious. "Good to know."

James nodded, then exited.

As he looked back down at Nina's name brightly lit on the cell phone screen, his chest tightened. After everything they'd gone through together, what would he say? She'd told him she loved him, but were those words spoken in the heat of the moment?

His own feelings had yet to clarify. On the mountain, when he'd struggled to find her, something inside him had shifted. Even now, he still wasn't sure what the change meant. Only one way to find out.

Colin hit Dial and listened to the ringing tone twice before she answered.

"Hi, James. How's Colin?"

The sound of her voice, so sweet and pure, left him struggling for breath. The tingling sensation in his body couldn't be blamed on the morphine. He cleared his throat. "It's not James. Hi, Nina."

Silence greeted him. For several seconds, his heart stopped.

Then, she sighed. "Colin."

"James loaned me his phone." He paused. "I wanted to let you know I'm feeling as good as new."

She chuckled. "Oh, I don't believe that for a second. Hey, does he have FaceTime on his phone?"

"Yeah. But you don't want to see me right now." He patted the almost bald side of his head.

"I do. Call me back on FaceTime."

"All right, but don't say I didn't warn you. Hang up, and I'll call you right back." He waited for her to disconnect before he went to the home screen and into the video chatting app. Where was a mirror when he needed one? His gaze landed on the cell phone—the Swiss army knife of technology. He turned on the camera, put it in selfie mode, and cringed. Worse than he thought.

Well, at least he'd find out if she was only into him because of his good looks. He pressed the Call button. Within a second, Nina's picture popped up on the screen. She was absolutely gorgeous. *How had a brute like me snagged such a gem?*

Nina covered her mouth with her hand. "You look... ummm." She gazed at him through the phone with wide, honey-colored eyes.

He braced himself for an honest and emotional reaction. Yeah, he looked like crap. He looked like he'd battled a fire-breathing dragon.

Nina wiped a tear from the corner of her eye. "You look like a hero. My hero."

A lump formed in his throat. He'd give away the world to hold her right now. He wanted to run his fingers through her silky hair and over her smooth skin. And kiss her lips like they had the power to heal him, body and soul. "Seeing you does me good. In the cabin, when I didn't think I'd make it out, I focused on keeping your face in my mind. You were the only thing I wanted to remember when I took my last breath."

"And now here we are." Tears streamed down her face. "I wish you weren't so far away."

"When I get sprung from this place, James has a room for me to crash." He itched around the top of the bandage on his neck. "He said he invited you to come up to Chicago."

Her gaze dropped to her lap. "He did."

"Stay in Polaris, Nina. As much as I want you here, you should be home where you feel safe and secure. Plus, you have your student recital coming up. Those kids need you." He hesitated, pushing back his own desire. His heart ached with her absence. "We'll keep in touch this way. I'll get a new phone, and we can talk every day. As soon as I feel up to it, I'll be on a plane to Salt Lake City."

"You saved my life. How can I not drop everything to be by your side?" She blinked back more tears.

"You saved yourself. I would never have found you if I hadn't seen the smoke from the fire."

"You would have never been out there in the first place if—"

"If it wasn't for Erich," he finished her sentence. "He's gone. We're still here. You take back the life he tried to steal from you. Teach your music students, get ready for their recital, and be happy."

"I'll try." Nina lifted a tissue to her face and blew her nose. "But only if you do the same. Take back your life. You have a new job in Hawaii starting in January, right?"

"Only if I get cleared to go back to work. Which reminds me, tell Bea to keep up on her exercises. I want to see a video of her dancing the jive at Luke and Celia's wedding reception."

"Will do." A faint smile lifted her lips.

Though the paths of their futures were uncertain, one thing he knew for certain was what he wanted from her. "I have one small favor to ask you."

"Anything, Colin."

"Take out your cello and play again."

She pressed her lips together. The silence lasted for several seconds. "I'm not sure I can."

Carefully shifting his body, he sat straighter and stared directly into the phone screen. "You can. If not for yourself, then for me. Don't let him steal something you enjoyed." He thought about Nina and his feelings for her. Was it love? How could he be sure?

"I'll try." She nodded. "I'll try for you."

"Good." He smiled his first genuine smile since waking up in the hospital. "I believe in you." More than he ever believed in himself. When he'd healed and his time in Chicago ended, where would he go next? Carry on with his lifestyle, hopping from one job to the next? Or head straight back to Polaris, ready to put down roots.

ina trailed her fingers along the curve of her cello case. She'd conquered the first step—bringing it up from the basement. The case sat in the middle of her living room floor. Ariel sniffed around the carbon fiber exterior. *Sorry, girl, but this is too big to add to your collection.*

Today, she'd dressed and showered before ten a.m. A win. Gabs had also gone in for her shift, leaving Nina home alone for the first time since the kidnapping a week ago. Another win. Because Nina had woken up that morning with a burning desire to shrug off the depression weighing her down.

She was determined to get out of the house today. Maybe take a walk downtown and stop at Downhill Delectables for a sandwich and a cup of tea. The high tourist season would start very soon, and the quiet streets of Polaris would fill up with skiers and snowboarders here to enjoy everything the town had to offer. Later in the afternoon, she had a series of music lessons scheduled to take place at the grade school. She owed it to her students to have one last lesson before the recital.

The final thing she was determined to do today was follow through on her promise to Colin. She'd play again because she owed him her word. Her playing wouldn't be perfect, but for today, the quality didn't matter. Only that she reclaimed something she'd locked away for many years. Erich had poisoned playing the cello, making both the memory and the act anxiety producing. Colin wished she found joy in it again. Was that possible now that Erich was forever gone from her life?

Maybe.

Nina flicked open the locks. As she lifted the top, the hinges creaked. Inside lay an item that at one time had been the most important thing in the world. "Hello, old friend." She wrapped her fingers around the neck of the cello and lifted it. Smooth wood slid underneath her palm, and she stopped her hand to rest above the S-shaped cutouts flanking the row of strings.

Next, she took the bow and freed it from the clasps holding it in place. She gently curved her fingers around the end and closed her eyes, letting muscle memory take control. The natural feel of the bow in her hand was like a friend from her childhood. One whom she hadn't seen for many years.

She stood and took both cello and bow into the kitchen. Once seated on the edge of a kitchen chair, she set the body of the instrument between her knees, pressing in to hold it steady. She took hold of the neck with her left hand and leaned the cello into her body.

In her head, she pictured herself as she once had been, dressed in a ball gown and playing onstage for a full performance hall. She'd been confident and passionate. Her love for music and the sound she created while playing fed her soul. She'd been a woman whose hopes, dreams, and goals were wrapped inside this very cello.

And now, could she possibly recapture some of the magic? She had to try. Not only for Colin but for herself. And most importantly, her music students. Wouldn't they benefit from seeing their teacher live what she preached during every lesson?

After taking a few deep breaths, she ran the bow across the arch of the strings. The sound produced was deep and full of longing. She wanted more. Pushing down her anxiety, she placed her fingers in first position, knuckles bent, and played a long D note. She flew through a two-octave scale next, savoring the vibration underneath her hands. Her brain and body buzzed in response to the ascending and descending tone. With a few turns of the pegs, she improved the tune of the instrument.

She used to love practicing. In her younger years, Nina would go for hours and lose track of time. Her mother scolded her for missing dinner, and she'd go to bed a hungry but happy girl.

Again, she closed her eyes and let her mind drift to the past. The melody of Cello Concerto in E minor, Opus 85, by Sir Edward Elgar floated inside her. Nina swayed as the melody played in her head. She set her fingers on the neck and hovered the bow over the strings, and then released a flood. Her fingers and wrists were stiff and slightly sore from the long-ago abandoned movements.

She lifted her chin and let her body sway with the song's cadence. About a minute in, she fumbled, forgetting the musical sequence, but after a few seconds, she picked right up again. She must have played this song hundreds of times between practices and performances. The Elgar, as she like to think of it, was one of her favorite pieces. The composer had managed to capture both hopefulness and yearning—both darkness and light. A perfect reflection of her heart.

Nina plucked the final notes and exhaled as the piece ended. She rotated her wrists to loosen the joints and muscles. Her skill had grown rusty, but overall, her little kitchen performance hadn't sounded half bad.

Even Ariel, who normally didn't like loud noises, sat in the doorway and listened. She made the perfect audience for Nina's first run at playing the cello after a long absence.

Placing her cello and bow inside the case, she noticed more pressure had lifted off her chest. Erich's effect on her life was shrinking, though it would never go totally away. He'd left a permanent stain, but the more she scrubbed, the lighter it grew.

Playing right now didn't mean she was ready to embrace performing. She might never feel comfortable at center stage. Though that wasn't what Colin had asked. He simply wanted her to play. In doing so, she stepped towards the light, leaving Erich's memory in the shadows.

Her heart burned at the thought of Colin, so far away. They talked multiple times a day, yet for her, that wasn't enough. She needed to touch him and feel his hand holding hers. A week ago, she'd declared her love. During their conversations since, neither had broached the subject. She was too afraid to ask if he'd heard her. If he didn't feel the same way, she couldn't take back her words. Maybe he didn't want to hurt her after what they'd both just survived.

Whatever happened between them, she was grateful for his presence in her life. He had gifted her with a new belief in herself. She now saw a future filled with love, and hope renewed her spirit.

~ ˅ ~

Colin slipped on a clean compression shirt, careful of his new skin graft, which was as tender as an infected tooth. But he was healing. The compression shirt stimulated blood flow to his wounds. His doctors were pleased with his progress. Even so, no one was happy when he'd told them he was leaving Chicago tomorrow.

On the dresser sat the program for Nina's music recital. Gabrielle had mailed it to him with a short note inviting him to attend. Once he'd seen the recital date, only two days away, he knew his next step. What would happen after, he wasn't sure. But sitting in Chicago while his body healed did nothing for his heart.

A knock sounded at his door. Since James's kids were at school and Jenna, his wife, was at work, he had a safe bet on who was on the other side. "Come in."

The door opened a crack. "You decent?"

"As decent as I'll ever get." He grabbed a long-sleeve athletic shirt off the bed and put it on—a painful task given the state of his upper body.

James entered the guest bedroom Colin had used for the past few nights. "You want to meet for lunch later?"

"Don't know. Have to check my schedule." A joke, since James hadn't allowed him to work during his recovery. He had ideas for how to improve the Angels' Grant program, but since he couldn't go to the office, he'd spent hours typing out his proposals on his laptop.

James wandered over to the dresser and lifted the music recital program. He glanced through the pages before setting it back down. "You sure leaving now is the right thing to do? Your doctors don't."

"Polaris has doctors. Good ones. I'm not hanging around Chicago until some MD gives me a pass to leave." He sat on the edge of the bed. "I need to be with her."

James grinned. "Should I start looking to hire your replacement?"

Despite his desire for Nina, he remained unsure which path was right for his future. "Don't know. I mean, I don't want to leave Health Shield and nursing. I enjoy my job and the opportunities it provides."

"But when you fall in love, priorities change."

"What does it even mean to fall in love?" Colin paced the small room. "My own parents didn't love me or each other. How am I supposed to know what love feels like?"

"Nana Rose loved you so much, she let both of us hang out at her house and eat her food through our teen years." James ran a hand down his teal-blue tie, smoothing the shiny fabric. "You loved her enough to devote your life to caring for the elderly. The Angels' Grant was your idea, don't forget."

"Okay." He raked his fingers through his short hair. "That was family. How do I know if I love Nina or if what I feel for her is an attraction that will fade over time?"

James stood and placed a gentle, stilling hand on Colin's shoulder. "Love is action. Think about how much you both were willing to sacrifice for the other." With a smile on his face, he walked toward the door. "We on for lunch?"

"Yeah." He nodded. "And start looking for my replacement. Someone else will need to cover the Hawaii job in January."

"Will do, man. Hate to lose you, but I'm happy you found a good woman." James closed the door behind him.

Colin sat as memories of his time racing down the mountain to find Nina flashed in his mind. He remembered the panic he felt knowing she was trapped with Erich and in danger. He'd been willing to risk his own safety, his own life, in order to protect her. And if she had died, he'd die too, because if he lost her, he could live a hundred more years and never recover.

For thirty-six years, he'd lived like a bird, with only temporary nests to call home. And just like a bird, he flew by instinct, following his own internal compass to his next destination. He was ready for a permanent home, with walls and a roof, filled with love, family, and music.

He'd waited a long time for his wanderlust to be replaced with a longing for permanency and a desire to set down roots—on a plot of land with a purple house and a yard full of flower gardens, set in a valley, surrounded by majestic mountains, and owned by the most beautiful woman he was lucky enough to love.

CHAPTER 26

*N*ina *checked her watch.* The recital started in less than an hour. Thanks to the help of Gabs and Celia, the stage was decorated with potted plants and flowers. Hung above the stage were hundreds of feet of sparkling twinkle lights.

She had to admit the high school auditorium stage looked as nice as some of the grand performance halls she'd played in.

"You need anything before I run home to change?" Gabs asked as she strode down the aisle to where Nina stood.

"The way you're dressed is fine." She looked over Gabs's blue jeans and sparkly sweater. "This isn't a night at the Met."

"No, it's even better." Gabs grinned. "Have you heard back from Colin?"

Thinking about him sent her heart racing. "Not since last night. I told him I was ready to buy a plane ticket to come see him, but he said to wait."

"Did he say why?"

She wrapped her arms around her body. "No, just that

he was excited to see me and he'd get back to me soon with what dates would work best. And something about checking his schedule."

"Weird." Gabs scratched the side of her head. "I'm so glad you're willing to take the leap and fly to Chicago. Tells me how much he means to you."

"What if he really doesn't want me there?" The thought had crossed her mind, despite their many wonderful conversations.

"Doubt it. Don't think about that now. Focus on your students and their recital. Fuss about Colin later."

Good point. "Fine. I'll delay fussing for the time being and banish all worries about Colin." No promises, but she'd try. "Is Celia still backstage?"

"Last time I checked, she was tidying up." Leaning over, Gabs gave her a gentle hug. "I'm so proud of you. I can't wait to see you play."

Nina's gut hummed with nerves. Earlier, when she'd packed her cello in the trunk of her car, she'd experienced a moment of panic. Her plan was to play one song at the end of the recital as a surprise for her students. Without the constant encouragement of Gabs and Celia, she would have backed out. But her cello was here, waiting backstage, ready to once again be heard. "I hope I don't screw up my piece."

"If you do, no one will even notice. The important thing is you're getting up there and proving to your students that fear can be conquered. They're all scared and nervous too, and seeing their teacher play in public for the first time in over a decade will be very inspirational."

Gabs's words calmed her heart. "Yes. I do want to show them you can be afraid and not let fear keep you from doing something you enjoy."

"Go backstage and take a few deep breaths." Gabs

started toward the rear of the auditorium and the door. "I'll be back in a few."

"Did you bring the chocolate chip cookies you made for the reception?"

"You leave those alone, Nina Pettit." Gabs's loud voice echoed through the room. "You'll be in big trouble if I come back and find chocolate chip cookie crumbs all over your face."

Laughing, she climbed the stairs at the end of the stage and walked into the small alcove to the right. The space now looked tidy, with all her plastic totes stacked up against one wall. Wonder where Celia had gone?

Sitting on top of one tote was the container filled with Gabs's cookies. Surely she wouldn't miss one. As Nina lifted the lid and reached inside, the sound of footsteps startled her. With her heart pounding like she'd just been caught stealing a diamond from a jewelry store, she turned to see Luke standing behind her, wearing a large smile.

"Give me one, and I promise not to snitch."

"Deal." She took out two cookies and handed one to Luke. For all Gabs's lack of domestic skills, she sure baked a mean chocolate chip cookie.

"Celia told me you're playing at the end of the show."

Nina nodded and brushed crumbs off her bottom lip. "I finally worked up enough nerve to get out my cello and play at home. Today's the next step."

"Good." He finished off his cookie in two bites, and then hooked his thumbs in the front pockets of his pants. "How are you doing?"

"I feel better every day. Some days, I wake up after a nightmare and can't shake Erich's ghost for the rest of the day." She gazed off toward a dark corner at the other side of the stage. "He did so much damage, and I don't know how long I'll take to fully heal."

"As much as I want him to pay for his crimes against you and Colin, I'm relieved you finally have closure." He rubbed the side of her arm. "The Erich you have to overcome now is only a memory."

Emotion bubble to the surface—sorrow, gratitude, regret, and a deep love for her friends. "I still struggle to accept that."

The lines between his brows deepened. "Soon, you'll watch your music students play pieces you taught them. And by taking back your love of the cello, you're showing them superheroes are real. I'm so proud of you."

Nina stepped into his hug. "Thanks, Luke."

"You can thank me by saving a few more of those cookies." He nodded toward the container.

"Will do." She chuckled, and the sound released the lasts tendrils of her anxiety.

Forty-five minutes later, Nina was surrounded by a multitude of girls in fancy dresses and boys wearing dress shirts and crooked ties. Celia, being a seasoned teacher, had volunteered to help keep everyone corralled until showtime. Then Nina would lead them out to their seats at the front of the auditorium.

All the students' instruments were lined up in order of performance, with her cello placed at the end. She'd done everything she could to prepare. Now she crossed her fingers that no one would get a bad case of stage fright and refuse to leave their seat, including herself.

She counted heads and noticed one student was missing. Where was Garrett?

As the question crossed her mind, Carrie Ann burst into the room with Garrett following meekly behind.

"I'm sorry we're late," Carrie Ann said. "Garrett had a case of the nerves at home."

"Mom," Garrett groaned and moved toward the group of students.

Nina glanced at Carrie Ann and smiled. "I'll take his violin. You get seated. He'll do great." She gave Mom a gentle push in the direction of the auditorium.

All her students were here. She was ready to watch them shine. Excitement built, making her giddy. "Everyone line up." She raised her voice to be heard over the children's chatter. They gathered before her in a semi-straight line. "You all have family and friends out in the audience who came to watch you perform, and I couldn't be prouder of how far you've all developed in your skills. Don't worry if you make a mistake or lose your place in the music. Play with your heart, and your song will be perfect."

~ , ~

Colin waited for the sound of applause before he entered the darkened auditorium. The students walked across the stage, with several stopping to wave at their parents in the audience. His breath stopped when Nina appeared at the tail end of the line. Even at a distance, he felt the impact of her like a thud against his chest.

She wore a black dress that molded nicely to her upper body and billowed past her waist, the hem brushing the tops of silver high-heel shoes. Her honey-blonde hair was left down and flowed over her shoulders in loose waves.

If he didn't keep a tight hold on his self-control, he'd storm the stage right now and kiss her in front of her entire music class and their families. Life had taught him to be patient, so he'd be patient, at least until the end of the recital. Once he had Nina alone, his cool composure would be replaced with hot and eager desire.

He located Luke, who'd taken a spot in the back, and Colin seated himself in the chair beside him, leaning slightly forward to spare his sore back from contact with the seat. "Hey," he whispered.

Luke glanced over at Colin before returning his attention to the stage. "If this isn't a test of your devotion to Nina, I don't know what is." He handed Colin a folded program.

He'd read over the one Gabrielle had sent him, so he knew exactly what he was in for—twenty-five students multiplied by three songs each equaled seventy-five or more minutes of sitting quietly and listening to each one while trying to stay awake. "I'm fully committed to seeing this through. Why are you here?"

"Celia has some students in the recital and wanted to be here to support them. I'm here for her." He grinned.

"Where is Celia?" Colin glanced around the dimly lit room, examining the backs of heads for Luke's fiancée's dark hair. He saw Bea seated near the stage and looked forward to catching up with her.

"She wanted to sit toward the front. I'm in back just in case I'm needed at the station. And to make sure you really show up."

"I'm offended." Colin watched as the students marched down from the stage and took their seats, with the exception of one girl who stayed behind, silver flute in hand.

Once the girl found her spot at center stage, Nina set pages of sheet music onto the music stand. Then, she walked off, and the girl began playing.

Luke leaned over. "If your big reunion doesn't go as planned, I have a spare guest room for you tonight."

He snorted quietly. "Thanks, I think. If I do end up at your front door, you'll need more beer."

"Got plenty, but I can always make a run for the hard stuff. Don't want your tears ruining my nice woodwork."

"You're real funny," Colin whispered. "If you hadn't saved my life, I might want to take this outside." Although, he'd be happy to live the rest of his life without hitting another human being.

As the little girl with the flute finished her first song, Luke smiled. "Honestly, a good fist fight sounds real appealing right about now."

For the next hour and a half, Colin listened to song after song. At some point, Luke had dozed off. He sat with his head tipped back, mouth hanging open.

Colin was too full of nerves to fall asleep. Every time he saw Nina, he got a jolt to the heart, like he'd shuffled his feet across carpet and touched a metal door handle. Finally, just when he thought he'd go mad with anticipation, the final student finished his last piece. He wanted to jump up and pump his fist in the air.

Instead, he politely clapped along with the rest of the audience. They continued to clap as all the students took the stage for a final bow. But Nina was absent. Shouldn't she be standing up there with her students? Their recital was as much her accomplishment as theirs.

Once the clapping subsided, one little girl with curly black hair stepped forward. "Thank you." She folded her hands and smiled. "We have a special surprise for you today. One last performance."

Inwardly, Colin groaned. He looked over at Luke. The cop's face was wide-awake and alert. He even seemed excited.

"Our teacher, Ms. Pettit, has shared her passion for

music with all of us," the little girl continued. "She played the cello for many years and was so good, she even played at Carnegie Hall in New York. And today, she will play a song just for us."

Colin sprang to his feet, all pain in his body forgotten. As Nina walked onto the stage, carrying her cello in one hand and bow in the other, Luke tugged on his arm.

"Sit down," he hissed.

Lowering himself back to his chair, he watched her get seated.

She settled the cello between her knees and took a deep breath. Then, with a flourished glide of the bow, the most beautiful sound filled the room—her music. Nothing could have prepared him for hearing her live. Her performance left him in awe. She was perfection. She was his.

When her last note faded out, Nina stood and took a quick bow. Her students rushed the stage, all clamoring for a hug. She set aside her cello and wiped away tears with one hand.

"That's your girl." Luke nudged him with his elbow.

"I know." Colin's throat clogged with emotion.

"You have a very rare jewel, Colin. Treat her with care." With his Stetson in hand, Luke stood and exited the auditorium.

While he watched her greet parents from the back of the room, a wonderful peace filled him. After everything they'd been through together, everything they'd survived, he didn't doubt the powerful love they'd built. A love that pushed a man down the side of a mountain and into a burning building. A love that brought Nina to him when he'd been kidnapped and beaten down. A love he was now ready to declare to Nina and to the world.

Once the last group of parents departed with their children, he stood. Nina's back was to him as she set her cello back inside its case. Colin strode toward the stage. He stopped at the end of the aisle. "Nina."

She stilled, and then spun to face him. Her hand flew up to her mouth. In an instant, she raced down the steps and into his arms.

Exactly where he wanted her for the rest of his life.

CHAPTER 27

is arms tightened around her. Tipping her head back, Nina visually drank him in. Still gorgeous, despite the bumps, bruises, and missing hair. His blue eyes held the twinkle of mischief she'd loved so much when they'd first met two months ago.

He set her back on her feet. "Surprise!"

"Why didn't you tell me?" She went to swat his arm but stopped, not wanting to cause him pain.

"That would have ruined the surprise." He grinned and pulled her back into him.

She inhaled through her nose. *Ahhhhh.* He wore her favorite cologne. Which was her favorite because he wore it. Stepping back, she let her gaze roam over his body and stop at the bandages on his neck. "Where do you hurt?"

"Everywhere." He laughed. "But holding you makes me feel a million times better."

Tears filled her eyes. She fought the desire to wrap her arms around him with the intention of never letting go.

"Don't cry. I'm fine." He cupped her chin in his hand and

tilted her face so she met his gaze. "Only a few more scars to add to my collection."

"You're a tough guy. I forgot." She sniffled.

Colin took her hand and led her to the stairs, then up and onto the stage. "You were wonderful. Breathtakingly good. Almost couldn't believe my eyes when I saw you take the stage."

She glanced at her abandoned cello case and smiled. "You were the one who asked me to play again."

"I know." His arms encircled her waist, and he kissed her neck. "You took back something that meant a lot to you."

With care, she wrapped her arms around his broad shoulders. "I wanted to play for my students. They worked so hard and were so brave to get up in front of an entire room full of people. They inspired me to follow their example."

"Your music today sounded genuine." Colin tucked a piece of her hair behind her ear. "Simple, but I don't mean easy. I guess I should say your music touched my heart—a man who is as far removed from classical music as you were from South Boston."

She warmed in his embrace. Now that she had him back, how would she say goodbye when the time came for him to leave again? "Do you always know the perfect thing to say to a woman? I swear, you can melt me into a puddle of sentimental goo within seconds."

He tipped his head back and laughed. "You bring out the best in me."

"Ditto." She watched his smile turn to a more serious expression. Should she be worried?

The sound of a door opening at the back of the auditorium made them both turn their heads.

The man took two steps, then quickly spun around.

"Sorry," he shouted before the door clicked closed behind him.

Nina giggled. "My students and their families are probably wondering where I am."

"Luke, Celia, and Bea are managing the reception." He held her gaze. "I needed you all to myself for a few moments."

"We can talk more after everyone goes home." She unhooked her fingers from behind his neck. "What if we go back to my place after I get cleaned up here?"

He shook his head. "I have something to say that will not wait."

Her heart drummed inside her chest, slamming against her rib cage. She felt light-headed. *Don't pass out.*

Colin brushed a light kiss across her lips. "I love you."

She jerked back, blinking. Had she heard him right? "What?"

"You lose your hearing?" One side of his mouth lifted. "Read my lips...I love you."

Her hand flew up and pressed against her heart, which was thumping at an alarming rate. "At the cabin, when I said those words to you..." She swallowed. "I meant them."

"I know." He rained kisses on her forehead. "I'm here to prove that I do too. And I'll prove it every single day we're together."

Nina worked to slow her breathing. Cautious joy permeated every cell in her body. Despite their feelings, several big obstacles still stood in the way. "We both know loving someone doesn't mean a future together. I won't move away from Polaris."

"Don't ask me to stop traveling the world."

Her heart sank, along with hope for a future with Colin.

"Don't ask me, because I've already decided where I

want to live for the rest of my life." Colin's thumb ran across her tear-dampened cheekbone. "See, there's this cute ski town in Utah called Polaris, and I've always wanted to become a professional skier."

"Stop." She bit her lip. "You're too old to be a professional skier."

"Well, that's disappointing. Guess you'll have to do." Colin tapped the tip of her nose.

"What happened to your wanderlust?" She had to make sure. Giving up a lifestyle he enjoyed was a big sacrifice. One she didn't want him to regret years down the road. "Don't you have parts of the world you still want to see?"

"Nina Pettit." He cupped her face and smiled. "You are my world."

The kiss he started was not soft or gentle, and she drank him in. Her fingers gently roamed his arms, shoulders, and chest. When she came up for air, she sighed in contentment. Colin had come home. "I want to see the world, someday soon, with you."

"Whenever you're ready." The fingers on his uninjured hand entwined with hers.

"I should really get to the reception. I want to introduce you to my students." Pulling his hand, she led him towards the door.

"And what will you introduce me as?" He set his heels, halting right before the door, and pulled her in for another deep kiss.

"Hmmmm." She disconnected her lips from his and sighed. "I'm thinking of a lot of terms totally inappropriate for children."

Colin ran his tongue over his bottom lip and laughed. "How about we stick with boyfriend, then, for now?"

"Sure, for now." Nina grasped his large, calloused hand

and squeezed. "I have a very cute boyfriend." She stood on tiptoes and nipped at his earlobe.

"Keep that up and you'll have a fiancé sooner than I'd planned."

Love had her walking on air. "I could live with that." And she would live—for the first time—fully and without fear.

EPILOGUE

A *month later,* Nina reached under the table and took Colin's hand, giving it a quick squeeze. "They look so happy." She sighed at the sight of Luke and Celia Veldkamp kissing for the hundredth time tonight. The sounds of clinking glasses and hoots and hollers filled the banquet room.

Luke and Celia's wedding had been small and intimate. A Christmas affair of the heart. On either side of the couple sat their combined children, Andrew, Marco, Alejandro, and Kenna. Several months ago, Celia's son, Alejandro, and Luke's daughter, Kenna, had combined into their own family and were expecting a little one in only a few short months.

"Luke looks like he's ready to throw his new bride over his shoulder and run out the door." Colin's grin traveled all the way to his sparkling eyes. "I know that's exactly what I want to do with you right now, my dear." He pinched her thigh.

Giggling, Nina gave him an innocent peck on the cheek. More to come later. "You're both men of little patience.

We've only just finished dinner. Celia's family wanted a dance, so she hired a Cuban band and flew them in from LA. From what I heard, they're so good, they'll get even the most reluctant dancer out onto the floor."

"I've been practicing my moves." Colin swayed his upper body, dipping one shoulder and then the other. "Hope you can keep up."

She stared at him, eyebrows arched. "Keep up?"

"Yeah." He chuckled. "I don't talk about this often, but I took dance lessons as part of my boxing training. Learning to move to a rhythm helped coordinate my footwork with punches."

"Interesting." She turned her attention from her attractive date to the side of the room where the band was setting up. Out of the corner of her eye, she noticed Luke give Celia a kiss on the head before heading over to the band leader. What was he up to? She smiled as she remembered catching him practicing salsa dancing alone in his office. "I see Bea is getting warmed up."

Standing next to the dance floor, Bea swayed her hips—her new and improved hips. The woman looked ready to jive as soon as the band dropped the first beat.

"Hey." Colin tilted his head toward the doors leading out to the lobby. "You want to catch some fresh air before the real party starts?"

"Yes." She stood and took Colin's hand, following him out of the ballroom.

The resort lobby was decorated for the Christmas season, with trees covered in white twinkle lights filling every corner. Fires burned in the fireplaces scattered around the massive space. Nina still couldn't be near a fire and not cringe. The memory of smoke and heat caused a visceral reaction.

She stopped next to a thick support log, which was wrapped in evergreen garland sprinkled with red bows. "Before we grab our coats and go outside, I want to ask you a favor."

"Anything." He rubbed a lock of her hair between his fingers. "You know I'd do anything for you."

She'd spent years wondering if true love would ever find her, and now here he stood—the perfect embodiment of selfless devotion. How had she gotten so lucky? Nina took a deep breath. "Meg called yesterday and invited me to Boston. Her daughter has a dance recital at the end of January, and I'd like to go." She squeezed Colin's hand. "I hope you'll come with me."

"That's wonderful." His lips lifted in a wide grin. "I wouldn't let you go without me. I'm glad you and your sister are working toward mending your relationship."

"I know. We've been talking a lot on the phone, and my brother called the other day. I feel like I'm close to getting part of my family back." She still hadn't spoken to her parents, who were in Europe for the holidays. They'd be overseas for the next two months, which was fine with her. If she was taking the big step to travel to Boston in order to reconnect with her siblings, she'd rather the main source of her distress stay far away. Reconciling with her parents could wait for another day.

"Let me know the dates." Colin led her to the coat-check closet. He handed over their tickets to the attendant. "Jimmy is really pushing the expansion of the Angels' Grant program. I'll take my laptop, so work won't be an issue."

Nina accepted her coat, and then accepted Colin's help as she put it on. "I think it's great what you and the company are doing with the program, and I'm extra happy you found a way to stay working with it after you moved to Polaris."

She kissed his smooth cheek and inhaled the wonderful scent of his spicy cologne. Her blood warmed. *Can't wait to get him alone.*

Hand in hand, they stepped outside. The wind had died down, leaving the falling snow gently drifting to the ground. Fat flakes fell from the sky and coated every unprotected surface, including Colin's black hair, which had grown back nicely. They walked along a sidewalk next to the building.

She reached up and brushed snow off the top of his head. A useless effort, but she still took pleasure in touching him. And with her body so close to his, she filled with desire. Maybe they wouldn't make it to the end of the reception. Surely Celia and Luke would understand.

The resort's driveway was flanked by tall spruce dusted with snowy white powder. They reminded her of the miniature trees that accessorized a Christmas village scene. Actually, the whole town looked like a Christmas village. In the valley below, lights sparkled through the fog of snow.

Nina stuck out her tongue and gathered several snowflakes. She giggled as Colin did the same.

While she did a quick twirl, arms outstretched, Colin laughed. When she stopped, he stood before her with a small box resting on his palm.

"I wasn't sure if tonight was the right time to do this, but after witnessing so much love and how happy Luke looked watching Celia walk down the aisle, I knew asking you now would be a perfect ending to a very good day."

She covered her mouth with her hands. Her pulse quickened, and her legs turned into licorice.

"Nina, baby, I waited a long time to fall in love. With you, I fell hard, and it was such a beautiful fall." He dropped to one knee, and it sank into an inch of freshly fallen snow, which didn't appear to faze him one bit. With his thumb, he popped the top of the black jewelry box. "I want to spend every day of the rest of my life with you. I want to laugh with you and cry with you. I want to make a baby with you." His serious face split with a grin. "Will you accept the gift of my heart and marry me?"

Dropping down to the ground next to him, she wrapped her arms around his neck and ignored the cold, wet snow on her legs. "Are you serious? About wanting a baby?"

He cupped her face in his hand and gently kissed her mouth. "Is that all you got out of my speech?"

Instead of answering, she deepened their kiss, savoring every second. Finally, she peered up into his brilliant blue eyes. She imagined their child, so perfect and loved, and could almost smell that sweet baby scent in the air. "I hope our baby has your eyes."

Colin lifted the sparkling diamond ring from the box and flashed it in front of her face. "Focus, Nina. Will you marry me?"

Blinking, she gazed down at the ring and then back up at the love of her life. "Yes." She laughed. "Yes. A million times...yes. Ariel's already given you her blessing."

The ferret had grown on him, and he'd come to enjoy evenings watching TV with Nina with the furry animal curled on his lap. "Don't let Ariel run off with this." He slipped the ring onto her finger and kissed the inside of her wrist. "My world." Taking her hand, he pulled her up to stand. His arm wrapped around her waist.

"Let's keep this to ourselves for the time being." She rubbed her thumb over his knuckles. "This is Luke and Celia's special day."

"You're glowing. I need sunglasses to look at you." He held her tighter as they walked back into the lobby. "No way people aren't going to notice the new bling on your hand."

Sighing, she glanced down at Colin's ring, which was both beautiful and very large. "Okay." She blew out a breath. "Let's play this cool, and if people notice, just tell them to keep things on the down low until the end of the reception."

Colin pulled her off into a quiet corner of the lobby and proceeded to kiss her until she couldn't stand. Luckily, she was held up by his strong arms. "You're not helping distract me from thoughts of all things baby."

"I'm thinking more of the stuff that comes beforehand." He nipped her neck.

"Come on." She pulled his hand. "We need to get back for Luke and Celia's first dance. He's been practicing the salsa for months."

"Fine. But promise me one thing first." Colin placed a hand on her lower back.

"Name it."

"Whenever you feel afraid, or anxious, or disappointed, you come find peace in my arms." He gazed into her eyes. "To my very last day on this earth, I'll be your shelter from any harm and your accomplice in joy."

"I promise." She stood on her tiptoes and kissed him tenderly on the nose. "To a lifelong partnership." And with that assertion, her heart was forever placed securely into his care.

ACKNOWLEDGMENTS

Like Colin, I too have a hint of wanderlust. My love of travel began as a child. Each summer, Mom and Dad would load up their pop-up camper and us kids, and head out on a summer vacation. We had many adventures. I'm very grateful for the opportunity to see so much of our wonderful country.

Special thanks to the following friends who helped with A Beautiful Fall. To Stacey Kraus and her musical expertise. To Matthew Dietzler for helping me come up with the best way to do away with the bad guy. To Liza Korry for the name of the bakery, Downhill Delectables.

I'd like to acknowledge all those who like Nina have broken free from abusive relationships and those struggling to find an escape. Your strength and resilience inspires me.

ABOUT THE AUTHOR

 Laurie Winter's head has always been full of stories. Then a dream gave her the inspiration to put her thoughts into written words, sharing a part of her heart and soul. Now, she creates authentic characters who overcome the odds and find true love. She lives in Wisconsin with her husband, daughter, and rescue dog.

Please connect with me on Facebook, Twitter, Instagram, and Bookbub.

ALSO BY LAURIE WINTER

The North Star series: Purchase now

THIS CHRISTMAS

Warriors of the Heart series: Purchase now

HOME FIELD

TRUE HORIZON

AFTER ALL

WINNER TAKES ALL

KNOW YOU BY HEART

Single titles: Purchase now

HARMONY